BORN TO BITE

Books by Hannah Howell

ONLY FOR YOU * MY VALIANT KNIGHT
UNCONQUERED * WILD ROSES
A TASTE OF FIRE * HIGHLAND DESTINY
HIGHLAND HONOR * HIGHLAND PROMISE
A STOCKINGFUL OF JOY * HIGHLAND VOW
HIGHLAND KNIGHT * HIGHLAND HEARTS
HIGHLAND BRIDE * HIGHLAND ANGEL
HIGHLAND GROOM * HIGHLAND WARRIOR
RECKLESS * HIGHLAND CONQUEROR
HIGHLAND CHAMPION * HIGHLAND LOVER
HIGHLAND VAMPIRE * THE ETERNAL HIGHLANDER
MY IMMORTAL HIGHLANDER * CONQUEROR'S KISS
HIGHLAND BARBARIAN * BEAUTY AND THE BEAST
HIGHLAND SAVAGE * HIGHLAND THIRST
HIGHLAND WEDDING * HIGHLAND WOLF
SILVER FLAME * HIGHLAND FIRE
NATURE OF THE BEAST * HIGHLAND CAPTIVE
HIGHLAND SINNER * MY LADY CAPTOR
IF HE'S WICKED * WILD CONQUEST
IF HE'S SINFUL * KENTUCKY BRIDE * IF HE'S WILD
YOURS FOR ETERNITY * COMPROMISED HEARTS
HIGHLAND PROTECTOR * STOLEN ECSTACY
IF HE'S DANGEROUS * HIGHLAND HERO
HIGHLAND HUNGER * HIGHLAND AVENGER
HIS BONNIE BRIDE * BORN TO BITE

Books by Diana Cosby

HIS CAPTIVE * HIS WOMAN
HIS CONQUEST * HIS DESTINY

Books by Erica Ridley

TOO WICKED TO KISS * TOO SINFUL TO DENY

BORN
TO
BITE

HANNAH HOWELL
DIANA COSBY
ERICA RIDLEY

KENSINGTON BOOKS

KENSINGTON BOOKS are published by

Kensington Publishing Corp.
119 West 40th Street
New York, NY 10018

Compilation copyright © 2012 by Kensington Publishing Corp.

All Kensington titles, imprints, and distributed lines are available at special quantity discounts for bulk purchases for sales promotion, premiums, fund-raising, and educational or institutional use.

Kensington and the K logo Reg. U.S. Pat. & TM Off.

ISBN-13: 978-1-62090-313-1

Printed in the United States of America

CONTENTS

DARK SECRET

Hannah Howell

Prologue

Spring 1514
Scotland

The two crosses were simple, the letters carved into the wood neat but obviously done by an untrained hand. It would not be long before the words were stolen away by the wind and rain. A shiver went through Murdina Dunbar, and she knew it had nothing to do with the bite of chill in the wind. Her aunt and uncle had been buried in unconsecrated ground.

Murdina sighed and fought the urge to weep. It was not so much grief that caused the sting of tears in her eyes as it was a crushing disappointment. She had traveled so far to find her aunt and uncle, hoped for a cousin or two as well. Every step of the way she had prayed that she would soon be part of a family again. Instead, she found herself still alone. Utterly alone.

"If ye be looking for their demon spawn, ye are too late. She and that bairn she hid are gone."

Demon spawn? Murdina turned to look at the man who had spoken to her, annoyed with herself for being so lost in self-pity she had not heard his approach. He was short, filthy, and had a belly that revealed he ate too well far too often. The intuition that had cursed her for her whole life immediately marked him as ignorant and brutal.

"What do ye mean by demon spawn, sir?" she asked, and knew her anger over his words had seeped into her tone, for his muddy brown eyes narrowed with wary malice.

"The mother was a witch, aye? What else could she have been

with all her potions and love of the night, eh?" He scratched his belly. "We took care of the lassie's witch of a mother, but no one wanted to hurt the lass, too. She was a healer like her mother, and we didnae want to be left with no healer at all, did we? Then wee Adeline, their demon spawn, took in that cursed bairn. Wheesht, there was nay denying that the bairn was Satan's own. Anne herself said so when she tried to be rid of the bairn that demon had begotten on her, but the lass saved it. We tried to get rid of the lad ourselves after that, but she ran off with him. Young Adeline guarded that lad as if he were her own."

Good for her, Murdina thought, proud of her cousin. "Where did she run to?"

"Why do ye care? Ye are weel shed of the likes of her." He looked her over. "Though, now that I get a good look at you, I see ye have the look of her and her fool da. All that cursed red hair, too. Blood will tell, aye?"

"Will it? Then ye will be verra pleased to learn that I dinnae intend to linger here. As soon as ye tell me where Adeline went, I will leave."

"Dinnae ken where she went, do I? Some of our men chased her, but they didnae return. Another lot of fools went out ahunting for her, and they did stop here for a wee while. One of their men was hurt. They said the lass had taken up with one of those demons one hears tales of. MacNachtons the mon called them. One of them demons was helping the lass protect the bairn, and they were all headed toward the far hills," he said and nodded, pointing toward the north.

Murdina sighed, picked up the reins of her sturdy pony, and started to walk in the direction he had waved his short, dirty finger in.

" 'Tis said no one returns from those hills," he called after her.

"I certainly willnae be returning, whether I go to those hills or nay."

Her heart was choked with grief and sympathy for her cousin. Poor Adeline, Murdina thought, although she was pleased to discover she had a cousin and the cousin's name. Adeline was as alone as she was, however. All her cousin had was a bairn that fools like that filthy man behind her wanted to kill. Her cousin would need help to protect the child, she decided. The man marked as a demon by superstitious fools might not have stayed with Adeline. All Murdina had to do now was find her cousin.

As she looked toward the distant hills, she hesitated and shivered, but quickly stiffened her spine. The hills were shrouded in a heavy mist despite the fact that it was a bright, sunny day. It made her uneasy, but she shook off the tickle of fear that tried to take root in her heart. If she had to track her cousin into those ominous mists, she would do so. Now that she knew she had family left, she would allow nothing to stop her from finding Adeline. Not even wild, frightening talk of demons.

Chapter One

"We have an important guest, and ye have been chosen to be his maid."

Murdina glanced up from the linen she had been scrubbing clean to the plump Mistress McKee and then back down at her work. "Ye told me I was to be the laundry maid only this morn."

"Weel, Jeanne will be the laundry maid now. She isnae the sort of lass we want to be maid to such a fine gentlemon. Too dirty, too rough, ye ken."

And too quick to lift her skirts, thought Murdina as she dried her hands, stepping away from the laundry tub so that a flushed, scowling Jeanne could take her place. "Ye say he is an important mon?"

"Aye." Mistress McKee grabbed Murdina by the arm and pulled her out of the laundry room that also served as the bathing room for men of lesser rank. "Ye also speak far finer than our Jeanne does."

It was strange to be chosen for something that would only rouse spite or suspicion amongst the other servants of Dunnantinny. Murdina made no complaint, however. Acting the maid for some fine gentleman guest had to be easier than scrubbing pots or washing linen. Unless, she mused, he was the sort of man to think all maids working in a keep were his for the taking. Since she would never tolerate being treated that way, there was a chance that this new position within the keep could land her in enough trouble to be thrown out. The laird would not take it kindly if she insulted or injured his guest. Being tossed out would actually be the most merciful of the punishments she could face for such actions, and the laird of Dunnantinny was not known for his merciful nature.

Accepting the heavy bucket of heated water Mistress McKee thrust at her, Murdina wished she had traveled a little farther before stopping. The bucket was heavy enough that the rope handle cut into her palm, but it was better than having Mistress McKee still touching her. The cold rigidity of the woman had begun to seep into Murdina. Unfortunately, she could not tell the woman not to touch her, so she simply braced for that chill every time it happened.

Being close to so many people all the time was a strain as her curse often made her all too aware of the feelings of those around her, especially when they touched her. She had learned almost nothing about her cousin Adeline, either, despite how close the keep was to the village where Adeline had been the healer. Nor had she collected much coin with which to continue her journey. In truth, all she had collected were bruises, blisters, and backaches as well as far too much knowledge of the venality of some of the keep's residents. She was no stranger to hard work, but being a maid in a crowded keep was a lot different than being a blacksmith's daughter. If she had learned more than just evil gossip about her cousin, she might have considered it all worthwhile, but she still had little more than what that filthy man had said as she had stood over the graves of her aunt and uncle. Only a need for coin kept her at Dunnantinny now.

"Greetings, Sir Baldwin," said Mistress McKee, pulling Murdina free of her dark thoughts and aching disappointment. "I had the maid bring ye up some hot water. I suspicion ye would like a wash after your long journey." She pulled Murdina into the room. "Fill up the ewer and bowl, lass."

Smothering the urge to push back, Murdina went to do as she had been told. She only half-listened to Mistress McKee and Sir Baldwin talk. The man had a very attractive deep voice, she thought as she checked the drying cloth near the washing bowl to be sure it was clean and dry. Listening to him speak made her belly tense in the oddest way. There was a soothing calm about him that eased the chill Mistress McKee had infected her with, but beneath that calm was a shadow, and she suspected he had a few secrets.

"Murdina will be your maid during your stay here," Mistress McKee said. "Lass, make your curtsey to the mon."

Murdina turned and curtsied, careful to keep her gaze respectfully lowered. It was as she began to rise up out of her curtsey that she chanced a look at Sir Baldwin and nearly stumbled. It took all of her willpower to keep her expression one of calm and respect and not rudely gape at the man.

Men were not supposed to be beautiful, she told herself. Yet, *beautiful* was the first word that came to mind. No wonder Mistress McKee had sounded close to cooing sweetly when she talked to the man, a touch of warmth actually invading that rigid chill the woman carried. He was more than handsome. He had to be at least two hands taller than her. His body had the long, powerful lines of the finest of stallions that had passed through her father's shop. Thick, gleaming black hair hung to the middle of his broad back, two warrior braids framing his face.

And such a face, Murdina mused, unable to look away. A strong jaw, well-defined cheekbones, and a sharp blade of a nose with no hint of the bump so many men had, the remnant of a nose too often broken. He was smiling at her, his slightly full lips parted just enough to reveal a glimpse of strong, healthy teeth. Yet, she knew deep in her heart that his heartbreakingly beautiful face could harden into a look any predator would be proud of. A look that even that enticing mouth would not soften.

His eyes, however, were what firmly caught her attention. The color of pure amber, they were nicely spaced, neither too large nor too small, set beneath tidy, arched brows, and encircled with lashes so thick and long they would cause every woman who saw them to suffer sharp spasms of envy. Those eyes beckoned, tempted, enthralled. Murdina knew that one heated look from them would be enough to seduce even the most pious of women.

When his smile widened a little, Murdina knew he had detected her fascination. She fought against blushing like some tiresome girl and looked to Mistress McKee as if awaiting the woman's next command. It would be one she would obey immediately, especially if it got her out of Sir Baldwin's bedchamber. The way the man made her feel, an odd mixture of nervous and excited, made her anxious to get far away from him. She considered asking to be relieved of her duties as his maid, but only briefly. Not only did she not wish to try and explain why she asked for such a thing, she refused to allow one too handsome man to make her a coward.

"The evening meal willnae be set out for a few hours yet, sir," said Mistress McKee. "Would ye like a wee bite of something to take the edge off your hunger until then?"

Murdina wondered why that perfectly reasonable question should make the man look so amused.

"That would be most kind of ye, Mistress McKee," he replied.

"Go, lass, and fetch the mon a tray of food and drink."

It took more effort than Murdina liked to simply walk away. She wanted to run. There was something in the way the man looked at her, the way that look made her feel, that urged her to run. Run like a deer scenting a pack of wolves, she thought as she made her way down to the kitchens.

Foolishness, she scolded herself. The man offered her no threat. She would have sensed it if he had, one of the few good things that came of the gift she had been cursed with. It was not his fault her heart pounded when she looked at him. He had done nothing, said nothing, to entice her. The proof of that was in the calm respect Mistress McKee treated him with, that faint wisp of warmth she revealed. If the man had tried to immediately seduce the maid Mistress McKee had chosen for him, the woman's mood would definitely have soured. Mistress McKee had a very rigid set of morals that often amazed Murdina, considering the somewhat widespread lack of morals within the keep.

What astonished Murdina even more was how one look at Sir Baldwin had slashed at the foundations of her own morals. She reluctantly admitted to herself that she had wanted to touch, to taste, that far too tempting mouth of his. She had wanted to rouse the heat of passion in those mysterious eyes. That was so unlike her, so against her vow to touch people as little as possible, for she truly did not want to know what they felt, that she decided it was why she had become so anxious to get away from him. With that admission, however, she grew calm. Now that she knew what her weakness was, had recognized it as no more than a woman's response to a far too attractive man, she could control it. As she collected the food to bring to him, she strengthened her resolve and reminded herself that she was not at the keep to find herself a man but to learn what she could about the Mac-Nachtons and then find her cousin.

Gillanders smiled as he stripped to his braes and began to wash the dust of travel from his body. Mistress McKee was a rigid woman, proud of her high place in the keep and undoubtedly fighting a losing battle with her attempts to keep the maids under her rule as pious as she so obviously was. Most maids in a keep like this were eager to earn an extra coin or two now and then by warming a man's bed, especially if that man was young, hale, and reasonably handsome. Of course, if dear Mistress McKee found out he was no Baldwin but one of the much whispered about MacNachtons, she would be worried about far more than the fact that her maids had few morals when it came to bedding a man who looked as if he had that coin or two to spare for them.

The thought that the young maid Murdina was of that ilk made him frown. He was not sure why it troubled him to think she was one to give her favors to any man who tempted her with a coin or a smile. That made no sense at all, for he was hungry for a woman. It had been far too long since he had lost himself in the soft heat of a woman. All that should concern him was how much she might think she was worth.

He could already feel the silk of that thick, blood red hair against his skin. He ached to see those beautiful eyes, a strange blend of blue and green, turn hot and liquid with passion. Small, long-fingered hands were undoubtedly calloused and a little rough from work, but he was certain that her fair skin would be soft elsewhere and as sweet as the cream it resembled.

His body grew hot and hard as images of Murdina beneath him, naked and flushed with desire, filled his head. Gillanders tried to shake the images from his mind but was not surprised when he failed. Even in her ill-fitted gown he could see that she was all he desired. The faded wool could not hide the fullness of her breasts or the sweet, womanly curve of her hips. She also had height enough to offer him the delight of long legs, limbs perfect for wrapping around him as they sought their pleasure in each other.

She was trouble, Gillanders decided. The need she roused was too strong, clutched at him too swiftly, and was difficult to shake free of. It would be wise to stay away from her, but he knew he would not do so. Since the first time he had rolled about in the heather with the butcher's daughter, a greedy, buxom wench who had gleefully rid him of his virginity, he had not known such a hunger for a woman. There had been a spark of interest in Murdina's lovely eyes, and he knew he would not be able to resist the temptation to use it to draw her into his bed.

There was a soft rap at the door, and he heard her husky voice announcing that she had brought him his food. Gillanders glanced down at his near naked body and grinned. His desire was no longer blatantly visible through his braes, so he bid her to enter and waited.

Murdina entered the bedchamber and nearly dropped the tray she held. The man was as good as naked. It took all of her willpower not to slam the tray down on the table near the fireplace and bolt from the room. With what she prayed looked like calm disinterest, she walked to the table and set the tray down on it. It was not easy, for she could feel both his amusement and his interest in her as a woman.

It was an effort to keep her gaze firmly on the food she set out. She did not understand why she so badly wished to look at him. Despite being the only child of a very protective father, she was not a complete stranger to the sight of a man's body, yet none had held more than a passing interest for her.

Then again, she mused ruefully, none of those men had been quite so fine to look at. She had been right about the long, lean, powerful lines of his body. There was no softness to the man, his strength clear to see beneath the taut skin, skin that held the light, golden tone much like one can get from the sun. That smooth, unmarred flesh made her palms actually itch with the need to touch him.

"Ah, just what I needed."

That deep voice sounded right in her ear, his warm breath caressing the sensitive skin there. Murdina bit the inside of her cheek to stop herself from squeaking in alarm. Her eyes widened as he reached around her, his strong, elegant hand picking up a thick chunk of cheese. She could feel the heat of his body all along her back. When the urge to lean back a little, to brush against his tall body struck her, Murdina grabbed the now empty tray and quickly sidestepped away from him. She fought against blushing when he looked at the tray she held up before her like a shield and quirked one dark brow at her. The amusement in his eyes made her want to hit him with the heavy wooden tray. They had not actually touched, but she had been close enough to catch the want that afflicted him, a desire for her that she found all too tempting.

"If that will be all, sir?" she asked, pleased with how calm and serious she sounded.

"I suppose it must be. For now."

"Then I will leave ye to dine. Please send for me if ye need anything else."

"Oh, I most certainly will. And my name is Gillanders."

I did not run, Murdina told herself as she shut the door behind her and hurried back to the kitchen. *I but left the room with swift efficiency.* She was not surprised when a small part of her heartily scoffed, but she ignored the tiny mocking voice in her head.

The man affected her like the most potent of wines. She had heard such subtle flirtatious remarks before, as well as many that were not so subtle. Not one had made her insides clench with the temptation to reply in kind. His amusement tickled her anger to life, but everything else about him left her as breathless as some cow-eyed maiden with little sense of the danger she was in, a maid too foolish to see beyond a handsome face, playful words, and a fine, strong form. When he drew close his desire had warmed her, and she knew it would be a mistake to touch him, to open herself up to the full strength of such a feeling.

His name was Gillanders. It should be Dangerous. He should wear some marking to tell women to beware, she thought crossly. It would be best if she found as many ways as possible to avoid the man.

Murdina was so lost in her thoughts she almost walked into the laird. She stumbled to a halt and looked up at the tall Sir Ranald Dumfries. He was so thin she often wondered if the man was ill. What she was certain of, however, was that he was a man it would be wise to avoid. He made her skin crawl with the way his too pale eyes fixed on her. She did all she could not to even brush against the man.

"How is our guest?" he asked.

"Weel, m'laird. He has been given the water to wash away

the dust of travel, and I have just taken him some food to tide him o'er until the evening meal is served."

"Good. Keep a close eye on the mon."

"M'laird?" She could not hide her uncertainty, wondering exactly what the man meant. There was a lot of lewd and violent behavior at Dunnantinny, but she had not seen that any of the maids were actually ordered to service anyone. Most were more than willing to do so without being asked. Murdina could think of no other reason the laird would ask her to watch Sir Baldwin, and she wondered what could happen to her if she refused.

"I wish for ye to tell me all he says or does. How he acts or any odd habits he might have. Do ye understand me?"

"Aye, m'laird," she replied, praying he would not press her to openly swear that she would do as he asked.

"Good lass. And if ye cannae find me, tell all to Egan or Donald."

The moment the laird was gone, Murdina softly muttered every curse she knew and then heartily wished she knew more. Her laird wished her to spy for him. If that was not appalling enough, he wanted her to keep *a close eye* on the very man she had just decided she would be wise to avoid as much as possible. Perhaps, she thought, it was past time to continue her search for her cousin.

Chapter Two

The door to Sir Gillanders Baldwin's bedchamber loomed in front of her like the gaping maw of some huge dungeon. Nay, Murdina thought, a torture chamber where the weapons used to break her will were a fine, manly body, enticing words, beautiful eyes, and a beguiling smile. Each time she approached the room she found herself both reluctant and eager to cross the threshold.

She had been his maid for a week, and the only time she saw him fully clothed was when he was outside his bedchamber. The man had not one drop of modesty in his blood. It puzzled her that he spent so much time shirtless or wearing only his braes. The castle was not a warm place. Most everyone else dressed very warmly to fend off the chill and damp.

And every time she left his bedchamber the laird or one of his men appeared to ask questions about Sir Baldwin. Murdina could sense their frustration with her lack of any useful information. She could hardly tell them that the man was flaunting his beautiful, broad chest and making her heart pound and her hands itch to touch all that taut, golden skin. It had already been hinted that she should crawl into the man's bed to try and gain whatever information they were so eager to learn. She was not about to let them know that she found Sir Gillanders very desirable. Nor could she ever explain that it was not just her virginity she was protecting by not getting intimate with any man, even one that she desired more every day.

Murdina took a deep breath and rapped on the door. The anticipation that heated her blood when he called out for her to enter irritated her. She was a grown woman and should be able to control such feelings. The man was playing some game of seduction with her, and she should have the strength to resist.

She stepped into the room, took one look at Sir Gillanders sprawled in his bed, and nearly ran right back out of the room. He was propped up against the pillows, that chest she so admired in full view all the way down to the edge of the fine linen sheet that barely covered his groin. One long leg was outside of that cover, begging to be admired.

That leg was worthy of admiration, she thought as she forced herself to move and put the tray down on the table by the bed. Long, well shaped, and sleekly muscular. The candlelight favored his skin, making its golden color almost glow with warmth. Murdina wondered a little crossly if the man was aware of that. Either he was so vain he thought he could pull her into his bed just by flaunting his body or she had somehow revealed her attraction to him and he believed it fair to try to tempt her into acting upon it.

And why were the candles lit? she wondered and glanced around. The heavy drapes were pulled close over the window, barring the daylight from entering the room. A fire burned in the hearth, making the room comfortably warm, and the day was not a cold one. It seemed a sad waste of candles when the sun would light the room very nicely. Consumed by that puzzle she was able to look at Sir Gillanders without being immediately distracted by his smile.

"Shall I open the drapes, sir?" she asked. " 'Tis a fine, sunny day today."

"Nay, leave them shut." Gillanders saw her confusion and groped for a reason to keep the drapes closed that would ease her obvious suspicion. "I have eyes that are verra sensitive to the bright light the sun can cast. I will open them when it no longer shines right into the room."

Although she had never heard of such an affliction, Murdina supposed it could be true. He did have eyes of a very unusual color. She realized she was staring into those beautiful eyes, her thoughts slowly clouding, and quickly turned her attention to pouring him a tankard full of the cool cider he preferred.

Gillanders watched her very closely. He could almost smell her attraction to him, and it fed his own. It pleased him that she was not one of those maids who readily tumbled into a man's bed, but it also frustrated him. The need she stirred inside him refused to be placated by any other woman. There had been several women in the keep who had indicated that they would be more than willing to warm his bed, but he had no interest in them. That troubled him a little for, as his mother liked to say, the men in the Callan line did their best to live up to the randiness of the tomcat in their blood. The MacNachton half was not one to deny itself pleasure, either. Turning away a willing woman who met his meager qualifications of reasonably clean and comely was not his usual habit.

"So, tell me, Murdina, how do the laird and his men fare this fine morning?" he asked as he helped himself to the bowl of honey-sweetened porridge she held out to him.

"They have been up and at work for some time now, sir."

"Ah, but I keep verra late hours. Sensitive eyes, aye?"

"Oh. Of course. They are just doing as they always do, but they have requested that I try and discover when ye might be ready to join them."

"Soon." He smiled at her. "I also suspect they wish ye to discover far more than that." He nodded when she blushed. "Dinnae look so guilty, lass. Most lairds would do the same. Do I nay always ask ye questions, too?"

"Aye, and I do wish all of ye would just stop," she snapped, and then grimaced. "I beg your pardon, sir."

"Nay, dinnae apologize. Ye are being forced into the middle of a game not of your choosing. Just because such things are done all the time doesnae make it right." He set aside his empty bowl and then studied her closely for a moment. "Most maids are weel accustomed to such games, but I am thinking ye have nay been a maid for verra long."

She shook her head. "Nay, I grew up as the daughter of a blacksmith. Lost my parents to a fever and there was naught left in the village for me."

"So ye came here to scrub floors or worse?"

"I came here because, when my father was dying, he said he had a brother in the village near here, and I sought my aunt and uncle. Sadly, they, too, are dead, but I have discovered that I have a cousin. I am seeking her now."

"Ye think she may have come here?"

Murdina hesitated, but there was such honest curiosity on his face, and all her instincts told her that was all it was; she could find no sound reason to hold fast to her tale. "I dinnae think so, but this laird rules o'er the village where she lived. She had to flee the place because of fools who allowed superstition and lies to rule them. I had hoped some word of her could be found here but have discovered verra little. All I hear of her from the people here is the same vicious rot I heard from a wretched wee mon at the gravesides of my aunt and uncle. Now I but try to gather some coin to continue the hunt for her. I cannae blame Adeline for taking her wee bairn and running from this place, but I hope she can be found."

Gillanders nearly choked on the cider he was drinking. "Adeline?"

"Aye. Adeline Dunbar. Do ye ken who she is?"

"The name seems familiar to me, but I may have just heard a few things said about her and that is what stirs a verra small twinge of recognition."

Murdina sighed, the sudden loss of hope she had just experienced leaving her feeling weary to her very soul. "Ach, weel, I am sure I will find her soon enough, and a wee bit of coin in my pocket when I resume my search cannae hurt." She had caught the brief sense of a lie, but it had come and gone so quickly she decided she had been mistaken, for he had no reason to lie about such a thing.

The sadness on her face struck him to the heart. Gillanders caught her by the arm and tugged her closer. The way she stared at him with a mix of fear and desire was all he needed to act upon his sudden desire to kiss the sadness from her face. He brushed his lips over hers, and she trembled. To his astonishment so did he.

He placed his hand at the back of her head and held her close as he teased at her mouth. A quick, sharp nip on her full, soft lips was enough to part them, and he took quick advantage. The only clear thought he had as he explored her mouth with his tongue was that he had never tasted anything as sweet.

Shock held Murdina still when he first touched his mouth to hers. Desire swept over her so swiftly she shook from the force of it, and she was unable to tell how much of it was from him and how much of it was her own. She did nothing to halt him when he deepened the kiss, the way his tongue stroked the inside of her mouth sending pure fire through her veins. It was not until the urge to crawl into the bed with him became so strong she actually reached for him that she began to come to her senses.

A little horrified at how quickly she had succumbed to his allure, she pulled away and stared at him. The warmth in his eyes nearly pulled her back to him. She quickly grabbed what little food remained on the tray, set it on the table, and fled the room. It was cowardly and graceless, but at that moment she did not care.

Once outside the room, the door separating her from the temptation of him, she paused to catch her breath. Her mother had warned her about the temptation of men and their kisses, but she had decided it was just the words of a woman deeply in love with her husband. The few kisses she had experienced had offered no temptation at all, the feelings she had gleaned from the men who had touched her only making it worse. Now she knew there had been some truth in her mother's warnings. There was no cold calculation in his kiss, just desire, and even that shadow that lurked within him had done nothing to dim it or taint it when she had sensed it.

And what about his wound? she suddenly thought. Everyone had spoken of how he had been wounded in the sword practice late yesterday, yet she had seen no sign of it. Perhaps she should have given in to the urge to rush to his side when she had first heard about it, but Mistress McKee had then talked of how the man had walked away and shrugged aside any help. He had even declined having Murdina aid him in tending his wound or bring him the late night drink he always asked for. Her father had been the same when he had hurt himself from time to time, not wishing her or her mother to fuss over him, so she had stayed away. Yet, with even a small wound there should have been at least some sign of a bandage, and she had seen none at all. She had not even felt an echo of discomfort from an injury when she had been touching him. There was something very strange about that.

"Learn anything yet?"

Murdina looked up at Egan, the sight of his battered, homely face almost enough to cool her still heated blood, and she took a step back from him. Only once had she accidentally touched him, and she now made an effort to never do so again for the man's emotions were all dark and twisted, making her stomach churn. She thought about his question and how to answer it. She could hardly tell him that she had learned that Sir Gillanders could lead a lass into sin with but a smile and make her enjoy the journey with but one kiss.

"Nay," she finally said, unwilling to tell the man anything of interest even if she had anything to tell. "In truth, I dinnae ken what ye wish me to discover about the mon. He eats, sleeps, bathes, and keeps late hours. I fear that is all I have learned aside from what he prefers to eat."

"And what does he prefer to eat?"

"Porridge sweetened with honey, cool cider, meat, bread, and cheese. He is also verra fond of apples, but they are nay at their best after a winter of storage."

"He says naught about why he is here?"

"I dinnae think any mon of his ilk would discuss his business with a mere maid, sir."

Egan scowled at her. "Ye have been in and out of his rooms for a sennight and that is all ye ken about the mon?"

She suddenly thought of how Sir Gillanders avoided the sun but decided that was not something Egan or anyone else needed to know. Having such sensitive eyes would be seen as a weakness, and no man liked others to learn that he had any weakness. Telling Egan about that carried the sour taste of a betrayal of trust. So would mention of how Sir Gillanders did not seem to be suffering from any wound.

"Aye, sir."

"Weel, it may be time to send in another maid, one who kens how to sweeten a mon's humor until his tongue runs freer."

She watched him stride away and bit the inside of her cheek to keep from ordering him not to do that. The mere thought of one of the other maids taking her place made her heart hurt. Any one of the others would be climbing into Sir Gillanders's bed so quickly she doubted he would have time to lift the covers for her.

"I hope he means that, for I would be fair pleased to be the mon's maid."

Murdina scowled at Jeanne as the maid paused by her side,

carrying two slops buckets. "Egan has no say in such things. 'Tis Mistress McKee who decides who does what about here." Jeanne stank of envy and a deep anger, and it was so strong, Murdina did not even have to touch the woman to feel it.

"Mistress McKee will do as she is told."

As she watched Jeanne walk away, it took all of her willpower not to hit the woman over the head with the tray she still clutched in her hands. It was jealousy burning inside of her now. Murdina did not understand why she had such feelings concerning a man she had known only a sennight, one she saw only a few times a day. She knew she ought to get away from Dunnantinny before she did something very foolish, took a step she could never back away from, but she knew she would not do that either. At some time during the sennight in which Sir Gillanders had been spinning his playful web of seduction, she had become firmly caught.

She looked at the door and thought about going back in there to tell him he had to cease his games with her. Murdina actually took a step toward the door before good sense prevailed. If she went back in there right now while the heat of his kiss still warmed her mouth and her body, the very last thing she would be doing was telling him to leave her alone. The fact that she could touch him, could enjoy his kisses and feel nothing but desire despite her cursed gift made him a temptation almost too large to ignore. She needed time away from the man to try and regain her strength. The next time she stepped into that room she wanted to have enough willpower and sense to be able to look at him without remembering how skillfully the man could kiss. Or how much she had liked it.

Gillanders moved away from the door and began to wash up. He would make sure no one tried to send him a new maid. Murdina was not telling the laird or his men anything she had seen. She had not even mentioned anything about how he kept the room as dark as a tomb. It was a weakness he should not have allowed her to see, but the fact that she had not shared that with anyone pleased him. They may have told her to spy on him, but she was not obeying them.

He also wanted to get her in his arms again, he thought and grinned. Her kiss had been sweet if inexperienced. The way she had trembled in his arms, leaned into him as the kiss had deepened, and had flushed with desire made him eager to continue his seduction of her.

A pang of conscience struck him as he dressed. There was a very good chance she was a virgin. It was not exactly kind of him to work so hard to steal what was her only dowry. Gillanders also knew that pang of conscience would not stop him from trying to do just that. He had never wanted a woman more.

A woman who was the cousin of Adeline—the much-loved wife of his cousin. He grimaced and cast a rueful glance at the door. He should tell Murdina that he knew exactly where Adeline Dunbar was. Unfortunately, to do that, he would have to confess that he was not who he had told everyone he was. Murdina was holding fast to any information she had about him, but he doubted she could hide the truth if she knew it. Murdina was no practiced liar. Egan or the laird would be able to see that she held some truth about him back with but one look at her very readable face.

As he headed down to the great hall, Gillanders swore that he would not leave Dunnantinny without telling Murdina about her cousin. When the thought of leaving without Murdina herself at his side caused him a sharp pang of regret, he softly swore. A woman twining herself around his heart and mind was not a complication he needed right now.

One step into the great hall was enough to have Gillanders wishing he could turn around or, even better, go home. Mistress McKee obviously did her best to keep it clean, but the laird and his closest men-at-arms were pigs. Not surprisingly, all the others in the great hall followed their lead. The smell of unwashed bodies was also strong. And, while Gillanders was able to eat food, even enjoyed it despite its inability to give him all he needed to survive, Dunnantinny needed a better cook.

He obeyed the laird's call for him to join his table and tried to hide his weariness with the game he played. Gillanders was not finding out what he needed to know and doubted he would. The laird was an uncivilized brute in many ways but he was canny. Too many pointed questions and the man would grow even more suspicious than he was now.

Gillanders sat down, looked at the overcooked, greasy meat set on his trencher, and inwardly sighed. It was time to go hunting, he thought, as he smiled at the young boy serving him. He was just not sure he could do so without being discovered, but he needed something to keep up his strength, and he was tired of relying on only the blood-enriched wine he had brought with him.

Out of the corner of his eye he saw Murdina slipping through the shadows at the far edge of the hall, heading toward the kitchens. She was a temptation he could not seem to resist. It was as if her allure and the one kiss they had shared had become a tether keeping him at Dunnantinny, at least until he could have more of her. He was either going to have to sate himself on her in his bed, or push her from his mind, if he ever wanted to get out of this place.

Then again, he mused with an inner smile, he could always take her with him. He had something she wanted, or rather, he knew where it was. The lure of family might just be enough to pull her along with him when he left. She did hold a strange allure for him, but he was well practiced in avoiding that. The ride to Cambrun would also be a lot more entertaining with her at his side. It was something he had to take some time to think about, without the fear that he might be getting tangled up too tightly with the woman. He shook her from his mind and concentrated on his host, still a little hopeful that the man would finally say something to make the long time spent at Dunnantinny worthwhile.

Chapter Three

The laird needed better spies, Gillanders thought as he stood upon the battlements, sipping mulled cider and watching the moonrise. He knew the laird and his men were Hunters, or worked with his clan's enemy when the opportunity arose. He was also certain that they had the blood of his cousin Arailt on their hands, but even after nearly a fortnight of enduring the company of such men, he had yet to gather any proof of that. With each day that passed, there was less chance that he would gather that proof and an ever-growing chance that he could be the next MacNachton who never returned from a journey to this land.

It was time to leave. There could be no further business with Sir Ranald unless a swift meting out of justice was required. Gillanders wondered why he still lingered when even that small flicker of hope he had had over a sennight ago had faded. Then he cursed when his mind produced an image in response to his silent questioning of himself. Murdina Dunbar naked on his bed, her blood red hair a blanket beneath her fair, comely body, and her slim, strong arms open to receive him.

She was still why he lingered despite how all his instincts were shouting at him to leave. That both alarmed him and intrigued him. Gillanders knew it could just be because his lust for her was so strong, but he suspected it was more. The need to discover how much more, before his manly instinct to escape such a trap overtook him, was what held him at Dunnantinny.

"Enjoy the night, do ye?"

Gillanders sipped his mulled cider and looked at Egan as the man stepped up beside him. The laird's two men, his right and left hands as Gillanders silently called them, had begun to shadow his every step. " 'Tis a fine, clear night. Stars shining, the moonlight strong, the land quiet. Weel, at least it was quiet until now."

Egan grunted, clenched his big hands into fists, and lightly pounded them on the top of the wall. "Aye, weel, I am thinking ye like the night a wee bit too much."

"Truly? Ye are thinking?" Gillanders knew the man badly wanted to hit him. Could scent the fury Egan fought to control. "And why wouldnae anyone like the night? Think, if ye are still in a humor to do so, of all one can do in the night that brings naught but pleasure."

"Wheesht, if ye talk of tupping, ye can do that any time ye want."

"Ah, I see. Weel, some of us like to do a wee bit more than shove a lass against a wall, toss up her skirts, and grunt o'er her."

"Ye seem to have healed verra quickly. I thought the wound I gave ye was more than a mere scratch."

"I have always healed quickly, and it was nay so deep, just bled freely. Ye need nay fear that ye did me any serious harm."

It did not surprise Gillanders to see suspicion darken the man's eyes. People did not heal as swiftly as he had. It was a wondrous gift, but one that could not be hidden well if it happened around others. Even Murdina had looked at him strangely, undoubtedly wondering why there was little sign of a sword cut on his body after so short a time. Fortunately, he was certain she had not shared that knowledge with anyone else. It was yet another reason, however, why he knew his time at this keep had to come to an end soon.

"Why are ye here? Ye talk fine, but naught happens save that ye eat our food, drink our wine, and bed our maids."

"I havenae bedded a single maid."

"Ye havenae settled anything with the laird, either. Talk, talk, and more talk. Nay more than that. Ye said ye wished to treat with us, for your clan, that ye thought we might be able to do some business with each other. Dunnantinny could use some trade, e'en an alliance or two, but I dinnae see that happening."

Gillanders turned to face Egan directly and said, "I dinnae think 'tis your place to *see* anything. I deal with the laird, nay one of his men."

He spoke with all the cold haughtiness of a prince. Gillanders knew that tone would have had his cousins and siblings rolling about laughing heartily and flinging insults at his head, but it worked to silence Egan. From the look in the man's eyes, it also worked to enrage him, and Gillanders wondered just how he might pay for that later.

"Then mayhap ye can try harder to make me *see*," said the laird as he stepped out of the shadows.

Giving the laird a charming smile, Gillanders then took another drink of his mulled cider. It gave him a moment to consider the laird's skill at creeping up on a man. The more he considered the matter, however, the less he believed that he had been that unaware of his surroundings. Either the laird had already been close at hand, this meeting and inquiry by Egan well planned, or the man was blessed with some unusual skills as a hunter. Gillanders briefly savored the thought of getting the laird alone and forcing the truth out of the man. He was sure that Sir Ranald had had something to do with Arailt's murder, and torturing the man a little to get the truth would help ease his grief over the loss of a good man. It was increasingly hard to continue to play games with the man, especially when Gillanders knew his time at Dunnantinny was fast running out.

"A decision might be reached more easily if one kenned exactly what terms needed to be met," Gillanders said, breaking the taut silence.

"Just as terms can be set more easily when one kens exactly what may be gained," replied the laird.

"Agreed. Mayhap 'tis time we spent more time talking with more serious intent and less in playing the games of courtesy."

Gillanders then spent an uncomfortable few minutes arranging times for the more detailed talks the laird was pressing for. It felt as if hours had passed until he was able to get away from the man, because Gillanders had no real trade to offer the laird nor did he have any intention of arranging a treaty with such men. He was finding it increasingly difficult to keep talking to the laird without actually promising or agreeing to anything.

Seeing a woman lurking near his bedchamber door as he approached it, Gillanders enjoyed a brief flare of anticipation, only to have it rudely doused when he realized that it was not the woman he ached for. It was the maid Jeanne. The maid had already cornered him several times since his arrival at the keep, offering herself to him. Despite the ragged state of her gown she had obviously made an effort to clean herself up this time. The unsatisfied knot of lust he carried around like added weight still did not respond to her blatant invitation to make use of her fulsome body. That hunger could be satisfied by only one woman. Gillanders did not like it, but he was not one to ignore the truth.

"What are ye doing here, Jeanne?" he demanded, his cold voice offering no hint of welcome.

"I but wish to ken if ye are weel served, Sir Baldwin," she replied, smiling as she sauntered closer to him.

"Has someone suggested that I am nay pleased with the maid I already have?"

Her smile faded a little. Gillanders knew she had finally sensed his utter lack of welcome despite the vast amount of bosom she revealed to him, the neckline of her gown tugged down as low as possible without actually baring her breasts for all to see. He suspected she was rarely refused and lacked the wit, or was too vain to realize that that had little to do with her charms. Many a man would bed her simply because he had an itch. Gillanders admitted to himself that he might have, too, if his body was not itching for one particular redheaded woman.

"She suits me weel, but I thank ye for your concern," he said. "Best ye get back to the duties ye have now."

Jeanne's smile completely disappeared. She was not so comely when she was angry, he decided.

"Ye do ken that she has been told to inform our laird of all ye do and say, dinnae ye?"

"Aye, the poor lass, ordered to bore the men each and every day with the tedious details of how I eat, sleep, and wash." He stepped back from her. "If ye think to tell me that ye wouldnae be ordered to do the same, ye would be a liar."

"Jeanne! What are ye doing up here?" demanded Mistress McKee as she marched up and grabbed the younger woman by the arm. "I hope she hasnae been troubling ye, sir."

"I was but asking Sir Baldwin if there was aught he needed," said Jeanne, trying to look innocent and subservient and failing miserably.

"Aye, I suspicion ye were. Go back to your work."

The venomous look Jeanne gave the woman before striding away should have left Mistress McKee trembling in fear, but the older woman was clearly made of steel, mused Gillanders. He hoped the woman did not think he had lured Jeanne to his chambers. Mistress McKee ran the keep, and he got the best of all that could be offered to a guest. She could easily make his stay vastly uncomfortable if she became disappointed in him.

" 'Tis nay your fault, mistress," he said. "Ye are but one woman and cannae be expected to ken everything the many people under your guidance are doing every minute of every day."

"Thank ye, sir. It can be most trying at times. Have ye need of anything else ere ye retire for the night? I can find Murdina for ye."

"I wouldnae mind a wee bit more of this fine mulled cider, mistress."

" 'Tis a fine drink to end the day. That it is. I will see to it."

After she left, Gillanders entered his bedchamber. He stoked the fire, shed his shirt, and sprawled in one of the large chairs facing the fire. It had been four long days since he had kissed Murdina, but he could still taste the sweetness of her mouth. She had become very adept at staying out of his reach, however. This time she would not slip away from him so easily. If naught else, he was eager to see if her kiss tasted as sweet to him a second time.

Murdina scowled at the door. She had been about to go to sleep when Mistress McKee had dragged her out of bed to bring Sir Gillanders some mulled cider. Just because the man liked to stay awake half the night did not mean everyone did. She could not sleep until the middle of the day as he did. She rapped on the door, wishing she could tell him just what she thought of his calling for drink at a time when most of the keep was sleeping soundly.

When she entered the room and saw him seated before the fire, flaunting his fine, broad chest again, she almost rolled her eyes. Her heart still pounded and her palms still itched with the need to touch him, but she was becoming more accustomed to the sight. It was not something she would ever become tired of seeing, she mused, but it no longer made her react like some shy child. The fact that there was no sign of any sword cut after but a short time of healing did trouble her a little, but she easily shrugged it aside. The man could be blessed with a stout con-

stitution, and the wound might not have been as serious as some
had thought it to be.

She could feel his gaze on her as she hung the small pot of
mulled cider over the fire so that the drink would keep warm
and scent the room with its spices. After filling a tankard, she
turned to hand it to him and tried not to let her annoyance be
banished by his smile. The man was too handsome, too skilled
at beguiling a lass for his own good, and he knew it.

When she held out the tankard to him, he took hold of it by
firmly wrapping his hand around hers. Not wishing to spill hot
cider over both of them, she tried to carefully slide her hand free,
but he held fast to her as he raised the tankard to his mouth.
Murdina struggled not to fall into his lap and ended up tucked
firmly between his long legs. There was a glint of humor in his
eyes that made her long to hit him, but everything else about
him told her that he was going to try and steal another kiss, maybe
more.

Murdina wanted to order him to release her, to end all his se-
ductive games for she was not a woman who could be had so easily, but the words would not come. She began to suspect she could
be. Everything about Sir Gillanders drew her to him despite all the
very sensible lectures she gave herself. Even reminding herself that
he saw her as no more than some maid he could use and then toss
aside did nothing to dim her deep attraction to him. A wicked
part of her was nearly begging to be used.

" 'Tis a fine cider," Gillanders said as he tugged her even closer
until her nose nearly touched his. "The blend of spices near as perfect as any I have ever tasted. Have ye e'er had a drink of it?"

"Nay, sir, 'tis too rich for a maid to be offered it," she said.
"Now, sir, I would ask ye kindly that ye . . ."

"Let ye taste it? T'would be my pleasure."

He kissed her just as she tensed to pull away from him, and
immediately Murdina lost all urge to do so. The soft thud of the
tankard's being set down on the table by the chair caught her attention, but the thrust of his tongue into her mouth scattered her
thoughts again. He tasted so good, and the lingering flavor of the
mulled cider had little to do with it. Despite the voice of caution in her mind that warned her it would be a grave mistake to
touch him, she did. The warmth of his smooth skin beneath her
hands as she stroked the broad chest she had admired so often

burned away what little control she had over her rising desire. She could feel his hunger for her, and it made her own yearning grow by leaps and bounds. The fact that such a man desired her was intoxicating.

It was his soft groan, one filled with desire and approval of her touch, that pulled her out of the passionate haze she had stumbled into. This was no dream. She was pressed against his body so tightly she could feel his hard length against her body, feel it pressed close to the very place that ached for it. The realization that she was thinking about rubbing herself against that hardness was enough to bring her to her senses. Murdina wondered why she did not feel better about herself as she pulled away from him.

"Nay, I told ye, sir, that I willnae be your plaything whilst ye stay here," she snapped and, without taking her leave as she should, she ran out of the room.

It was a graceless retreat and, far worse in her mind, she knew she would not stay away. Her duties would bring her back into the reach of that temptation again and again until Sir Gillanders went away. While the sensible part of her said his leaving would be for the best, the part of her that was so fiercely drawn to the man ached with sorrow at the very thought of his going away. Murdina prayed that a good night's rest would restore her good sense, but she feared her sleep, when it finally came, would be filled with the dreams of all she now craved. She had not only tasted a deep desire for the first time in her life, but she had tasted the depth of his for her as well, and that was certain to haunt her dreams for a very long time.

Gillanders cursed as he stood up, so hard with need that the mere act of standing hurt. It would be a long time before he could sleep. He had no doubt what he would be dreaming about, either, if he were blessed with any sleep at all. The hunger he ached with now would be tormenting him all night long.

He also had to deal with that touch of guilt for attempting to seduce a woman who was obviously a virgin. Gillanders could almost hear his mother's *tsk* of disappointment in him. She paid little heed to the women the young men dallied with, only warning the men to be certain they left no child behind and unprotected, but she heartily disapproved of seducing the innocent. All of the men at Cambrun now heeded to warnings about being certain they left no child behind. No one liked to think of how many might have died because they had believed for so long that they could not have children. The discovery of the Lost Ones, people with MacNachton blood left to fend for themselves and too often being killed by superstitious fools, had been a hard lesson they had all taken to heart. Seducing the innocent was one lesson taught, however, that only some of them tried to heed.

The thought of the children they had lost and the ones they had found had Gillanders thinking of his own children yet to come. When the images in his head revealed a small girl with blood red hair and eyes a mix of blue and green, he cursed. It could be the result of his hunger for Murdina, but he had the sinking feeling that it was much, much more.

He was going to have to try and get her to travel to Cambrun with him and not just to meet her cousin. The more he thought of the way he wanted her, teased her, and thought of her all the time, the more he began to think she might be the gift that all MacNachton males wanted to receive. Murdina Dunbar could be his mate.

A mate who had not one tiny drop of MacNachton blood in her, he thought as he began to wash up before seeking his bed. He did not think she had anything different about her; she even seemed lacking in some of the strange gifts that made some women such perfect mates for the MacNachton men. Such gifts gave them the ability to accept what he and his kin were, what they had to do to survive. They had tasted the poison of the superstitious fears of others and also knew that there were things and people in this world who were different.

"Weel, she will have to learn," he told himself as he crawled into bed. "Her cousin is married to one of us, and if she wishes to be with her own blood again, then she shall have to accept the family that kin has joined."

Easier said than done, he thought. He would have to tread warily, easing her toward seeing the truth. Gentle steps were needed or she would run from him as fast as she could. The mere thought of how she might look upon him with horror when she found out the truth struck him with a deep, sharp pain in his heart, and he sighed with resignation. Murdina had already become more important to him than a woman who could give him some pleasure during his stay at Dunnantinny. The trip to Cambrun was going to be long and hazardous, and not just because some of the laird's men might try to follow them. Every step he would be taking could well decide his future.

Chapter Four

"He is one of them, of that I have nay doubt."

"Nor do I, Egan, but he gives us no proof of it at all," grumbled Sir Ranald. "The mon makes my innards clench with anger every time he speaks, and I would enjoy cutting out his clever tongue, but I willnae declare him the one of the ones we seek until I am certain. I have no wish to be made a fool of because I acted too quickly and was wrong."

Murdina paused near the door of the laird's tiny ledger room. She had been ordered to bring the man some wine and had worried with every step toward the room that she would be punished for being too slow to obey the command. It was not her fault, but she knew men like Sir Ranald would not care about that. He was the sort of man who expected immediate obedience even if the one he had commanded had to crawl over broken glass to accomplish the chore. The only thing that had delayed her was the need to find Mistress McKee to let her into the room where the wine was kept, deep in the underbelly of the keep.

Curiosity about what the two men were saying stopped her now, all thought of possible punishment pushed aside. She knew they spoke of Sir Gillanders. He was the only one at the keep who could be said to have a clever tongue. He was also the only one she could think of who would inspire caution from Sir Ranald. If they needed proof of something from anyone else, she was certain they would just beat it out of the man. Or woman. Murdina had quickly seen that the men of Dunnantinny were not at all hesitant to raise a fist to a woman.

"The Dunbar lass isnae giving us much news of the bastard."

"Nay, but I suspicion he gives her little to see or hear. Those MacNachton demons havenae survived for so long by being fools easily beguiled by some bonnie lass."

"Many a clever laddie has fallen into trouble atween a pair of fine, white thighs," said Egan.

"True enough." The laird laughed, and Murdina shivered as the cold, raspy noise scratched at her ears. "But, I dinnae think he has e'en bedded her."

"That is strange, is it nay? She is a fair piece and a fine armful for a mon."

"True, but he might ken weel how easily he could reveal his true self to a lass sharing his bed. Ye are keeping a close watch upon all our people, aye?"

"Aye. He hasnae attacked anyone. If 'tis true that his ilk needs blood, he isnae taking it from our people."

"The animals? Horses? Cows?"

"Nay them either. Cannae see any sign of it."

"He should have sought some out after ye wounded him."

"A wound I ken was deep, yet he suffered little trouble with it. It healed as if by magic."

"Which should have been because he got some blood somewhere."

"Are ye sure that is true? The blood drinking and all?" asked Egan.

"The Laird says it is," Sir Ranald replied, his tone one of a man quoting the words of some great prophet. "He has been hunting the MacNachtons all his life, has seen proof of their fiendish ways and vile hungers with his own eyes. One of his men saw this mon and swears he is one of them. Aye, I doubted all The Laird said, but recalled that mon from the village, the one who bedded Anne Drummond, bred a little beast on her, and then tried to return to his clan. This mon has the same look, the verra same reluctance to face the light of day. He claims to be here to see if we will ally with him in trade or in war but says little about what he wants and why. I think we have played this game with him long enough."

"So we kill him?" asked Egan, eagerness in his voice.

"Nay unless we must. The Laird wants the mon. The Laird searches for the secrets of the strengths and weaknesses of the

MacNachtons. He needs live ones. So we secure the bastard and then send word to The Laird. He will let us ken when and where to send our sly demon."

"Shall I take some men and see to that now?"

"We will give the mon one more night to play his games, fill him with wine, and then catch him in his sleep. Pick five strong men to help us."

"Five?"

"If The Laird speaks true, we will need at least that many to secure our captive."

"Jesu! What *are* these people? Six men to take down one? Is The Laird sane?"

"Verra sane. These are demons, Egan. Satan's own. That mon who bred a wee demon on Anne Drummond killed four men with his bare hands. And his teeth. Ne'er forget that, Egan. He killed armed men with his teeth. He ripped the throats right out of the men. I have his skull. I saw the teeth. I have found two others as well, and so, aye, I believe him. They are naught but monsters. Animals in men's skins."

Murdina glanced at the wine she had brought and thought that Sir Ranald did not really need any more drink. To speak such nonsense he had to have had more than enough already. Quietly, she backed away from the door and then walked up to it making certain that the men in the room could hear her footsteps. She used the time to calm herself and to keep all knowledge of what she had just overheard from her face. After taking a deep breath and letting it out slowly to further calm herself, she rapped on the door, entering the room the moment after the laird called out to her. She almost stepped right back out, for the whole room smelled of fear, anger, and violence, all directed at a man she kept dreaming of kissing.

"Ye took long enough, woman," snapped Sir Ranald as Murdina set the tray down on his writing table and poured a tankard of wine each for the laird and Egan.

"It took some time to find Mistress McKee and the key, m'laird," she replied, deciding it did not hurt to at least try and explain her tardiness.

Sir Ranald grunted and took a long drink before asking, "Any news of our guest?"

"He is resting, m'laird," she replied.

"Resting? 'Tis the middle of the day."

"He keeps late hours, m'laird." She shrugged. "He reads of a night, works on papers or letters, cleans his weapons, and such as that. If my father was called to tend to something that kept him working late, he, too, would rest during the day if his work allowed it. Mayhap Sir Baldwin keeps such hours when he is at home and thus has fallen into the habit of it all."

She quickly stopped talking when she saw how closely both men eyed her. Either her tone or her words must have hinted that she was doing more than just babbling; she was stoutly defending Sir Gillanders. She had been, but that was the very last thing she wanted these two hard-eyed men to think. Murdina did not wish to lose her place as Sir Gillanders's maid, nor did she want them to grow as suspicious of her as they were of him.

"So he avoids the heart of the day and thus the sun," said Sir Ranald.

" 'Tis difficult to rest beneath the harsh light of the sun, m'laird, but, aye, he does darken the room. I did question it once when he said he didnae wish me to open the drapes, but he explained his reasons for that."

"Did he? And what did he say?"

"That his eyes are verra sensitive to the strong light of the day." Murdina hoped Sir Gillanders would forgive her for revealing that, but she was compelled to try and ease the suspicions the laird held. "He does have eyes of a most unusual color. It wouldnae be so strange if they had such a weakness."

"Nay, I suspicion it wouldnae be so strange for his eyes to have such trouble. Ye may go now."

Accustomed to the laird's abrupt dismissals and eager to get away before he thought of more questions to ask, Murdina strode out of the room. She considered lurking outside the door to see if she could hear more of their plans for Sir Gillanders, but shook the idea from her head. If the laird and Egan wished to continue their discussion, they would now check to be certain she was gone. As quickly as she could without actually running, Murdina went to the kitchens.

Her heart was thundering, stirred by all the wild thoughts running through her mind. She did not know what to do about all she had just heard. Sir Gillanders was in danger, yet should she risk her own life for a man she barely knew, a man who shamelessly taunted her with his beauty and kissed her without permission? A man who could take a sword thrust and healed from it as if touched by an angel? This was not her trouble. She was only a lowly maid who both the laird and Sir Gillanders had tried to use as a spy. Sir Gillanders was definitely playing some game with the laird.

But has he done anything he should die for? she asked herself. The answer was an immediate no. Sir Gillanders Baldwin, or whatever his true name was, might be a seducer, a man with neither morals nor humility, but he was certainly not the monster the laird thought he was. Murdina was certain she would have seen the demon in Sir Gillanders after so many days of serving him. She had touched evil before and knew its chill. Touching Gillanders had never given her the same feeling. With her gift, it would be very hard for a true demon to hide himself and all he was from her.

There was one thing that strongly roused her suspicions about the man. If he was the MacNachton Sir Ranald thought he was, why had he not told her anything about her cousin? The man by the graves of her aunt and uncle had been certain Adeline had left with a MacNachton. Sir Gillanders had to know something about her fate, yet he had said nothing, had acted as if he did not really know the woman. Perhaps he was hiding the fact that poor Adeline had been killed by his clansman.

After a moment's thought, she sighed and shook her head at her own foolishness. She was allowing the fear and suspicion of Sir Ranald and Egan to affect her. Sir Gillanders could not speak of Adeline or admit to knowing who the woman was if he was truly a MacNachton. He was here under false colors for some reason, and telling her he knew about Adeline would rip aside the mask he hid behind.

"Murdina!"

She turned to face Mistress McKee, almost glad to be distracted from her thoughts. Sir Gillanders had one more night. She did not need to make a decision on what she should or should not tell him right this minute. Although she already knew she would warn him, she needed a little time to decide how much to tell him about what Sir Ranald believed. This would be her home for a while longer, and she needed to tread carefully or find herself tossed out.

"Aye, mistress?" Murdina moved out of the pantry where she had gone to idly sort the goods on the shelves and have some privacy to think.

"I need ye to go to the laird's chambers."

"Ye do?"

"Dinnae look so worried. The mon isnae in his chambers but has just ridden out to see if he can hunt down some venison for the table. I cannae do the cleaning there as I had planned to. My daughter is about to give birth, and I need to be with her."

"Of course ye do, mistress. I wish her a safe and easy birthing."

"Thank ye, lass. Ye are a good child. Now, ye dinnae have to scrub the place down. Just change his linens and clear some of the dust. Mayhap clean out the hearth if needed."

Murdina agreed, fetched the things she would need to do the chore, and made her way to the laird's bedchamber. Being a maid who was allowed into the upper chambers was a lot better than being given work in the kitchens or the laundry, she decided. The work was hard, but she worked alone most of the time and that suited her. Then she stepped into the laird's bedchamber and grimaced. The room was soaked in the man's anger and cruelty. She felt as if her skin was crawling with it. As she shut the door, she glanced toward the hearth to see if it needed cleaning and gaped. Three clean skulls were set upon the mantel.

Fighting back the urge to flee the room, she set down the bucket of water she had brought and cautiously approached the hearth. The closer she got, the more she saw that they were real, not some strange carvings. A shudder went through her as she wondered what the people had done to have their bodies treated with such disrespect. Taking a step closer she frowned, for there was something not right about the skulls. It took her a moment of staring hard at each one to realize that there was something wrong with the teeth. It looked as if the ones who had been killed had had fangs like some wolf.

She took a step back and then told herself not to be a fool. The ones who had lost these heads were long dead. Murdina was not sure why the skulls had such teeth, but they looked real enough. She was not prepared to think these were the heads of some demons, however. People were born all the time with some oddity, the same oddity running through entire families. Had her mother not told her that her gift was one that had been in her family for a very long time?

What the gruesome display did tell her was that Sir Gillanders was in grave danger. If this was how anyone with that strange style of teeth was treated, he was a dead man, for she had noted in passing during one of his heady kisses that he did have some very sharp teeth, ones that could be mistaken for fangs. The mere thought that his skull could soon be sitting on some man's mantel made her stomach roll with horror. This barbarity decided her. She needed to warn him of the danger he was in as soon as possible and do so with great secrecy.

Murdina forced her gaze away from the skulls and hurried to clean the room. She was not sure she should tell Sir Gillanders about the skulls. If he was what the laird thought, a MacNachton, he might know who the heads could have belonged to. The news that these heads sat up on a mantel like some macabre decoration would only hurt him. Although she had not noticed that he had teeth as large as those displayed in the skulls, perhaps not every MacNachton got them, or it could be something that became apparent only after death, only when the skull was cleaned of all skin and muscle.

She quickly shook all thought of the skulls from her mind, sickened by the act of displaying such things as if they were prized plunder of some just war. It was a cruel, harsh world they all lived in, but she doubted many men would do such a thing even to their worst enemies. Now that she knew what Sir Ranald was truly capable of, she would have to be very careful when she went to warn Sir Gillanders. She would also have to do her best to make the man believe her when she told him he was in danger. It was going to hurt to send him away, but she could not bear the thought that he might stay and suffer the fate the three men whose heads sat upon the mantel had suffered.

It was not until she finished cleaning the hearth that she looked at the skulls again, each glance easing the horror she had felt upon first seeing them. Now she just felt pity for the men whose ends had to have been brutal, their bodies not allowed to rest in peace. One of these could be the man whose son her cousin had protected. From what she had heard the laird say, she knew for a fact that one of these men had done nothing worth being murdered for, his body then desecrated.

Clenching her hand into a fist so tight her nails dug into her palm, Murdina wondered if she should touch one of them. She had never touched the dead even though she had been sure that her gift would never work once a body's soul had fled, yet, once, she had gotten a feeling from something not alive.

Murdina shivered with cold remembrance of the time when she was barely eight, had picked up the cooper's hammer, and had known, without doubt, that he had killed his wife with it. Her father had heeded her and done well in keeping her away from the man until the truth came out in another way. Her mother had insisted that she should not fear touching everything, that she had seen the vision because there was so much strong emotion left within the hammer. That had been proven true, but it had taken her a very long time before she had dared touch anything with a naked hand. She wondered now if that would hold true for bone, if strong emotion could have sunk straight into the man's bone and still linger.

" 'Tis best to ken it now," she whispered and, her hand shaking, reached out to touch the middle skull.

So many emotional images rushed through her mind that she became nauseous. One thing stood out within the chaos, however: the man's love for his son. And his grief. The pain of knowing he would never see his child grow up to be a man, or be able to make sure he was safe and loved until he did. The wet heat of a tear running down her cheek pulled Murdina free of the hold of that memory, and she yanked her hand back.

"Oh, sir, I think 'tis your son my cousin cares for," she whispered as she brushed the tears from her face. "She will care weel for him. And, although I dinnae ken exactly who ye are, I think your kin is here, and I will see that he doesnae join ye on this mantel."

Murdina gathered the things she had brought to the room and the soiled linen from the bed, and hurried to get rid of it. As soon as that was done, and knowing no one would be looking for her until morning now, she slipped upstairs and hid in a small alcove at the end of the hall where Sir Gillanders's bedchamber was. It was late before the keep grew so quiet she felt it safe to go to his door, and she began to fear it would grow too late to warn him. She rapped softly on the door, keeping a close eye out for anyone approaching. It swung open, and before she could say a word, she was yanked inside, the door shut and latched behind her.

Chapter Five

"Why are ye here?"

Murdina stared at Sir Gillanders. She had been right the first day she had seen him. That far too handsome face of his could look frighteningly predatory when he wanted it to. It astonished her that she was more fascinated than terrified. She also noticed that he was fully dressed in his bedchamber for the first time since she had become his maid.

"I have come to warn ye, Sir Gillanders," she said, frowning when he began to back up toward the bed with her still held tight against him. "I am thinking it might be wise if ye leave this place."

"Why would ye think that?"

There was a hint of suspicion darkening his fine eyes, although his hold on her was neither punishing nor painful, simply firm. That touch of suspicion stung, however. Murdina did not think she had done anything to deserve it. The man knew she had been told to watch him closely, something she had readily confessed to, and he had declared this a common practice at keeps. He had to know she had told the laird nothing of importance as well for, as far as she had seen, he had revealed very little about himself.

"Because I have just heard the laird and Egan talking about you," she replied. "Weel, nay just heard. A wee while ago, as it took me some time to get here since I didnae want anyone to see me do so when ye hadnae called for me. They are certain ye are nay who ye say ye are and that ye are nay here to treaty with them or do trade with them."

"Aye, I had gleaned that much but a short while ago."

"Had ye now. Weel, did ye also *glean* that they think ye are something evil, some demon? They are even watching all of their people and animals to see if ye are drinking blood from them. They truly believe ye are some monster."

Gillanders inwardly cursed. He was glad he had heeded his father and brought a goodly supply of blood-enriched wine with him. It had kept him from seeking some blood elsewhere after he had been wounded in that bout of swordplay with the laird's men, men who did not appear to understand that practicing one's skill with a sword usually meant you did not attempt to kill or maim your opponent. That the laird had kept a close watch on all sources of blood he might have sought confirmed Gillanders's suspicion that the laird knew exactly who he was, might even have encouraged his men to wound him to test him in some way. Giving the man nothing to confirm those suspicions was obviously not enough anymore.

"A strange thing for them to accuse a mon of," he murmured as he sat on the edge of the bed, forcing her to step between his legs.

"That is not all that is strange. They think ye are one of a clan named MacNachton and truly believe that ye are some demon. Called the whole clan demons, animals in men's skins. And, Egan wished to kill ye right now."

"I should like to see him try."

Murdina ignored that bit of manly boasting. "The laird doesnae want that. He wants ye captured and held for someone he calls The Laird in awed tones. 'Tis strange that he would call another mon simply The Laird when he is one himself."

"Mayhap he doesnae ken the mon's name." Gillanders wondered if she was aware of how easily and quickly he could have her sprawled beneath him on the bed, a place he had ached to have her since the first time he had seen her.

"That would be strange as weel since he means to hand ye over to the mon. He must ken something or he wouldnae be able to send word that he has something the mon wants. And it seems one of The Laird's men lurks about here freely, for he is the one who recognized you and spoke to Sir Ranald about you. And why should this laird be so concerned with getting ye alive if he is an enemy of yours? 'Tis what Sir Ranald said, that The Laird wants any of your ilk one can find delivered to him alive so that he can discover the secrets of your strengths and weaknesses. Ye have a most powerful enemy, Sir Gillanders, and one who sounds most insane. From all I heard, ye dinnae want this strange laird to get his hands on you."

"Nay, that is true enough. Yet, I might still find out what I came here to learn if I am careful."

"What did ye really come here for?"

"To discover who murdered my cousin Arailt. He had a lover here, bred a son, and was slaughtered here as he tried to get to us so that we might help him protect his son."

"Oh. Was his lover Anne Drummond?"

"Aye. They mentioned her, did they?"

She nodded, a chill snaking down her spine as she recalled all they had said. "Your cousin is the reason they intend to send six men to capture ye and take ye to the dungeon. Sir Ranald said the mon who was murdered killed four men with his bare hands and his teeth. Sir Ranald was told of it by this laird. He believes it for"—she grimaced and looked at him, unable to hide how much she wished she did not have to tell him all she had heard— "he has your cousin's skull. He says he saw the teeth."

Gillanders swore and prayed he might have the chance to make Sir Ranald pay for that desecration of his cousin's body.

"Egan still questions The Laird's sanity, and I think he is right to do so. Yet, for all that, there will still be six men coming after ye to take ye captive. Ye have but one more night to, as Sir Ranald says, play your games. For all I ken, they may weel have counted this night as that one more. So ye must see that ye have to leave this place as quickly as ye can."

He was touched by her concern. The news that Arailt had put up a good fight and taken some of his killers down with him eased some of Gillanders's grief over the loss of a good man, but none of his fury over the killing. The pleasure of that knowledge was somewhat dimmed by Murdina's disbelief in all Sir Ranald had said. The fact that she did not believe what she had heard, undoubtedly thought Sir Ranald and Egan fools for heeding a strange man known only as The Laird, did not bode well for him. At the moment, however, it served him well, for her disbelief had helped to make her run to him with a timely warning.

"I had already begun to think it was time to leave," he said, bringing her face closer to his and brushing his lips over her mouth. "Howbeit, I do thank ye for the warning."

Murdina told herself to break free of his hold, but good sense had fled the moment his lips had touched hers. All she could think of was that he was going to leave, that the first man to ever stir a woman's fire within her was about to go away. The thought of never seeing him again made her reckless and greedy. She had nothing in her life, not even family. It would be wonderful if, just for a little while, someone would make her feel wanted, cared for. She slipped her arms around his neck and pressed her mouth more firmly against his, savoring the hot sweetness of his kiss and letting the heat of it flood her body.

Gillanders knew the moment she gave in to her desire. Her whole body softened against him, the faint stiffness of uncertainty fleeing her small, lush figure. He pushed her down onto the bed and deepened the kiss. Desire was a fire in his veins, an ache that loudly demanded to be satisfied.

As he stroked the inside of her mouth with his tongue, softly growling his approval when she began to respond to the caresses and thrusts of his tongue with some of her own, his mind cleared of all thought save that of feeling her flesh against his. He ran his hands over the soft curves of her body and then unlaced her gown as he kept her drugged with his kisses. Tugging her bodice down, he pressed a kiss between her breasts, fighting the need to immediately feast upon the plump, rose-tipped curves. He also had to fight the urge to nip at her long, slim throat, the sight and sound of the rapid pulse in the vein there clouding his mind with the dark hunger the MacNachtons were cursed with.

"Ah, lass, ye are beautiful." He licked the hard tip of each breast, her soft gasp of pleasure music to his ears. "And ye taste as sweet as the finest honey."

Murdina was briefly shocked when he covered the aching tip of her breast and sucked on it like a bairn, but a fierce desire brutally banished her hesitation. She thrust her fingers into his hair, the thick silk of it a soft caress on her hands, and held him close. The way he covered her breasts with kisses, strokes of his tongue, and the skillful touch of his hands soon had her squirming beneath him, her body eager for something more.

In a small, still sane part of her mind she was aware of him tugging up her skirts, but she did not stop him. It was not until he rubbed his hand against her woman's flesh that shock dimmed a little of her pleasure. This was not what she had come here for. Yet, his touch and the way it made her burn caused her thoughts to scatter. It was not until she felt the hint of anger and cruelty invade the sweetness of her pleasure in his arms that her senses returned. She pushed at him, trying to get him to move off her.

"I think someone approaches your bedchamber," she whispered when he frowned at her.

She was just thinking that his eyes were even more beautiful when darkened by a desire she had stirred within him when he leapt up, grabbed her by the arm, and silently urged her to get beneath the bed. From her hiding place she watched as he walked toward the door, reaching it just as a hard rap at it announced a visitor. Murdina was not surprised to see Egan, although it did shock her a little to realize that the man had such strong feelings toward Sir Gillanders she could sense them even before he reached the bedchamber door.

"Why do ye disturb my rest, sir?" Sir Gillanders asked in a voice that made Murdina shiver.

"I was wandering the hall and thought ye might wish to share a drink," said Egan, holding up a jug of wine that Murdina strongly suspected had some dangerous herbs in it.

"Kind of ye to think of me, but, nay. I am still a wee bit weak from our swordplay the other day. It may have been an insignificant wound, but it bled freely, and I find I still tire easily."

"Of course. Then I bid you a good rest, sir."

Gillanders frowned at the door after he shut and bolted it. "Now why did he come to me, I wonder."

As she crawled out from beneath the bed, Murdina asked, "Do ye think they ken that I might have heard their plans for ye and come to warn ye?"

"Nay. I think he but wished to see if I was armed whilst in my bedchamber. Mayhap e'en see just how late I remain awake."

"They planned to make ye drink a lot of wine to be certain that ye went to sleep and slept deeply."

"I did notice how readily they filled my tankard when we dined this evening, and now comes Egan with more. I think they must plan to make me insensible with drink ere they try to take me."

"And they mean to try that tonight."

"It would appear so." He walked to the other side of the bed, picked up the bags he had packed, and set them on the bed.

"Oh. Ye were already planning to leave here." She told herself it was foolish to feel so hurt, but that did not ease the pain that gripped her at the thought of his departure.

"I was. They played their games weel when we dined, but nay so weel that I didnae scent the threat. And I think ye ought to come with me."

She blinked, stunned by the invitation, and not daring to take it as a promise that he cared for her. "Why should I do that? Do ye think I might be in danger, too?"

" 'Tis possible as it willnae take them long to look to you as the one who warned me. But, also, I ken where your cousin is."

"I had wondered when I began to think ye were nay Sir Baldwin but Sir MacNachton. She is with your clan?"

"She is. She has wed my cousin, and they raise Arailt's wee son as their own."

"Then she doesnae truly need me to join her. She begins a family of her own."

Gillanders walked up to her, gently tugged her into his arms, and kissed the top of her head. "Ye are her only living kin just as she is yours. Of course she will want ye to come. And, when all is said and done, do ye have any other place ye can go?"

"Nay." What she wanted was for him to say he wanted her to come with him, for himself, but she beat down the yearning. "Then I shall come. I but need to gather a few things."

"Then hurry, lass. We need to be away from here as quickly as possible if we are to put distance between us and Sir Ranald's men."

"Ye think they will try to chase us down?"

"Aye. If all ye say he believes about me and mine, his awe of that laird, is true, he will wish to capture me ere I can get to Cambrun."

"And how do we flee unseen from a crowded keep? Many are abed, but there are all the guards to worry about."

"I ne'er stay anywhere without finding out exactly how to flee unseen if I must. Trust me in this, I ken exactly how to get out of here with nary a one seeing us leave."

She nodded and stepped away from him. "I just wish I could

pack my wee pony," she mumbled as she started toward the door. "Poor beastie doesnae deserve the fate of being left in the hands of men like these."

Gillanders stared at the door as it shut behind her. They would be taking her pony, but he would let her discover that later. It would not be as fast as a horse, but it would be better than one horse trying to travel a long way, perhaps at a fast pace at times, with two people and all their belongings packed on it.

He frowned as he thought on how she had known Egan approached before he himself had even heard the man's steps. It was hard to believe she could have better hearing than a man like him with both Callan and MacNachton blood in his veins. Nor did he think she was a trap set by Sir Ranald. Yet, she should not have been able to tell that someone was approaching them as she had. It was something he was going to have to ask her about. There was a chance that little Murdina had a secret or two of her own.

Murdina shoved her meager belongings into a sack she had taken from the kitchen. She already had bread, cheese, and wine in there. It had been difficult to overcome the abhorrence of stealing, but she had done so, deciding that men like Sir Ranald did not deserve loyalty.

Her heart pounded with an uncomfortable mix of fear and excitement. She was about to mark herself as the one who had warned Sir Gillanders, the one who had helped the prize Sir Ranald sought to slip out of his grasp. When compared to that crime, a little theft was nothing. She would never be able to come back this way, however. She knew the laird had a long memory when it concerned people he believed had wronged him.

Some of her fear, and also the excitement she could not quell, came from the fact that she was about to embark on a journey with a man who made her blood heat with desire. Murdina knew they would become lovers once they were away from the keep. She also knew she ought to be alarmed by that, for she would be giving away her only dowry to a man who gave her no vows or love words. That did frighten her but not enough to make her turn away from it.

She could touch him. It all came down to that simple fact. She could put her hands on the man and feel only calm or desire. If he had any evil in him, it was well buried. Even the shadow she could sense beneath the calm, beneath things like loyalty, love for his clan, and honesty, carried no tinge of evil.

"Ah, Mother dear, your lass is about to become a fallen woman," she whispered as she gazed upward to the ceiling. "I but pray that, if ye are watching, ye will understand and forgive. I can touch him, Mother. 'Tis such a wonder that I cannae turn from it. And, aye, I do believe I may be in love with the fool."

She collected her things and walked toward the door of the tiny room she had been given once she had been given the chore of being a maid to an honored guest. The room was dark, cold, and often damp, little more than a niche in the wall with a thin door, but it had been hers alone for a short time. After being crowded in with all the other maids who did the lowest and dirtiest of the chores, it had been a pleasure to have the tiny space. She hoped there would be a tiny space for her somewhere at Cambrun.

"I begin my adventure now, Mother," she whispered. "Please watch over me and Sir Gillanders. Even if he isnae the mon who will stay with me, he is still a good mon."

She slipped out of her room and headed toward Sir Ranald's bedchamber. There was one more thing she had to pack to take with them. This time she had no hesitation about the theft she was about to commit.

Chapter Six

Gillanders picked his pack up, tossed it back down on the bed, and resumed pacing his room. He had wavered between waiting a little longer for Murdina and simply leaving without her. It was easy to convince himself that a much needed stealth was the reason she was taking so long to return, but it was also easy to convince himself that she had changed her mind and was not going to ride to Cambrun with him. The latter possibility troubled him far more than he wanted to admit.

He finally sat down on the edge of the bed, crossed his arms over his chest, and stared at the door. If she did not appear soon, he would hunt her down. Murdina thought she had been unseen when she had come to warn him, but he was not so certain. Since she had no skill at stealth, had never been trained to it, she could have been seen but simply not known it. The reason she had not joined him yet could be because Sir Ranald or one of his men had caught her warning him or even caught her as she was trying to join him now. His stomach knotted at the thought of Murdina's facing an angry Sir Ranald.

The sound of a soft footstep just outside his door brought him to his feet. He was standing at the side of the door, dagger in hand, as it was eased open. Murdina's scent came to him first, but he remained tense until he was absolutely certain there was no one with her. The moment he was sure she was alone, he tugged her into the room and shut the door. Relieved that she was safe and with him again, he pulled her into his arms and kissed her.

Murdina let the heat of his kiss melt away her fear, but before she sank beneath the fog of desire he could so easily rouse in her, she backed away from him. "We dinnae have time for that, I think."

"Nay, true enough. A shame that." He frowned when he realized she carried two sacks. "Do ye wish me to carry one of those? They look to be quite a burden."

"Oh, nay. One contains what little I own and some food. And, the other? Weel, the laird is spending time with his mistress in the village as is his habit, ye ken. So, I went into his bedchamber and took the skulls," she confessed, her voice slowly fading away to a whisper. "I wasnae sure what ye would do with them but, if they are your kin, I thought ye would at best wish them removed from Sir Ranald's mantel. I think one may be of the cousin ye lost."

"Why would ye think that? Because he was murdered near here?"

It was very tempting to tell him that she had merely guessed, as he suggested, but she fought against giving in to that cowardice. The man had a right to know the truth, even if it changed his mind about taking her with him. If he pushed her away now, at least she could slip back to her little bed. Once on the journey to Cambrun she could find herself deserted in the middle of a strange land. Murdina did not think he would do such a cruel thing, but she had never faced anyone squarely and told him the truth about her gift.

"I touched one." She sighed when he looked at her in confusion. "I have always had a strong intuition about people. S'truth, ye are the first person I have willingly touched in many a year, aside from my own parents. When I touch a person I can feel a great deal about who they are, what they feel. Ye just feel calm but with a wee shadow behind it all. Sir Ranald feels angry and cruel. So does Egan."

"And ye felt that when he approached. 'Tis how ye kenned he was coming to the room."

"Aye. Once I did get a feeling from a hammer the cooper in my village used to beat his wife to death. So, I do all I can to touch no one and to touch very few things, especially things like daggers and swords. That has nay been easy to do in such a crowded keep."

"Ye touched the skulls."

Relaxing a little when she sensed no revulsion or fear in him, she nodded. "Just one. I got the feeling of deep grief, the grief of a mon who kenned he would ne'er see his son grow to be a mon nor be able to protect that child as he grew."

"Did ye see who killed him?"

Murdina realized that Sir Gillanders was no stranger to such gifts, his calm as she spoke one of utter acceptance. "Nay. I dinnae truly *see*, I just *feel*. 'Tis true that, at times, it is as if I see something, but it comes from the emotion's being verra, verra strong. 'Tis difficult to explain, but, with the hammer I spoke of, I could feel the woman's pain and the cooper's fury and hate."

He nodded. "So it was nay so verra hard to ken just what he had done with that hammer." He took the bag holding the skulls from her. "We will take this because, aye, I suspicion they are the skulls of my kinsmen, and they should be returned to Cambrun. Mayhap, when we reach my home, ye can touch them if it doesnae repel ye, and discover enough that we may ken exactly who has been returned home."

"I can try but 'tis just the skulls. Are ye certain your clan will want them returned?"

" 'Tis more than we have of them now. So, come, lass, 'tis time we left this cursed place."

Stunned at how easily he accepted something she had hidden all her life, Murdina silently followed him. There was a chance the MacNachtons had more oddities in their blood than a tendency to grow very sharp teeth. If that was true, if some of his people had gifts such as she had, for once in her life she would be able to cease fearing that someone would discover what she could do and decry her as a witch.

Murdina forced herself to concentrate on following Sir Gillanders as carefully as she could and not getting caught. The man slipped from shadow to shadow with ease as he led her down into the bowels of the keep. He had not been boasting when he had claimed he already knew how to slip away without being seen. The bolt-hole he led her through was long, narrow, dark, and damp, but she caged her fear.

Once out of it and in the stables, she wondered how they could silently escape with his horse. That was not an animal one could easily hide in the shadows. Before she could ask, he had readied his horse and her sturdy pony, secured their belongings to the saddles, and was leading his mount toward the back of the large stables. She grabbed the reins of her pony and followed him.

"Another bolt-hole?" she whispered as he opened a thick wooden door to reveal a large, ironbound one.

"Sir Ranald obviously plans to flee on horseback if pressed to it. I wondered when I saw how the stables were built hard up against the curtain wall. It did take a while to be able to open both doors and the iron-gate though. On the outside is a steep hillside, difficult for an enemy to descend unseen by men on the walls, so this proved not to be the weakness I thought it to be. It is, however, a way to leave this place unseen with a mount to help us put a lot of miles between us and this cursed place ere we are discovered to be gone."

It all worked just as he said it would, but the fear that they would be caught did not leave Murdina until they were several miles away. She could no longer see the keep, and there had been no outcry, so she began to believe that they had actually succeeded in escaping. It would be several hours yet before the laird left his mistress's bed, returned to gather the six men he thought he needed to subdue and capture Sir Gillanders, and found only an empty bed. Murdina wished she knew exactly how much effort the man would exert to hunt them down. She rested her head against Gillanders's broad back, closed her eyes, and prayed the laird simply accepted his loss and stayed at Dunnantinny.

The sun was barely peeking over the horizon when Gillanders found a place for them to rest for a few hours. One thing he had gained from his mother was far more tolerance for the sun than many another MacNachton. The height of the day was still dangerous, however. During those hours, especially if the sun shone brightly, he could be seriously weakened and would need blood to recover his strength. That was something he wished to avoid.

He nudged Murdina awake, smiling at the way she rubbed her eyes then blinked sleepily as she looked around. As soon as he dismounted he helped her off her pony and pretended not to notice how she winced. A blacksmith's daughter might know a lot about horses, but he doubted she had ridden one very often.

Her pony was probably one the family had had to pull a cart or help at the forge.

"A shieling?" she asked as she walked around in a small circle, attempting to ease the stiffness in her legs, and studied the small stone and thatch building.

"Enough shelter for us to rest for a wee while," he said as he tended to their mounts. "Aye, and to allow our mounts to have a wee rest as well."

"I am certain they are in need of one." She paused next to her pony and scratched at his ears, earning an affectionate nudge from the animal.

"Do ye think we will be safe here?"

"Aye. For a few hours. Enough to have a bite to eat, a wash, and a rest."

Gillanders spoke even as he walked into the shieling, and she quickly followed him. It was not until they had washed the dust of travel away, eaten a little, and prepared to take a rest that Murdina realized Gillanders was anticipating a great deal more than a rest. While she had cleared away what they had used to have their meager meal, he had set out their blankets. He had also stripped down to his braes and was now lying on the blanket, his arms crossed beneath his head, watching her closely. The desire he had for her was so clear and strong she could almost scent it in the air.

She hesitated only a moment before shedding her gown and slipping beneath the blanket they would use for a cover. He was the one she wanted. He was the only man she had ever been able to touch freely. In most people's eyes it would seem wrong of her to want to give herself to him when he had not even offered a future together for them, but she did not care. The ability to touch him without being drowned in feelings of every sort was a blessing she could not ignore. This might be the only time she could learn just what could be shared between a man and a woman. If she ended up alone, it would hurt, but not as much as having missed this chance to know the things that had made her mother smile whenever the woman looked at Murdina's father.

Gillanders turned on his side, wrapped an arm around her waist, and tugged her close. "I do heed a nay when 'tis said, lass."

"I ken it," she said, knowing she was blushing but trying to ignore it. "I find I am nay inclined to say it."

"I cannae tell ye how much it pleases me to hear ye say so."

He did not have to tell her, she could feel it. As he kissed her, his tongue stroking the inside of her mouth in a way that had her clinging to him, Murdina sensed his desire, and it fed her own. This would truly be a sharing, she thought, fighting not to tense with shyness as he rid her of her shift. The moment he pulled her back into his arms and their flesh touched for the first time, she ceased to worry about her decision. She was skin to skin with a man, and all she felt was desire, his and hers. She would be a fool to run from this.

Gillanders knew the moment she had shed all doubt, for her body nestled against his in a welcome that had his heart racing like that of some untried boy. He kissed her until that soft haze made her eyes the color of the sea and then began to kiss his way down to her breasts. As she stroked his back and arms, he could feel the faint roughness there, but the rest of her skin was as soft and sweet as he had thought it would be. He silently promised her that she would never have to suffer the roughness of hard work on her hands again.

The rose-colored tips of her breasts were hard and beckoning, and Gillanders feasted on them. He slid his hand down over her taut stomach and between her legs. She tensed a little but that faded as he caressed her. The damp welcome of her desire was quick to form, and he had to grit his teeth against the urge to thrust himself into her heat as quickly as possible. He eased a finger inside her, feeding that desire and readying her for his possession. By the time he slid a second finger into her heat, she was breathing heavily and arching to his touch. Gillanders wanted to kiss her there, to taste her passion, but beat down the need for she was a virgin. Some of the things a man and woman could enjoy in bed would be a little too frightening for one who had never had a man. He would save that pleasure for later.

Shaking a little from the strength of his own passion, Gillanders settled himself between her legs as he kissed her. Slowly he eased into her and met the proof of her innocence. Taking a deep breath to steady himself, he thrust deep inside, breaking through the barrier, and swallowed her soft cry of pain with his kiss. Sweat trickled down his spine as he held himself still so that she could adjust to the invasion, but he doubted he could hold still for long. He prayed the loss of her innocence had not killed all of her desire.

Murdina held tight to Gillanders as she caught her breath. The pain of the loss of her maidenhead was rapidly fading, an ache for more replacing it. She curled her legs around his lean hips, and he groaned, pressing his face against her throat. Murdina almost smiled, for she could sense his need as well as how fiercely he was fighting to control it. She shifted her hips, pulling him deeper into her body, and shivered with the pleasure of it.

"Has the pain eased?" he asked in a voice made hoarse with the fight to remain still.

"Oh, aye," she whispered, and kissed him.

A heartbeat later he began to move, and Murdina gasped from the ferocity of the desire that flooded her. She knew some of that was from him, but her own body was savoring the joining, reaching out for the joy he could give her. A strange tightness began to build low in her belly as she moved into a perfect rhythm with him. It was the bliss her mother had told her about when she had reached the age to notice men. Murdina reached for it, shifting her body so that he filled her completely with every thrust of his strong body. When that tightness snapped she was flooded with a joy that was tinged with a delectable pain and cried out his name. Even as she sank beneath the waves of pleasure washing over her, she heard him call out her name and felt the warmth of his seed flood her womb.

Still reeling from what they had shared, she barely moved as he fetched a cloth to wipe the signs of her lost innocence off of them both. When he returned to her side and pulled her into his arms, she nestled as close to him as she could, savoring the warmth of him, even his scent. She loved the man, of that she had no doubt. It was why she had been ready to take the risk and give away her innocence despite no words of love. It hurt a little that he had not filled her ears with promises of a future and words of love, but she shook that aside. She would win his love and, if she did not, she would still cherish what they had shared.

"I tried to nay hurt ye, lass," began Gillanders, rubbing his cheek against her hair.

"Ye didnae. T'was but a wee sharp pain that quickly faded."

"Good. Rest now. We still have a long journey ahead and one that might be fraught with danger."

"Because ye believe Sir Ranald will be chasing us."

"Aye. I must believe that so that I remain vigilant." He briefly tilted her face up to his, brushed a kiss over her mouth, and then tucked her face up against his neck. "Sleep. Ye, too, will need to be rested enough to remain vigilant."

She closed her eyes and enjoyed the way he ran his fingers up and down her back. There was a pleasure to be found in resting skin to skin with this man, all desire sated, and peace surrounding them. Danger might be on their heels but, for this moment, she intended to bask in the sense of peace and contentment he gave her.

Gillanders stared down at the woman in his arms. Despite her innocence she had gifted him with a passion he had never tasted before. He knew what that meant, just as he knew what the urge to mark her that had nearly overcome him as they made love meant. This woman was his mate.

No one was certain why it was so, but MacNachtons did not just marry; they mated. They marked that mate on the neck, the one bite wound that never healed. He ached to see his mark on her pretty neck. Gillanders sighed and had to admit that, if he was not already in love with her, he was very close to it. With most people that would be enough, but she did not know the truth about him yet. It was going to be even harder to tell her now, for the fear that she would turn from him now ran deep. The mere thought of it clutched at his heart.

When she moved her small hand over his heart, he fought against tensing. She was asleep, but he was obviously letting his feelings run so strong that she could sense them even as she slept. Perhaps her gift would be enough to make her more understanding of how different he was. He smiled briefly. It would certainly make her a wife one never lied to.

There was still time before he had to confront her with the truth. He had no doubt about her desire for him. Despite her innocence it had run as hot and wild as his. He would make sure she shared enough of that pleasure with him that it would aid him in getting her to stay with him. He wanted her to love him, but he would take what he could get in the beginning.

Chapter Seven

A fading, late-day sun shone through the trees and touched Murdina's fair skin and long, red hair with a warmth that made Gillanders harden with need from one breath to the next. She was beautiful and passionate, her innocence no barrier to her desire for him. The fierce urge he had to put his mark on her long, slim neck every time they made love told him that she was his mate. One time he might have been able to shrug it aside, but it had happened again. It would be impossible to convince himself otherwise now. The way she looked at him and made love to him told him that, if she were not in love with him now, she soon would be. However, he still faced the problem any Mac-Nachton did upon finding his mate outside the clan. How did he tell her about the need to taste her blood and mark her as his own?

He decided to wait until they were within reach of the gates of Cambrun. Her cousin was there, marked and mated. Adeline would help ease whatever fears Murdina might have about his clan and their ways. As he slipped beneath the blanket and tugged her into his arms, he dreaded the time he would have to tell her what he was, and dreaded it more with every mile they drew closer to his home. He had, at best, but one full night and day left to enjoy the peace they had found together, to savor her smiles and sweet loving, before he put it all to the test with the harsh truth of his existence.

The touch of her small hand on his chest banished his worry. Gillanders smiled when she opened her eyes to look at him, lov-

ing the soft, sleepy look that lingered there. She smiled back at
him, and he knew they would be lingering a while longer beneath the shelter of the trees. He brushed a kiss over her mouth
and felt the tips of her breasts harden against his chest.

"How fare ye, lass? Sore?" he asked as he kissed her throat.

Murdina could feel the heat of a blush stain her cheeks, and,
staring at the hollow at the base of his throat, answered, "Nay, I
am hale."

"Good."

She laughed when he pushed her onto her back, but her amusement faded when he kissed her, passion rising quickly to brush
it aside. Yet again she could sense his desire for her. It fed her
own, blending with it and enriching it. In this, the skill that she
had seen as mostly a curse became the gift her mother had always called it.

Every stroke of his hands added to the heat of her passion.
Murdina caressed him wherever she could, delighting in the
smooth warmth of his skin. She stroked his broad shoulders and
tangled her fingers in his hair as he kissed his way down her body.
It was not until his broad shoulders pushed between her thighs
that she became aware of where his kisses had been leading.
Shock cooled some of the desire racing through her veins, but
with only a few strokes of his tongue it faded away, and she
opened herself to his intimate kisses.

Just as she began to call to him, desperate to have him inside
her, he began to kiss his way back up her body. When his mouth
possessed hers, she wrapped her body around his, silently urging
him to join with her and end the aching need he had roused. She
gasped with pleasure when he thrust inside of her, filling her, and
clung tightly to him as he took them both to that sweet paradise
only he could give her.

It was not until he eased away from her, their breathing having slowly returned to a more normal pace, that Murdina became
all too acutely aware of just how intimate they had been this
time. She could feel a fierce blush burning her cheeks as she
looked at him. Just what did one say when a man gave her such
a sinful pleasure, and was she wrong to have enjoyed it as much
as she had?

Gillanders brushed a kiss over her forehead and idly began to
untangle her hair by combing his fingers through it. "Dinnae look

so worried, lass. I dinnae think we are about to be struck down by God."

His irreverent words and amused tone had annoyance conquering her embarrassment. "Nay having the vast experience ye do in such matters, pardon me if I need a wee bit of time to accept certain things. I am verra new to this game," she muttered.

" 'Tis no game I play here, lass. Trust me in that."

Before she could ask what he meant by that, he gave her a quick kiss, stood up, and began to don his clothes. Murdina took a moment to enjoy the sight of his long, lean body touched by the soft light of a setting sun. It astonished her that such a man desired her as he did. She just wished she was able to tell how deep that desire went and if there was more there than the simple lusting all men had for a willing woman who returned their desire.

She quickly shook away that thought, knowing her mind would prey on it until her head ached but give her no answers. In moments she had used a little water and a rag to wash up and donned her clothes. She dug into her sack for what she needed to clean her teeth and drank some of the cider Gillanders offered along with one of the last bits of bread.

"We may be able to get a few supplies in the next village," Gillanders said as he moved to ready the horses. "If we make good time we should reach Cambrun at sunset on the day after the morrow, but I certainly dinnae wish to go that long without something to eat, and we shouldnae pause to hunt down our food. It could take too long."

Murdina secured their rolled-up blankets to their saddles. "Ye still believe that Sir Ranald is hunting us?"

"I do. I think he will pursue us right to the base of the mountain Cambrun sits upon." He mounted and then looked at her. "Ye dinnae think so?"

"Oh, aye, I do," she replied as she mounted her pony. "I but pray that I am wrong. Yet, I can still hear how he spoke of the man he meant to send ye to. I think Sir Ranald would do most anything to win that mon's good regard."

Gillanders nodded in agreement and nudged his horse into motion, keeping the animal's pace slow so that Murdina could ride alongside him on her stout, placid little pony. He had thought to ease her worry about pursuit with a pleasant little lie, but had decided against it. It could prove dangerous, for it would cause her to stop keeping such a close watch for their enemy.

Travel proved slow for the sky was not clear and clouds often robbed the night of the light from the moon. Gillanders tried to ease the tedious plodding along by encouraging her to speak of her family, but they soon both fell silent. It was not easy to keep a careful watch on the path they took and talk at the same time. He also began to feel guilty over the way he evaded her questions about Cambrun and his clan.

He was going to have to tell her the truth before the sun set again. Gillanders knew he could not take her right up to the gates of Cambrun without preparing her for all she would discover there, no matter how much he would like to. It had been a coward's plan. He found he had far more sympathy than he had ever had before for the men who had struggled with the same problem when they had found themselves mated to an Outsider. Belief in such things as demons and a natural repugnance for creatures who saw one as food made it difficult to gain acceptance from any Outsider, and his clan had learned to accept that hard truth. It was impossible to accept, however, when that Outsider was the one you wished to mark as your mate.

"Gillanders!"

The urgency of her soft call drew him out of his thoughts, and he looked to find her staring at him in fear. "What is it, love?"

"I think they are near at hand. Sir Ranald and his men. They are close."

He wanted to deny it, if only out of pride. It was galling that he had not seen or heard the threat, but he shrugged that foolish vanity aside. She had a gift, and it was proving its worth right now.

"Close?" he asked as he dismounted and unsheathed his sword.

"It feels as if they are all round us. Ye cannae mean to stand and fight. We should run."

"If they are all round us, love, there is nowhere to run to. Dismount and stand with the horse. Go where the feelings ye are getting are nay so harsh and close."

She did as he said, bowing to his better knowledge of such things, but her heart pounded with fear. It was hard to know how many men there were out there, creeping toward them through the thick trees, but it was more than one man could face. Murdina tried to calm her fear for him by reminding herself that Sir Ranald had said Gillanders was to be captured, not killed. Sir Ranald's need to present a gift to the man he called The Laird could be what saved Gillanders, although she doubted she would be so lucky.

Her mind diverted by that thought, she began to plan how she might escape to get help for him if it looked as if he would be captured. His horse was strong, and she could tell by the look of the animal that it was also fast. Murdina decided she would mount the horse the moment it looked as if Gillanders was going to be captured. On her own she might be able to elude any pursuit until she could get to Cambrun and get help for him.

She was about to ask Gillanders if that was a good plan when the men broke through the trees and encircled him. They saw her, several glancing her way, but obviously considered her little threat and kept their full attention upon Gillanders. Murdina could not believe that he could face so many men and still hold that calm she could feel coming from him. The dark shadow she always sensed was a little stronger, but it was impossible to sense what it came from.

"So, ye are a cursed MacNachton just as I thought," said Sir Ranald, standing with sword in hand but making sure his men were between him and Gillanders.

"Aye, and this is one skull ye willnae be decorating your bedchamber with," said Gillanders.

"There are seven of us, fool," said Egan.

"Aye, and it would grieve me to get that much blood on my hands, so I will give ye a chance to leave now, to turn away and return to your home and hearth."

The men laughed, but Murdina shivered from a chill and that chill was coming from Gillanders. She looked at him and took a step back. His lovely amber eyes had changed to a more yellow shade. They looked like the eyes of a wolf. When he smiled, she glimpsed fangs and felt the first flicker of fear from Sir Ranald and his men.

The more she looked, the more the men with Sir Ranald edged toward Gillanders, the more Gillanders became different. His face changed to that of a pure predator, still beautiful, but now terrifying in that beauty. The hand that held the sword changed as well, his nails becoming more like claws, lengthening and thickening.

"The Laird wants him alive," Sir Ranald said, making no move to join his men.

"I am nay dying for that mon," said Egan as he charged Gillanders.

Murdina found herself trapped in a nightmare. Her fear for Gillanders faded the moment Egan's head rolled across the clearing without her even seeing Gillanders swing the death stroke. She stumbled back as the dying Egan's emotions slammed into her, adding to the fear she was already feeling from the men facing her lover.

Sir Ranald's men charged Gillanders, but he leapt clear of them with a skill and grace no man should possess, appearing oblivious to the wounds that were inflicted upon his body. One man knocked Gillanders's sword from his hand, but he quickly proved the weapon was unnecessary. With one swipe of his hand he gutted a man. With another he tore out a throat. Each man dying sent his last fierce emotions of fear, horror, and pain slamming into Murdina until she found herself backed up hard against a tree, still clinging tightly to the reins of their mounts. She released them, allowed the horses to back away from the blood and death filling the small, shaded clearing, and sank down onto the ground.

Gillanders had the last of Sir Ranald's men by the throat and threw him against a tree. The snap of bones hurt her ears, but she was so consumed by the emotion battering her mind, heart, and body that she barely flinched. She wrapped her arms around her stomach as if to keep her churning innards from falling out, prayed she could cling to her sanity during this onslaught, and watched as Gillanders stopped Sir Ranald from fleeing.

"Who is The Laird?" Gillanders demanded.

"I dinnae ken!" Sir Ranald replied as he scratched helplessly at the hand around his throat. "I swear I dinnae ken. He ne'er tells anyone. I dinnae e'en think any of his men have seen him."

"Yet ye all rush to do his bidding."

"We fight demons." His wide, terrified gaze flicked around at the bodies strewn upon the ground. "And ye are that, arenae ye. Ye are a demon."

"Nay, ye fool. I am but a mon. Different, aye, but still but a mon, and if ye had let me just leave ye wouldnae be facing death."

"I will keep your secret. I swear. I will say we ne'er found ye."

"Is that what ye told my cousin ere he died?"

"I didnae kill him!"

"Nay, but I believe some of your men aided in the murder. And I think ye found others and killed them, which must have angered The Laird. Ye had three skulls on your mantel. Three of my kinsmen whose blood stains your hands, e'en if ye didnae do the actual killing. And I suspicion ye sent others to their deaths or torture at The Laird's hands."

"Nay! Nay!"

Even through the maelstrom of emotions tearing through her, Murdina could sense the man's lies.

"Where is The Laird?" demanded Gillanders.

"I dinnae ken! His men come and take away any prisoners from those who get them. Or they arrange a place to take them to and someone collects them there. I cannae tell ye anything about the mon!"

"Then ye are of little use to me."

Murdina almost fainted when Gillanders bent his head and bit into the laird's throat. Sir Ranald's fear and horror pounded against her already battered senses as the man she had made love to but hours ago drank his blood. Through Gillanders's torn clothing, she could see the wounds he had suffered cease to bleed and begin to close. He was healing right before her eyes.

Murdina did not even have the strength to flinch when Gillanders lifted his head and with but one twist of his hand, snapped the laird's neck. The laird's last burst of emotion, tainted with his cruelty and anger, flooded her. She groaned from the force of it, the man's final pain becoming her own.

Shaking, sweating, and rocking back and forth where she sat, Murdina watched as Gillanders checked all the men to be certain they were dead and even helped himself to what little of value they had. She remained seated when he walked out of the clearing, leaving her alone with the dead. A moment later she heard the sound of horses running and knew he had taken the time to free their animals.

A part of her wanted to run, but she was unable to move. Never had she suffered such a battering from the emotions of others. It was too much, too hard to control, and too dark. Murdina wanted to empty her belly but held it down, knowing she would not be able to move away from the mess once she was done. All she could do was wait until Gillanders returned.

When he did, she watched him cautiously approach her and could see nothing of the beast that had ended the lives of seven men. His eyes were again the color of warm amber and held a look of uncertainty that sat ill on his face. His fangs were gone, his face and hands clean of blood, and he had even changed his clothing so there was no blood on him. Yet over the image of the man whom she had let into her bed, was the one of the man who had just killed so many men, drank Sir Ranald's blood, and healed before her very eyes.

The word *demon* whispered through her tortured mind, but she could not hold fast to it. Her heart refused to believe it even though her heart was being shredded by the death throes of so many men. Yet, Sir Gillanders MacNachton had not been honest with her. Murdina knew that, if she had the wit to think on that, could dig through the morass of others' emotions that still rampaged through her, she would be hurt by that. She had to wonder if the torment she was now suffering was making her mad.

He reached for her, and she heard herself whimper and pressed herself against the tree. She could not bear any touch at the moment, could not tolerate even one more touch of another's emotions or her heart would shatter. Perhaps even her mind. She sensed his hurt but, for the moment, was not concerned about how he felt.

Chapter Eight

"What *are* ye?"

Gillanders had never believed one's heart could break; yet her words hit him like a mallet to the chest. He had to tightly clench his hand to stop himself from rubbing at his chest to ease the sudden, sharp pain her hoarsely whispered question had caused. It was not easy, but he sternly reminded himself that she was unaccustomed to the ways of the MacNachtons. She had grown up amongst Outsiders. To suddenly discover there were others in her world, ones so different from what she had always known, had to be a hard shock.

He sat down in front of her, trying not to be hurt by the way she pressed herself back against the tree she sat next to. It was impossible to do when he could see how desperately she wanted to keep a distance between them. Her fear was so strong he could almost smell it. He ached to take her into his arms and soothe that fear away but knew that she would run if he reached for her now.

"I am a MacNachton. Sir Gillanders MacNachton of Cambrun."

"That isnae all."

"Nay, I am a Callan as weel." A brief flare of anger darkened her eyes, and he hoped it was a sign that her shock and fear were easing. "We MacNachtons are but a different breed of people. In some ways, so are the people of my mother's clan, the Callans."

"Different how? Those fangs?"

"Aye, all MacNachtons have them."

"To drink blood?" Murdina had to swallow hard, afraid the frantic roiling in her belly would make her sick.

"Aye, to drink blood, although it has been many generations since we drank only from people. I am nay a Pureblood, one who carries only MacNachton blood. My father wed a Callan. Her clan has its secrets, too. 'Tis believed that an ancestor of theirs was some Druid priestess who could change into a cat. In both our clans are people who also have gifts like yours."

Gifts like hers were no gifts at all, she thought, choking back a sob. None of the men who had died had been good men, but she had never wanted to feel the fear and pain they suffered as they died. Although she was no longer maddened by the sheer weight of it all, her skin still crawled with the remnants of it, and her stomach churned so badly she could feel the sting of bile in the back of her throat. The worst had been the horror each man experienced, as he had, at last, understood exactly what they had cornered. It had run so deep in each man's mind and heart she could still taste it.

"We are an old race, and our ancestors are the ones who stirred up all the dark tales about us. They were a brutal lot of men, arrogant in their power. They were called Nightriders, for they would ride down from the mountain in the dark of night to raid villages for blood and women. That ended many years ago, and then our laird decided we needed to breed out what made us different from all around us. He was the son of an Outsider, one who carries no MacNachton blood, and the old laird knew it could help us, for he could abide some sun upon his skin."

Her eyes were still glazed with that horror that struck him so deeply, but she was not shaking as badly as she had been, so he continued, hoping that his talking to her would continue to calm her. "We also were a barren clan. It had been over a generation since a child had been born and that one of an Outsider and my father. We had bred too much amongst ourselves and were slowly dying out. The laird wed a Callan woman and had twin sons. It was enough to tell the others he was right, to stir them to act and accept his plans to change what we were and more easily blend with Outsiders. It wasnae perfect, for the Callans do have many cat-like qualities, but his sons can also abide some sun. The dark hunger isnae as fierce in them, either."

"The dark hunger?" she whispered. "Ye speak of the drinking of blood?"

He slowly nodded. "We begin to think we will never fully change into Outsiders. Whate'er created us is strong, the needs insistent, but more of us can hide what we are much better now. We also dinnae hunt down people like cattle. Most of the time we need nay more than animal blood, often mixed with wine. 'Tis only when we have been sickened by the sun or badly wounded that we need more, and then 'tis offered freely by the ones within the clan or taken from the enemy we defeat."

"But ye nay drink down their souls."

"Nay! We have ne'er been able to do such a thing."

" 'Tis what those men thought ye would do, what they feared."

Gillanders nearly cursed aloud. She had felt everything the dying men had. It was a miracle she was not yet mad, her mind broken. He reached out to soothe her with a touch but she cringed, and his heart broke all over again. Taking a deep breath to ease the grip of that pain on his throat he tried to think of what else he could tell her.

"We have more of us now who can abide some sun," he finally said. "The sunlight steals our life, draws it out slowly, weakening us so that we cannae even move to hide from the verra thing that is killing us. Purebloods cannae abide it at all. The stronger the MacNachton blood, the more dangerous it is to be out in the sunlight. I can abide all but the middle of the day when the sun is at its strongest.

"Finally there are the Lost Ones. These are the children, or descendants, of MacNachtons and Outsiders. I fear our ancestors, thinking they could nay breed a child, especially with one nay of our ilk, ne'er watched to see if any lass they bedded bore them a child. The moment we discovered the first one, a search was begun for others. To our sorrow we ken weel that many have died over the years. The ones we have found have all had a hard life, were constantly threatened, and became skilled in hiding. That threat is even greater now, for we have an enemy who hunts us. Someone learned of us and has the coin and the power to send men hunting us down. They, too, seek our Lost Ones."

"The Laird."

"Aye, although we cannae be certain he is the only one."

"And the child my cousin Adeline took in is one of you."

"Osgar is Arailt's son, so, aye, he is one of ours. So is Adeline now, for she is Lachann's woman." He stood up and held out his hand.

Murdina did not take it. She knew that hurt him, could feel the stab of that pain, but she could not touch him. Not yet. So much of what the men he had killed had felt was still crawling through her veins that she feared his touch would be all that was needed to push her that last step toward madness. With one hand on the trunk of the tree, she pushed herself to her feet.

"Adeline still waits at Cambrun, Murdina," he said. "I swear that ye will be in no danger there."

"Then we had best resume our journey."

"Aye, let us leave this place of death," he murmured, and strode toward the horses.

Murdina slowly walked to her pony and mounted. She idly wondered if she was already mad, had broken beneath the onslaught of so many emotions. After watching Gillanders kill all those men, his eyes the yellow of a feral beast, his fangs stained with blood, it had to be madness that had her riding away with him. Despite all she was suffering, all she had seen him do, however, she could not see him as a threat to her life. She nudged her pony into motion and followed him away from the scene of battle, praying that she was not making the biggest, and perhaps the last, mistake of her life.

Gillanders watched Adeline escort her newfound cousin up the stairs to a room and sighed. The last of their journey had been trouble-free but a constant torment. She had spoken little and turned her back to him when they rested. All the warmth he had enjoyed in her smiles and her body was gone.

"She is the one, is she?" asked his father.

"Aye, but I fear she will ne'er come to me." He told his father all that had happened as well as why it had affected Murdina far more than it would have anyone else.

"Wheesht, laddie, ye are fortunate she is still sane."

"True. I but wish she would speak to me. Jesu, I but wish she would smile at me again. 'Tis as if she has gone all cold, pulling away from me even though she is right there before me."

"Give her time, lad. Let her be soothed by the women and enjoy finding the last of her family for a wee while."

"I will. It willnae be easy, but I will give her time."

Jankyn was watching his son walk away when his wife walked up and slapped him on the back of the head. Laughing softly and rubbing the back of his head, he looked at her. "What was that for?"

"Ye just sent him in the wrong direction. He should be wooing that lass."

As quickly as possible he told her all that had happened and why he had told his son to give Murdina some time to recover. "The lass is fortunately made of steel, for I can but wonder how she remained sane after that."

"And thus will make a good mate for our son. But he should-nae be leaving her alone too long. Once she calms from her ordeal, she will begin to wonder where he is and think too much on his absence from her side. I believe I shall fetch a soothing potion and take it to her for, if Gillanders stays away too long, someone will have to be able to convince her to go and hunt him down."

Murdina sighed with pleasure as she drank the tankard of heavily spiced cider Gillanders's mother served her. Finding out this young, vibrant woman was his mother had been quite a shock, too. There were obviously a few things about the MacNachtons he had neglected to tell her. No one had suggested that Efrica was a second or even third wife, so her claim to be Gillanders's mother had to be the truth, yet Murdina found it so hard to believe she decided to just ignore the puzzle for now.

As the woman took the empty tankard away, Adeline gently pushed Murdina down onto her back on the bed and pulled the coverlet over her. "Best if ye rest, cousin." She laughed. " 'Tis wondrous to say that. I thought myself utterly alone. Weel, until I found my son and then my husband. Ye have the look of my father, too, which warms my heart."

"I, too, thought myself alone." Murdina briefly clasped Adeline's hand, swallowing the urge to weep. " 'Tis good to ken I have kin still."

"And ye will have more once ye get o'er your journey and go fetch my son to your side," said Efrica.

Murdina blushed. "I am nay sure he will wish to be fetched,

and I am nay one of his people. And he is a knight whilst I am but the only child of a blacksmith."

"Neither are we of his ilk, and your birth is of no concern." Efrica sat on the side of the bed. "Nor are a few others like my sister, the laird's wife. My husband told me what ye suffered, how that gift ye havenae yet told us about made ye feel all that those men felt as they died. But, they meant to kill ye. Ne'er forget that. Aye, they might have captured my son and sent him to this laird we cannae seem to find, but he would have died, probably after many long months of torture. I dinnae think the killing is what troubles ye when ye look at him, either."

"Nay, but in a way he lied to me. I looked at what he could do, how he changed into a mon I didnae ken as he fought, and felt the sting of that lie. I am also nay sure if I can be the woman he needs, if he even wishes to keep me."

"Oh, he wishes to keep ye. I saw how he watched ye as ye walked away with Adeline. As for being what he needs? Of course ye are or he wouldnae be looking at ye that way. Now, my husband in all his idiot male wisdom has told Gillanders to give ye time. Take it, but if he keeps away once ye are over all ye suffered, hunt him down. If ye love my lad, Murdina Dunbar, then ye will find a way to be all that he needs." Efrica stood up and brushed down her skirts. "Rest. We can visit more later when ye wake and begin to recover your strength."

After the woman was gone, Murdina looked at her cousin. "'Tis verra hard to believe that young, vibrant woman is Gillanders's mother."

"Ah, weel," Adeline took Efrica's place on the side of the bed, "these people dinnae age as Outsiders do. There is a lot I need to tell ye about the MacNachtons, Cousin. But I will say this now, as I can see that your eyes grow heavy with sleep. They are good men. If Gillanders has decided ye are his mate, ye will ne'er find a better mon to love. He will protect ye and any child ye bear with his verra life, love ye until your eyes cross, and be a true soul mate, the other half of you that ye didnae e'en ken was missing."

"That would be nice. Yet, he didnae tell me who he really was before he . . ." She blushed as she realized what she was about to confess.

"Bedded ye?" Adeline laughed when Murdina blushed even

more. "They are a hot-blooded lot these MacNachton men. Dinnae look so shamed. Ye are in love. 'Tis the way of it."

"But I was in love with the other Gillanders, the one he pretended to be."

"Nonsense. Gillanders was Gillanders. All he hid was that which this clan has always hidden. And 'tis worth their verra life if anyone discovers what they are. Ye hid what ye are until the last moment, aye?"

"Weel, aye, but ye would think he would tell me ere he bedded me."

"He is a mon. He wanted ye, and since ye may weel be his mate, that wanting must have been fierce."

Thinking of how his desire felt when he touched her, Murdina had to agree. "I dinnae ken what to think save that I think Efrica's potion is beginning to dull what few wits I still had."

"Exactly what it was meant to do. Ye need to rest. Murdina, just what is this gift ye have?"

"I can feel what others feel. One reason I was so drawn to Gillanders is because all I could feel from him was calm. A wee hint of a shadow, but mostly a wonderful calm. Oh, and his desire. I kenned that was true, for I felt it each time it rose in him. When he killed those men," she added in a shaky whisper, "I felt all they did as they died."

"Sweet Jesu. All of them?"

"Aye. All of them. They were afraid, in pain, and utterly horrified, for they believed he would drink down their souls. I cannae explain how it was when all of the emotion came to me, but I do think 'tis a near miracle that I am still sane."

Adeline hugged her and then sat back while still clasping her hand. "It is. I am curious now. What do ye feel from me?"

"Happiness. Calm. Sympathy."

"That is utterly astonishing."

Adeline asked a few more questions but then left. Murdina closed her eyes. Her body was so soothed by Efrica's potion that Murdina doubted she could move, but her mind was slow to find its rest. The shadows of what the dead men had felt still preyed upon her mind, casting up images of the way they had died. She knew it would be a while before she could banish those shadows.

Gillanders also came to mind, but that did not surprise her.

He had occupied her thoughts a lot ever since she had first set eyes on him. Memories of their lovemaking were far better than the shadows of the dead men's feelings, but they carried a hint of sadness with them. She needed to accept that he had not lied to her, that he had simply been what he was, a man who had a lot of secrets he had been trained to keep, if only for the sake of his clan.

She still wanted him, still loved him. For now she would rest, shed herself of all those dark shadows, and regain her strength just as Gillanders's lovely mother had suggested. She would also learn all she could about the MacNachtons. It was clear to see that he had not yet told her everything. The knowledge of what she would share if she did stay with him would be important, for she realized she did not want to taste his pain again as she had when she had shied away from him after the battle.

The fact that she could hurt him like that actually made a flicker of hope rise in her heart. You could not hurt a man who cared no more for you than as a way to soothe his lusts. It was going to take a lot of courage but, if he did not come to speak to her, the moment she regained her strength, she would speak to him. Nothing could be settled until they talked. All she could do was pray that the talk would lead to his asking her to share his future.

Chapter Nine

"Where is Gillanders?" Murdina asked the far too beautiful Jankyn, still unsettled by how Gillanders's father looked young enough to be his brother.

"Out in the stables," the man replied, watching her so intently it made her uneasy even though she could feel no threat from him.

For two days she had seen little of Gillanders, mere glimpses of him as they passed in the great hall. He had been avoiding her as much as possible. When she recalled how she had reacted to the truth about what he was, Murdina was not surprised by that. Also, his father had told him to give her time, although she doubted the man had meant for Gillanders to utterly ignore her. She also thought that Gillanders was giving all she had suffered very little consideration. It hurt her to know she had hurt him, but seeing what he was in all its ferocious, bloody glory had been a terrible shock, especially when she had been so crippled by all the emotions she had been pummeled with.

"He plans to go ahunting for more Lost Ones," Jankyn continued. "Could be gone for weeks."

"Gone? For weeks? He ne'er said a word about that."

"Weel, I suspicion he didnae wish to interrupt your getting to ken your cousin."

Something about her reaction to the news that Gillanders was thinking of riding away and staying away for weeks was definitely amusing the man. She could not discover what it was, however, for she did not have the time. If she was to corner Gillanders for a long talk, she had to catch him quickly.

"Oh, aye, run away, will he?" she muttered to herself as she strode away. "Two days of hiding like a child expecting a scold just because I found the sight of him ripping out throats with his teeth a wee bit frightening. Wheesht, who wouldnae. But did he give me time to calm down a wee bit, to learn more about his clan? Nay, he hid. Weel, he cannae hide any more. I will tie the fool to a post until he talks to me."

She heard laughter and knew Jankyn had listened to her rantings, but she was too angry to care. Refusing to run after any man, Murdina nevertheless walked to the stables as swiftly as she could. If she did not stop Gillanders from leaving, it would be a long time before they could talk as they needed to. She also feared how he would behave if he left still believing she could not tolerate what he was.

The moment she saw him, she hesitated. Murdina knew only that he desired her and that she could hurt him. It was not much to plan a future on or to risk her heart on. Adeline was certain Gillanders wanted her for far more than as a woman to warm his bed. Even his own mother thought so. Yet, it would still take a lot of courage to speak her heart to him on no more than those assumptions. Then she watched him make a final check of his saddle and knew she had to grasp that courage right now. If she let him leave, every instinct she had told her that it would be a long time before they could return to that idyllic time before she had seen what he was, if ever.

"Going somewhere?" she asked as she walked over and looked at him over the back of his horse.

"Out to hunt for Lost Ones," he replied. "We all do it from time to time."

Gillanders studied her face. He could see none of the fear or horror he had seen that day in the clearing. She was clear-eyed and apparently angry with him. Gillanders felt a faint stirring of hope, but refused to let it rise. Murdina might now accept what he and his clan were, but that did not mean she would now wish to bind herself to him for what could be a very long lifetime or to bear his children.

"Did ye nay think to tell me?" She heard the faint tremor in her voice and silently cursed, but the chill she felt from him was breaking her heart.

"Nay. I felt ye still needed time to overcome your revulsion."

"It was nay revulsion," she snapped, welcoming the anger that pushed aside her timidity and fear.

"I saw the horror on your face, Murdina. Aye, and your fear."

"Of course ye did, but horror and fear are nay the same as revulsion. For sweet Mary's sake, I had just seen ye kill seven men all by yourself, and only one of them fell to your sword. I didnae come from a place where all kenned your clan, where whispered tales of ye are common. When Sir Ranald and his men encircled us, I thought we were dead for certain, or captured and wishing we were, and then suddenly ye are leaping about higher than any mon should be able to, snarling, tossing men about as if they weighed naught, snapping necks, ripping out throats, and drinking blood. Ye showed me, in a fierce, blood-soaked way, that those teeth I thought naught but some small oddity amongst your clan were, in all truth, fangs. Then, as I looked at ye splattered with their blood, I actually saw all your wounds heal before my verra eyes!"

Gillanders grimaced. The way she described it, he could understand why she had been afraid. It lessened the sting of the memory of the horror on her face.

"And," she continued, "did ye just forget what my cursed gift is? Mayhap what ye saw in my eyes was naught but what those men had filled me with when they died. I nearly broke apart from the weight of all their fear and pain."

"Ye stayed away from me for the rest of the journey here," he said, although he recognized the truth of what she said, one he had considered that very day but only briefly, while she had sat there trembling, pale, her eyes clouded with emotion.

"Which was but wee more than a day. It took nearly that long simply to shed enough of what those men had filled me with to think clearly." She started to pace, the strength and turmoil of her feelings making it impossible to remain still. "I didnae ken who ye were anymore. All I could think of was that I had given my innocence to a stranger, a mon who hid himself so weel e'en I ne'er saw the truth. Oh, aye, I sensed a shadow within you, but nay more than that. Certainly nay e'en a tiny hint that ye could leap about like a cat or tear a mon open with your fingernails that became claws right before my eyes."

She stopped and looked at him. "Once I fought through all the rest, I needed to think and get o'er my anger about that. Ye ne'er warned me, Gillanders. Nay once. One moment ye are the mon who likes to flaunt his chest and makes me blind with desire. The next ye are something else with claws and fangs. But, I didnae run, did I? I didnae flee your side. I still rode with ye to Cambrun, to a keep filled with more of your ilk. And all because ye swore I would be safe there."

He nearly gaped at her. It was true, and he had been too busy nursing his hurt to see it. She had remained with him. Despite the distance she had put between them for the rest of the journey, despite that lingering glint of fear in her eyes, she had followed him to Cambrun, ridden right into what must have seemed to her like the lion's den, just because he swore she would be safe. All he had needed to do was give her a little time to speak to the other women, to think over all that had happened, and to understand exactly what he was. Time to be rid of the vicious onslaught of others' emotions she had suffered that day. He also should have talked to her more. He should have sought her out until her fears eased enough for her to listen to him, and helped her to overcome what had to have been a horrendous burden thrust upon her by her gift.

"I but needed a wee bit of time, Gillanders," she said. "I grew up in a wee, quiet village, the cherished and weel protected daughter of the blacksmith. I have ne'er e'en seen men fight with swords. There was so much blood that day, men screaming, the stench of death all round me...." She stuttered to a halt when he took her into his arms. "It was ye I was afraid of and yet I wasnae, if that makes any sense to ye at all."

"It does." He kissed the top of her head and rested his cheek against her hair. "I saw that look upon your face and believed myself condemned as the demon some call me."

"Nay, I..."

"Saw the horror of battle, the cost of fighting for one's life, and swallowed the fierce, terrible emotions of dying men."

"Aye, but what troubled me most was that I felt ye had lied to me in some way." She looked up at him and touched her fingers to his lips when he began to protest. "*Lie* is such a harsh word, I ken it. Ye but hid a truth. Have I nay done the same for most of my life? It took me a while to accept that ye did nay more than I did."

"Ye told me the truth ere ye joined me on the journey to Cambrun. I meant to tell ye my truths as weel. I planned to do so ere ye rode through the gates of Cambrun. If I were a good mon, I would have told ye the truth ere we shared a bed, but I wanted ye too badly to risk ye running away from me."

"Oh, I have ne'er questioned your desire for me."

He grinned. "So ye ken it rises anew?"

She did and, as always, it stirred her own, quickly and fiercely. "I do." She pressed her cheek against his chest, enjoying the sound of the strong beat of his heart. "It awakens my own and strengthens it."

Gillanders put his hand beneath her chin and turned her face up to his. "Did Adeline tell ye of the marking?" He knew that if he made love to her now he would not be able to stop himself from marking her as his own.

Murdina blushed, silently cursing herself for how easily her fair skin did that. "Aye. She said it didnae hurt. She also said 'tis the mark a MacNachton gives his mate." She tensed, praying that he was speaking of the mark because he intended to mark her, to claim her as his true mate.

"I have ached to give ye one since the first time we made love."

"Are ye certain?"

"Verra certain. I love ye, Murdina Dunbar. I suspected I was caught from the first time I looked into those beautiful eyes of yours. The only thing in doubt is whether ye feel the same."

"Oh, aye, I do. I love ye." She gave herself over to his hungry kiss, enjoying the ferocity of it and returning some of her own. "I suspected it when I could touch ye and feel only calm," she said when he ended the kiss. "E'en when ye suffered from some less kindly emotions, they didnae trouble me as those of others do. Beneath it all I could still feel that calm."

Gillanders knew he could wait no longer to mark her as his own. He swiftly unsaddled his mount, returned the animal to its stall, and then grabbed Murdina by the hand. It was not until he heard her laugh that he realized he was nearly running to the keep. He slowed his pace but not by much, ignoring everyone they passed as he dragged her to his bedchamber.

Murdina did not think clothes had ever been shed as fast as theirs were once they were inside his bedchamber, the door latched securely behind them. When he took her into his arms and tumbled them down onto the bed, their flesh meeting for the first time in far too long, she did not think she could endure it if he spent too much time with kissing and stroking her. She wanted him inside her now, needed him to ease an ache that had been gnawing at her for days. Threading her fingers through his hair as he teased her breasts with strokes of his tongue and soft kisses, she knew she would not be able to play this game for long before she demanded what she needed.

"Love, I dinnae think I have the patience this time," Gillanders said as he covered her face with kisses. "I need ye now, need to make ye truly mine."

"I find I am in nay mood to play, either," she whispered against his ear and then lightly nipped at the lobe.

"Sweet Jesu, I dinnae think I have e'er heard sweeter words."

Her soft laugh turned into a gasp of pleasure as he thrust inside of her. Her body welcomed him greedily. Murdina held him close as he moved, each stroke deep within her sending her passion climbing higher until she trembled from the force of it. A tightness low in her belly increased until she knew she was close to tumbling into the bliss he could give her. There was a quick, sharp pain in her neck and she fell, crying out his name as pleasure swept over her in waves. A small, still sane part of her heard him cry out her name as he joined her in that fall.

It was not until she felt a cool, damp cloth bathe her between her legs that Murdina became aware of her surroundings once again. She opened her eyes as Gillanders walked away to rinse out the cloth he had used on her and quickly bathe himself. He was a beautiful sight to behold, she thought a little besottedly, as he walked back to the bed and slipped in beside her. She murmured with pleasure when he took her into his arms, holding her close and running his fingers through her hair.

" 'Tis done now, love," he said. "Everyone at Cambrun will ken that ye are mine now."

She frowned and touched her neck, surprised by the feel of a small mark upon her skin." 'Tis a scar already?"

"Aye. When we bite someone, if we lick at the wound afterward, it will heal. We dinnae ken why, but when we bite the woman we have chosen as ours, when we have fully accepted that she is our mate, that mark doesnae fade away as all the others do. If ye allow me to have a wee sip of ye now and then, those marks will fade ere we catch our breath." He brushed a kiss over her forehead.

"Catch our breath?"

"Weel, unless 'tis done for some dire need, most time 'tis done with one's mate as part of the loving."

"Ah, I see. Since I barely noticed it when ye did it this time, I cannae see that I shall object. All it did was make the pleasure e'en fiercer," she whispered.

"That it does, but we dinnae do it often. It wouldnae do to take too much blood, and the pleasure can be the sort to make ye want it too often if ye are nay careful."

For a moment she simply enjoyed being held in his arms, savoring the knowledge that this man loved her. Murdina could feel it, knew it would always comfort her. It was a very strange life she would be living now, but she found only happiness in her heart. She had all she could ever want, but there was still one small shadow on that happiness.

"Adeline told me that ye all live for a long time, that your ability to heal so quickly adds many years to your lives," she said. "I dinnae have that ability, Gillanders."

"Ye will." He pulled back a little and smiled at her. "We have discovered that that gift of a long life can be shared. Ye have seen my parents, aye?"

"Aye, your mother was good to come and speak with me several times." She did not think he needed to know that most of that was to encourage her to hunt down her son and make him mark her.

"My mother is four and fifty years old, and my father is eight and seventy."

"Nay."

"Aye, and dinnae look so horrified. My aunt has discovered that, if an Outsider drinks some of our blood, it works in them as it does in us by healing wounds and keeping old age away from the door."

She frowned, not completely sure she could stomach drinking blood, but then certain she could overcome any hesitation if it meant she could remain at his side for many years to come. "But, I dinnae have fangs."

"Ye dinnae need them. I can make a wound if ye can abide drinking from me now and then, or ye can drink the potion Aunt

Bridgit has made, one so full of rich wine and spices ye cannae taste the blood in it."

"Oh. Weel, that will do," she said, and was rewarded with a kiss that had her passion raising its sated head. But, a chilling thought suddenly occurred to her as he kissed her throat, and she pulled away to look at him. "The Laird kens that, doesnae he."

"We think he might, or will verra soon if we dinnae find him and kill him." He pulled her back into his arms. " 'Tis a dangerous time for us, but ye will be safe here."

"It wasnae my safety I feared for."

"Ye have seen that I am nay without skill in battle, my love. And our laird rarely asks the mated males to go out ahunting, for the loss of a mate is a verra hard thing for a MacNachton to bear, e'en one who has only wed into the clan. Be at ease. Dinnae allow the fears of what might happen to shadow all we can share."

"I love ye, Gillanders," she whispered, brushing a kiss over his mouth.

"And I love ye, Murdina MacNachton."

"Do I get a wedding?" she teased.

"Aye, and since one of the people who hailed us as I rushed ye up here like a fool blinded with his own need was my mother"—he laughed when she blushed—"I suspicion she has already begun the planning of it."

"I shall ne'er get used to how all in a keep seem to ken everyone's business."

"Aye, ye will, for this is nay like Dunnantinny. This is now your home and your family. We shall have us a fine life together."

"Even if it proves to be a verra long one? Can ye love the same lass for a hundred years?"

"Easily. For that long and far longer."

HIGHLAND VAMPIRE

Diana Cosby

*This book is dedicated to Eric, Stephanie, and Christopher, my amazing children, who are truly blessings in my life. I want to thank each of you for being who you are, and for your service to our country. I'm proud to be your mom. God bless. I love each of you so much. *Hugs**

Acknowledgments

I am truly thankful for the immense support from my parents, family, and friends. My deepest wish is that everyone is as blessed when they pursue their dreams.

My sincere thanks and humble gratitude to my editors, Alicia Condon and Megan Records; my agent, Holly Root; my critique partners, Shirley Rogerson, Mary Forbes, and Michelle Hancock. Your hard work has helped make the magic of this story come true. A huge thanks as well to Joseph Hasson for brainstorming *Highland Vampire* with me and allowing the magic of this story to breathe life. A special thanks to Sulay Hernandez for believing in me from the start.

And, thanks to the Roving Lunatics (Mary Beth Shortt and Sandra Hughes) and the Wild Writers for their friendship as continued amazing support!

Chapter One

July 1297
Medieval Scotland

Enter the stone circle.

At the deep burr echoing in her mind, Rowan Campbell whirled. Against the cast of moonlight, she peered between the massive towers of stone encircling a swath of land.

Naked, a lone man lay sprawled on his back within the circle. Black hair was strewn over well-muscled shoulders, the firm slide of skin angling to a taut, lean body, a body designed for war.

Had he spoken to her mind? Impossible.

Long moments passed.

The warrior remained still.

Had he been injured in battle? Or were the men who'd labeled her a witch responsible for his fate? On a shaky breath, Rowan searched the nearby forest for any sign of movement.

Not a breeze stirred or a stick cracked beneath the cloak of the night. 'Twas as if the world had stopped. Nay, stilled, as if under the sway of a greater force.

The air began to pulse with raw, primal energy. Expectancy curled around her, seeped into her pores. Beneath the silvery cascade of the fading moonlight, the man's body began to shimmer.

Terrified, she stumbled back.

No. Come closer.

Rowan whirled, scoured the night-blacked trees arching toward the sky with ominous intent.

No one.

She'd heard naught but her overactive imagination. Imagination? Nay, being branded a witch and on the run for a sennight would leave the stoutest man on edge. Exhaustion and fear fed her mind.

But neither mattered. If she didn't escape from the Highlands, she would be caught and burned upon a stake. On a sigh she studied the heavens.

Red ribbons of light streaked the sky like blood, announcing the oncoming dawn.

Weariness weighed upon her like a sodden gown. However much she wished to rest, with danger about, she could not tarry. Rowan tried to turn, but sensation halted her, then tugged her forward. Panic threatened, and she tried to step back.

The force dragged her closer to the timeworn stones erected centuries ago. Columns, Highlanders whispered, that held immense power.

"Release me!" Her cry echoed into the night. Merciful Mary, she was on the run. With her pursuers nearby, only a fool would call for help!

She struggled against the pull, but with her next step, her foot settled inside the circle of stones. Like a curtain drawn, the air around her grew thick, the silence rich. When she stood in front of the stranger, her body halted. Fighting for calm, she stared at the formidable man.

Morning rays continued to seep into the sky, its growing brightness silhouetting the warrior's figure. The paleness of his face surprised her, but the hard slant of his cheeks drew her gaze to his mouth, to lips pressed together in pain.

You must aid me to the cave nearby.

She turned to find who'd spoken.

Trees swayed in the breeze, a hawk flew in the distance, but she found no sign of another person.

This was crazy. Rowan tried to step back, but a force dragged her to her knees, drew her hands to encircle the intimidating stranger's waist. As her fingers skimmed across muscled flesh, a jolt rocked her, awareness so deep it shook her to her core.

No, she didn't want to do this! She fought against the compulsion, but her arms lifted him.

Without warning, his legs pushed with her. Then he stood at her side.

I must lean upon you.

Rowan refused to think, to analyze the strangeness of this moment. 'Twas a nightmare, one she prayed she'd awaken from posthaste.

Shafts of sunlight slid over the horizon, and the heat within the stone circle swelled.

Move!

At his low growl, Rowan hurried forward, amazed that even though his face was contorted in agony, he kept pace. They navigated through the break within the stones, and the air around them cleared.

Unsure, she hesitated.

To the cave!

At his harsh command, Rowan guided the dangerous-looking man forward, his weight as he leaned upon her increasing with each step. If he passed out, she could never lift him. What was she thinking? If he passed out she could escape!

Paces away from the blackened entrance, his breath left him in a hiss, and the stench of burning flesh permeated the air.

Rowan glanced over, stilled. Beneath the sun's newborn rays, slices of red clawed the stranger's shoulder, more pale flesh becoming scorched with each passing moment. God in heaven, what was going on?

On an oath, he jerked her against him, lunged toward the cave. They landed hard, but he kept her protected within his arms.

Her body caged against his, Rowan struggled to break free. "Release me!"

The stranger remained still, his chest unmoving, not a flicker of emotion upon his face.

Frantic, she shoved against his chest.

He budged a hand's width.

Heart racing, she pushed on his injured shoulder; he collapsed onto his side, his moan, low and chilling, echoing through the cavern.

Fear collided with her urge to heal. Ever since she was a child, she'd been skilled in helping others. This man's skin was ice. More, he'd not attacked her but had collapsed atop her from pain.

In the glow of morning light illuminating the land beyond the cave, she caught the pallor of his face, his teeth clenched in pain. Guilt tamped down her nerves. How could he harm her? He could nae move.

Many questions lay unanswered about who he was and how he had ended up naked and near dead within the stone circle, but she needed to focus on tending to him, not on her fear.

With a final tug, Rowan pulled herself free, the honed curve of his backside drawing her to look, appreciate his very male, very muscular form. His pale skin accented the hard angles of his body, highlighted every nuance that formed this incredible man. Fine he was to look at, a fact she had little doubt many a woman had noted.

Even battered and undressed, his body seemed that of a man used to being in charge. A warrior. A man who would normally fail to notice a common healer such as her.

Enough.

The man was suffering. From his shallow breathing, she judged he was near death, and here she was acting like a weak-willed lass, not one who'd aided in the birthing of many a babe and offered many a man succor as he'd drawn his last breath.

Frustrated with herself, Rowan glanced at his shoulder where she'd seen the streaks of red. No sign existed of his being wounded. She searched his back, then the other shoulder.

Naught.

Where were the marks? She'd watched them grow, could still smell charred flesh on the air. Uneasy, she fought for calm. Mayhap in her exhaustion, she had imagined both?

As if either mattered? With the men chasing her believing her a witch and wanting her dead, she must focus on the task at hand. Once assured the warrior would survive, she would leave.

With a gentle hand, she examined the warrior's body for any sign of injury and found nothing swollen nor any visible cause of his unconsciousness.

What had she missed? Something caused him immense pain. She leaned close to his mouth, inhaled his weak breath. No scent of ale or wine. Neither had she expected such. His scream earlier was that of a man in pain.

Poison.

Rowan half fell back, glanced toward the cave opening. Golden rays spilled inside the timeworn entry, illuminated the grass and the circle beyond. Above, tattered clouds filled the sky. She scanned the line of distant trees.

No human or animal lurked nearby.

Pulse racing, she turned toward the man. Nay, he'd not spoken to her mind, now or earlier. She was exhaus—

Eyes as black as the devil's flickered open. Their potent intensity held her, stirred within her a desperate need.

Awareness flashed within his gaze. Against the glint of the blood-red sun, his teeth began to lengthen.

What manner of creature was he?

Through the wash of agony, Aedan MacGregor, Laird of the Highland Vampire Coven, focused upon the beautiful woman caught within his hold. Terror streaked her wide turquoise eyes, and wisps of her plaited, wheat blond hair flew about her head as she struggled to break free. She appeared like a fairy caught outside the Otherworld.

"Release me!" she gasped.

Her rich burr spilled from her full lips and wrapped around him, cutting through the haze of misery. For a moment he lost himself in her throaty voice, imagining his hands upon her flesh, her cries as he took her over the edge. What in Hades? Never had a human woman tempted him.

Weakness swept his body. Aedan kept his hold upon consciousness—barely. Enough. He had little time or energy for these foolish thoughts.

"Come to me," he whispered, surprised a scan of her mind offered him naught. Always was he able to read a human's thoughts. 'Twas the herbs the traitor had slipped into his drink last eve that dulled his senses. Once the effects wore off, he would read her mind with ease.

She shook her head. "Pl-Please, do not kill me."

"Lass," he whispered, each word draining precious strength. "Never would I harm you. That I swear."

"Yo-You are—" She focused on his teeth, and a tremor rippled through her slender frame.

"A vampire." He struggled not to slip under, to keep her within his hold. Through sheer will, he managed both. "Trust me."

If possible, terrified eyes widened further. He shouldn't have expected otherwise. Humans created horrifying fables about what they did not understand, found relief in giving their fabricated creature a name, regardless of the truth.

"I am dying." He cursed his weakness, cursed the fact that he'd exposed his dire state to a human, one whose mind he could not read. Could he trust her? Did he have any choice? "I need a small amount of your blood."

Fingers, slim and strong, slid to her slender throat, trembled. "Do nae ask this."

"Use your dagger," he whispered, the last of his strength fading fast. "Slice your thumb, and let several drops fall within my mouth. 'Tis all I need to begin to recover."

Wary eyes studied him. "And then?"

"I will sate my hunger with another."

Her lower lip wavered. "Will you kill him?"

Did it matter how he acquired nourishment? Aye, to her it did. "He will nae be hurt, but will fall asleep. When he awakens, he will but find himself tired, with no memory of my being there."

Turquoise eyes darted toward the entry, shifted back.

Bedamned, he should take her blood and be done with it, but he could not risk scaring her. With his body so weakened, if she broke free and ran, he'd not have the strength to will her back or give chase.

After a long moment, she withdrew her dagger. "But a few drops."

"Aye."

Precious seconds passed. On an exhale, she slid the honed blade against the pad of her thumb.

A drop of blood beaded upon the sharp metal, and the rich scent filled the air, infused his every breath. His body demanded he take. He waited, preserved the last of his meager energy in case she decided to bolt.

Her eyes locked upon his, she held her thumb a hand's breadth above his mouth. The beads of red grew, wobbled upon the honed tip, fell.

The warm salty drops landed upon his tongue. Aedan savored sweetness unlike anything he'd ever tasted. He swallowed.

Strength flooded his body, and his senses heightened to a dangerous edge. A deep keening ignited within his soul, and a completeness he'd never experienced filled him.

He stilled. By the sword's blade, this woman was his mate!

With a steadying breath, she pressed her thumb harder, and several more drops landed upon his tongue.

In a brilliant explosion of light, his mind melded to hers. Images ignited: her tumble of terrified thoughts of what he would do to her, of being shunned throughout her life, and of the men who chased her and wanted her dead.

Questions storming him, he withdrew from the woman's mind.

As if sensing his increased strength, she pulled her thumb away, and pressed her finger over the cut.

He banked his body's demands to take her, to claim her as his rightful mate. "My thanks." With care, Aedan sat up, amazed by the increase in his strength from the meager amount of blood he'd swallowed. Was her being his mate responsible?

The beautiful woman stumbled back, the pulse at the base of her throat rapid.

He tried not to notice, to want her. Failed. "As I said before, I will not harm you." His words were truer than she would ever know. With their bodies merged through her blood, and their destinies joined, he would protect her always, even at the cost of his life.

Looking unconvinced, she watched him. On a shudder, she glanced toward the entry. Images of men with pitchforks, swords, axes, and other weapons chasing her flickered through her mind.

Anger stormed him. "Who threatens you?"

Surprise appeared on her face, then suspicion. "How do you know?"

"You have fear within your eyes," he replied, not wanting to overwhelm her further by explaining that he could read her mind. The time would come to impart that knowledge. As well, he dismissed his ability to read her mind earlier due to his weakened condition.

"You are a vampire; how can I not be afraid?"

It was only part of the reason she was afraid. Until she grew to trust him, she would tell no more. "Your name?"

She took a step back.

"Please tell me." He kept his voice soft.

"Rowan Campbell." She hesitated. "And yours?"

He sensed no treachery in her asking. "Aedan MacGregor. I belong to the Highland Coven."

"You are alone?"

Aedan nodded. "Aye."

Her fingers toyed with the sleeve of her gown. "I—I thought stories of vampires were tales crafted by the bards."

"We keep to ourselves. Unless we feed."

Her face paled.

Blasted wives' tales. "We harm none, take naught except what is necessary."

"And I am to believe you?"

A muscle in his jaw worked. "Had I wanted you dead, 'twould be long since achieved."

After a moment, she nodded, again glanced toward the entry.

"Fear not. I will protect you."

She turned, studied him a long moment. "Why would you?"

You are my mate, he wanted to explain. From this moment on her protection would be his first priority. "You saved my life."

"I did naught but give you a few drops of blood." She backed another step toward the entry. "I—I must go."

With their bond, he could not allow her to leave him. "Rowan," he said, liking the sound of her name upon his tongue. "If you depart now, you will place yourself in danger. While you are in my presence, none will harm you." He allowed compulsion to soften his voice. "Trust me."

Panic slid through Rowan as she stared at the formidable man. Man? Nay, a vampire. Could this day become more unbelievable? Aye, it could. Because she found herself wanting to do as he bade and offer him her trust. She needed sleep. 'Twould rid her of such ludicrous thoughts. Unsure, she looked past the stone entry, searched the forest looming beyond.

Trust me.

Rowan whirled to face him. " 'Twas you who spoke in my mind before." A smile edged his lips, one that inspired wanton thoughts of her within his arms, of his mouth moving over hers as he made love to her. Heart pounding, she shook her head. "Nay, none of this is happening. You are but a dream."

"Lass, I am very real."

Another vision of him laying her upon a moss-covered bank emerged in her mind. "Stop it!"

His face grew somber. " 'Tis not I."

"You read my thoughts," she accused.

"Aye," he agreed, "but they are images conjured by your mind, by your growing need."

Her growing need? Ridiculous. "Never have I had such indecent thoughts." She held up her hand. "Why am I trying to explain? None of this makes any sense."

"It is complex."

Complex? An understatement. Since she'd been chased from her home, her entire life had been turned upside down. Rowan attributed her wanton thoughts to exhaustion and turned her focus on finding a place where she would be safe. She eyed the handsome stranger. Though he'd vowed to not harm her, could she give him her trust?

His eyelids slipped closed, and he struggled to reopen them.

She glanced toward the sun rising in the eastern sky. Daylight, the time a vampire slept.

"Yes, soon I must sleep," he said, his voice rough with fatigue. "But I need your vow that while I rest you will not leave me."

"Why?"

"As I explained before, 'tis unsafe."

She almost laughed. And being cloistered with a vampire was safe?

"Aye," he replied, "I will protect you."

Anxiety edged through her. "How can you read my mind?"

He hesitated, and then sighed as if coming to a decision of great import. "Your blood now runs through my veins. Forever are we bound."

"Forever?" She shook her head. Nay, it could not be! "Remove the connection."

An arrogant smile slanted his mouth. " 'Tis impossible."

Was it? Or, did he choose to keep their mental tie for his own self-serving reasons? She'd been so caught up in her fear, her shock at learning he was a vampire, she'd not thought of the obvious questions. Why was he out here alone? Was he a thief, on the run, or had he murdered someone?

He grimaced. "Still your mind's mayhem. I am nae wanted, nor have I killed anyone."

"Nay? Then why did I find you half dead within the stone circle?"

Anger flashed in his eyes. "I was drugged and left there to die."

Chapter Two

Left to die? Rowan stared at the stunning vampire in disbelief. With his immense power and intelligence, he was dangerous. Whoever dared cross him was a fool.

"By whom?" she asked.

"Come," he said, his voice rough with exhaustion. "We both need sleep."

She paused. "You will nae answer my question?"

"It is unimportant."

"Unimportant?" Did he not understand? "As long as I am with you, if you are in danger, it affects me."

His jaw tightened. "As I said, as long as you are in my presence, I can protect you."

"As you protected yourself within the stone circle?" His face darkened, and she hesitated. Was she a fool to challenge him? If he wished, he could kill her in a trice.

"Lass, 'tis best if you do not know."

"For whom?"

"You ask too many questions," he said with quiet warning. "Do not invite danger.

"Why—" A heaviness weighed upon her, and she grew sleepy. Her legs walked toward him. "Stop making me tired. I wish answers."

"The time to talk will come later. Now, you will rest—with me."

Her mind blurred, and Rowan struggled for coherent thought. She needed to warn him. "Nor am I safe."

"Aye." He reached up, wrapped his strong hand around hers. "Now, lie with me."

As if 'twas that simple? She scowled at him, but found her gaze lingering on his naked magnificence. Heat stole up her face. "Lie with you? 'Tis indecent!"

" 'Tis only for sleep," he assured.

Hesitant, she settled onto the ground near him.

A smile touched his impossibly handsome face, a face crafted for charm and, as well, a face crafted for sin. "I sense you are a healer." He stroked the curve of her cheek. "Have you never seen a male unclothed?"

She angled her chin. "Indeed, I have tended many a man, but only when they are ill, which you are not."

"I was dying," he said, his face growing solemn. "Because of you, I live."

The sincerity of his words moved her, left her torn. Well she knew her place within the clan. Or, lack of. "Do not paint me heroic. It was you who summoned me to you."

"Mayhap, but it was your blood that saved my life."

He stared at her a long moment, the intensity of his gaze sizzling through her body, igniting a longing within her that left her aching.

"Aedan," he whispered, his soft burr wrapping around her like spun velvet. "I wish to hear you say my name."

"Why?"

He arched an expectant brow. "Must you challenge my every request?"

She remained silent, unsure why this moment seemed momentous.

"My name."

Stubborn he was. "Aedan."

He smiled as if given a precious gift, a smile of satisfaction, one that sent ripples of awareness sliding through her body. "Rowan," he said, his burr dark with need. "Lie with me."

"I . . ." She wanted to, but for reasons other than to pursue sleep. Foolish thoughts.

"I agree your thoughts are foolish."

His breath slid over her face like a soft caress. She hesitated. "Why?"

"Never mind." He drew her against his muscled body, her soft, flowing gown offering but scant separation.

Rowan expected to feel fear being so close to a vampire. Instead, she found his presence a balm of comfort. More unsettling, she wished for no barrier, to feel his naked flesh against her.

On a groan, he pressed a kiss against her brow. "Lass, do not think overmuch."

Simple for him, but her body ached in ways she'd never imagined. Another surge of tiredness swept through her. Rowan yawned, her indecent thoughts fading into a blur of exhaustion. Her lids grew heavy, and, against her will, she tumbled into the black void of sleep.

Aedan stared at Rowan asleep within his arms, the sweet taste of her humming through his mind, her erotic visions feeding his own. She was a virgin. When he took her, he would be her first. Never would another touch her.

Ever.

And they would make love, of that he held no doubt. Though she was an innocent, he'd sensed her growing excitement; her visions of them entwined were simple yet devastating.

He inhaled her scent, shaken by how much he wanted her. Sweat beaded his brow, and his fangs lengthened. With sheer determination, he willed away his desire to feed as well as the gut-wrenching need that demanded he claim her for his mate.

He must not forget the reason they'd met. Someone within his clan's trusted circle wanted him, their laird, dead. What had his enemy used to leave him in such a disabled state? Senses alert, he scanned his body. All but dissolved, a trace of foreign substance lay near his heart.

Foxglove.

A dangerous herb, but not strong enough to kill a vampire. A fact a vampire understood, and the reason why Aedan had been left within the stone circle. Unconscious, and with the circle of stones slowly drawing his power so that he would be unable to move if he awoke, he would have been burned to death by the morning sun's rays.

Sunlight washed the earth beyond the cave's entry, wrapping the roll of land within its warmth. Aedan's lids grew heavier. Aye, 'twas time to sleep. Whoever plotted against him would be seeking rest as well.

He settled more comfortably against Rowan, and her flaxen hair spilled from its hastily woven plait across the paleness of his arm as if fairy dust. A smile touched his mouth. Aye, he was a man enchanted. Intrigued, he lifted several locks of her hair, let the strands slide through his fingers to spiral back against her windswept mane.

Rowan, a fitting name. The rowan tree was a symbol of strength. The five-pointed star at the base of each berry was a symbol of protection to the ancients. The hearty white flowers that grew upon the sturdy limbs were a symbol of innocence, appropriate as the lass was innocent of a man's touch. He would not dwell upon the latter.

Another wave of fatigue settled over him. This day he would rest, but this night, once he'd fed, he would keep watch over the stone circle and wait. Whoever had left him there should return to ensure his body lay charred inside.

Then, the traitor would die.

Confident he would soon have vengeance against whoever had dared to try and kill him, Aedan cast an invisible shield upon the cave's entry, allowing no one to enter. With the scent of Rowan filling his every breath, he closed his eyes and gave in to much needed sleep.

A wisp of chilled air skimmed over Rowan. With a shiver, she reached for a blanket, and her hand scraped upon the cold dirt.

Dirt?

Where was she?

Memories flooded her, of running for her life after being branded a witch, of finding herself before the stone circle, then of helping save a vampire's life, of his unexpected tenderness, and of how he'd held her in his arms and pressed a kiss upon her brow as she'd fallen asleep.

She opened her eyes. Blackness engulfed her. Heart pounding, Rowan stumbled to her feet. "Aedan?"

From deep within the forest a wolf howled, the lonely sound macabre.

"Aedan, are you here?"

A gust, rich with the scent of the night, tumbled past.

On cautious feet she crept to the entry. She searched the midnight sky, thick with stars against the moonless night. Though he'd taken a few drops of her blood, hunger must have driven him to feed.

She listened, thankful the forest did not ring with the angry shouts of men in search of her. No doubt they were scouring the woods. Should she use the blanket of night to put more distance between them, head south where she could begin a new life? Or, should she stay and trust Aedan to keep his word to protect her?

Tingles of sensation edged up her skin.

Uneasy, she scanned the distant line of trees, found her gaze drawn to the stone circle, its sturdy columns black against the star-washed night. As she stared, a pulse filled the air, slow, steady, growing stronger. The need to move toward the ancient circle filled her.

Confused, she took a step forward.

Mist swirled around her; then fully dressed, Aedan stood before her.

Rowan jumped back. "How did you do that?" She held up her hand. "Nay, I do not want to know."

Black eyes held hers, their intensity stealing her breath. With a curse he caught her wrist, his hold gentle, then turned her away from the circle and led her toward the cave.

"Aedan, what is wrong?"

At the nervousness within her voice, Aedan relaxed his stance. She was perplexed; how could she not be? He was as confused. "The stone circle drew you, did it not?"

"Aye." A blush colored her cheeks. "Though it sounds foolish."

"Far from foolish," he replied. "To humans a stone circle is a place of power, a place for ceremony, but for vampires 'tis fatal." He took her hand, needing to feel the warmth of her skin against his own. "If a vampire is caught within, the stones draw his strength, and over time we become unable to move."

"And with the morn, you would be burned to death. Oh God." A shiver wove through her, and he folded her within his arms, their bond growing stronger with each passing moment.

Worry-filled turquoise eyes met his. "Aedan, why would I be drawn into the circle?"

He frowned. "Mayhap it sensed our bond." But, doubts lingered.

"Mayhap." She exhaled a ragged breath. "Do you have any idea who tried to kill you?"

He shook off his disturbing thoughts. "Nay, but I will find my enemy." He scanned the night-blackened stones, the shiver of starlight glinting off each. Majestic. Powerful. "Whoever dared such a traitorous act will return to ensure I am dead."

"What will you do then?"

Aedan remained silent. Soon he must explain he was laird of the Highland Coven, and that he could not allow anyone near him he could not trust. But he did not want to trouble her when she already had so much to worry about.

And what of her being his mate? When would the time come when he must share such critical information?

A stick cracked nearby.

Hands strong and gentle lifted Rowan. The earth blurred, and she found herself pressed within the shadows inside the entry of the cave.

"Stay!" Aedan whispered. With a swirl of mist, he vanished.

Heart pounding, she stared into the shadows of the night.

A wolf howled, closer this time.

Prickles slid up her flesh. Someone was watching her. Pulse racing, she scanned the looming blackness, the air growing cooler with each breath.

Mist engulfed her. "You are safe."

On a half scream, Rowan turned. The swirl of white cleared, and Aedan again stood before her, his body taut, his gaze searching the forest beyond. After a final scan, his eyes met hers.

Would she ever grow used to his appearing out of nowhere? "What did you find?" Nerves tangled her voice.

"Naught. Neither did I pick up any unusual scent. Most likely, a roebuck or another animal of the night passed nearby."

She should agree, assure herself all was well, but . . .

"What is it?"

At the edge in his voice, she searched the night-blackened land. "I am unsure, but it was almost as if I sensed someone was out there. Oddly, with the passing moments, the air grew colder."

"Foxglove," he said with a hiss.

"What?"

"Whoever drugged me did so with foxglove, which has dulled my senses."

A tremor rippled through her. "Another vampire is nearby?"

"Mayhap."

"But you are not sure."

Aedan shook his head, his frustration easy to read. "Nay."

"Most likely you are right; it was an animal," she said. "Or, if another vampire, he or she could have been far away."

"Do nae make excuses for me. I have sworn to protect you," he said, his voice grim. "If another vampire was nearby, I should have been able to detect him. I had not considered the drug's effects, a mistake I will not make again." His hands clenched into fists at his sides, then slowly released. "However much I wish to take you elsewhere to keep you safe, it is imperative that I remain here another day, mayhap two. If anyone returns to confirm my death, I must know."

"I understand."

"You do not, but you must trust that I will keep you from harm."

Touched by the depth of his caring, she laid her hand upon his forearm. "However irrational, I do."

Aedan drew her hand within his and pressed a kiss upon her palm, humbled to have found this amazing woman, one he wanted forever. " 'Tis not irrational."

"Is it not? All my life I have been told tales of vampires' viciousness, of their killing people in cold blood without thought. Yet, with you I find trust." She paused, her eyes searching his as understanding dawned. "But because you can read my mind you already know that, do you not?"

He stroked his thumb across her lower lip, wanting her, needing her forever. "Aye. "

If he could read her mind, was there more that he could sense or know about her that he hadn't revealed?

At her thought, he released her, turned and scoured the darkened woods. Judging from the stiffness of his body, he was upset.

Rowan's unease grew. "Aedan, what are you keeping from me?"

Silence.

"Aedan."

He turned, his face taut, his eyes torn between happiness and regret. "I want you."

Need infused her, a yearning so desperate she caught her breath.

His nostrils flared.

Pleasure shot through her. He was not immune to her either.

"Nay, I am far from immune. I want you overmuch."

"Never before have I wanted a man." Heat warmed her cheeks.

"Never have I lain with a man. But against all that I have been taught, against my beliefs, I want you."

"Rowan."

At the desire that roughened his voice, heat built within her. "Tell me."

He muttered a curse. "Never did I believe I would find you."

"Find me?" She frowned. "We have never met."

He gave a cold laugh void of amusement. "We have not, but our blood recognizes the other."

"You are not making any sense."

On a shaky exhale, his eyes held hers, a silent plea within. "Rowan, you are my mate."

Chapter Three

Against the backdrop of the night, shock veiled Rowan's face. "I am your mate? Impossible."

Hurt tore through Aedan at her disbelief, but had not his surprise at the discovery been as great? "Rowan, neither you nor I were given a choice. Our bond is a gift of nature neither of us can change."

"I . . ."

Bedamned. "Did you not say but moments ago that you want me?"

Her body trembling, she tried to step back.

Aedan held her, needed her to accept the attraction between them, one as natural as his next breath. "I am going to kiss you—unless you bid me to stop."

Eyes wide and unsure, she watched him.

However much she struggled to accept the fact, beneath her nervousness he saw need. He lowered his mouth to a whisper above hers.

"Order me to stop," he said as her scent infused his every breath, driving him insane, "before I touch you, before I taste you everywhere."

Her body shuddered against his. "I cannot."

On a groan he claimed her lips, hot, hard, demanding her response. Her actions would acknowledge what she refused to say.

"Aedan," she moaned as she returned his kiss, her own blistering hot.

His tongue slid between her lips, teasing, tasting, seducing her until her body melded against his. On a soft growl, he backed her against the cave wall and pressed his full length against her, wanting her to feel every inch of his need.

He lifted his head. "I am going to make love to you. Here. With naught between us but the stars and the night."

Another tremor whipped through Rowan. Until Aedan she had never known someone who made her want, who made her feel as a woman desired. Now, she did.

And he was a vampire.

However frightening the thought, she accepted it.

But, he believed her a woman with whom he shared a life-long bond. How she wished such a connection could exist between them. But she was human, while he was a vampire. She could not ponder the differences between them now. This stunning vampire, a man who sought to protect her, who found her beautiful and engaging, wanted her. However wrong, she wanted him as well.

Her lower lip trembled. "I need you."

"Aye," he said on a rough whisper, "I will fulfill each fantasy and more."

A cool breeze tumbled over her body. Rowan gasped. "I am naked."

"Aye. A vampire's speed has many a use." He slid his lips against the sensitive skin at her neck. "Worry not, I will nae rush the lovemaking."

The sultry promise in his voice left her breathless. How could he move her to such depths? How could he make her want him so much? If nothing else, she understood that he was a man of his word, one she found herself needing more than she could explain.

Rowan laid her hand upon his heart. "Aedan, make love to me."

Hands, tender and gentle, slid up her flesh to cup her breasts. "Only to you—forevermore. With a heated look, he lowered his head and drew a sensitive tip into his mouth, suckled.

Sensation poured through her as he teased, tasted until her mind blurred with desire.

"Aye, lass," he said, kneeling before her, " 'tis pleasure you feel, pleasure only I shall ever bring you."

His hands skimmed over her, and she struggled to speak.

"Feel me touch you," he whispered.

His fingers splayed her most private place, and cold air brushed against her. She gasped. "I—"

"Watch me," he said, hunger burning in his eyes, his mouth but a breath away from her, "while I taste you."

Merciful Mary! Should she allow this?

"Should you?" he asked as his finger slid deep within her. A groan echoed within his throat, and his gaze darkened. "You are so wet," he said, slowly withdrawing his finger. "Tell me, should you allow this?"

Her every fiber hummed. The air around her pulsed with a scorching heat. "Yes." Would she now be damned?

"Nay, never will you be damned." With a smile, he leaned forward, drew his tongue across her slickness, tasted her essence.

As with her breasts, he savored, his mouth a sweet torment. Her body trembled with each stroke of his tongue. Her mind blurred with emotion, a frenzy that devoured her until all she could do was feel.

"Now," he whispered as his lips pressed against her sensitive wetness, "let yourself go."

A slow tremor wove through Rowan before waves of heat swamped her. "Aedan!"

"Come for me."

Another burst of energy tore through her; her body stiffened, then soared. Colors exploded in her mind.

Her cries of pleasure fueled Aedan as he took, tasted, and cherished her release. Never had he met a woman so sensitive. Her eyes glazed with passion, and he watched her again spill over the edge. Satisfied, he swept her into his arms.

"Wh-What are you doing?" Her question stumbled out in a sated whisper.

"Making love to you."

A frown furrowed her brow. "I thought you already did."

He nuzzled her neck as he strode into the blackness of the cave, laying her upon a cloth he'd spread out earlier. "That was but the beginning."

"The beginning?" Rowan sighed, a satisfied glow upon her face. "Will I die?"

"Aye." He winked. "With pleasure."

"I think mayhap you are a wee bit arrogant."

"Aye," he said as he rested his body atop hers, his full length flush against her sensitive wetness, "very much so when it comes to you." He pressed his brow against hers.

"What?" she asked.

"The first time, 'twill hurt."

A smile filled with pleasure and sincerity touched her face. "As I have heard, the pain will last but a short while; then there will be naught but pleasure."

"Lass, I believe those are supposed to be my words to offer comfort to you."

She arched a playful brow. "I am a healer."

Need surged through him. "So you are." He slid against her swollen wetness and groaned. "When I take you, we will be joined by yet another bond forever."

"A bond I will cherish," she murmured, her mind overwhelmed with the wonders of her feelings.

Her response left him humbled, thankful for the gift of her being. Aedan drove deep, and Rowan cried out, the streak of pain shattering the warmth of her gaze, tearing him apart. Beneath him, Rowan's body began to glitter. Stunned, Aedan stilled. The ancient tale was well known. When one of the fey lost her virginity, her skin glittered.

Rowan was a fairy?

Impossible.

He'd scanned her thoughts. She had been raised in the Highlands by the humans.

The twinkles of light coating her body grew brighter.

Panicking, he scoured her mind. Naught. Aedan started to withdraw from her thoughts, but a dark shadow locked deep inside caught his attention. He wove through the matrix.

By the sword's blade, 'twas true!

"Aedan?" Rowan said, her voice unsure.

He tried to focus as his mind fought to understand. A fairy. Which explained her healing abilities, those natural to the fey, and why the Scots who chased her believed her a witch. How could she not know, not have any inkling of such life-altering information? He again scoured her mind for answers, found naught but innocence of the fact.

As if her knowledge of her heritage changed anything? Ancient laws forbid a vampire from changing a fairy into a vampire.

Though the fey's magic was strong, it was unknown if a fairy could survive the transition.

Neither was the threat to her life alone. Regardless of whether she was destined to be with him for life, if he dared try and convert her, the agony she would experience during the transition would be sensed by Ysenda, Queen of the Otherworld, whose retribution was foretold to be quick.

And lethal.

"Aedan, is something wrong?" Rowan asked, her voice anxious.

Wrong? Indeed. She was his mate. But to change her into a vampire was forbidden, and doing so now could invite death. "You are—were a virgin," he said, trying to absorb the enormity of the revelation.

A tentative smile widened her lips. "My body is adjusting."

"Indeed," he said on a groan. What should he do?

Rowan shivered against him, and her tight sheath wrapped around him causing tortuous pleasure.

What could he do? No longer was she a virgin. And, she was his mate, his, forever. Emotions swept him. Mayhap forbidden to change her into a vampire, but he would give her a woman's pleasure. The issues of her being of the fey, he would consider later.

Aedan took her mouth in a long, slow kiss, then lifted his head. "Now," he said, his voice a low rumble, "I will finish making love to you." With each stroke slow, he cherished the spirals of heat shooting through him, tempting him to let go, to drive into her until he found his release. Aedan kept up a steady pace. This time, her first time, would be for her.

Rowan's head fell to the side. "Aedan," she whispered, her throaty voice thick with wonder. "I know not if I can take much more."

"You can," he said as he slid his full length inside and proved her wrong.

Against the burst of starlight flooding the heavens, the stone circle stood like a black mark on the earth. Without warning, striations of cloud severed the sky, wisps that for but a moment held the struggling shimmers, and then faded into night.

Restless, Aedan scanned the land outside the cave.

A soft clatter echoed from the northwest.

He focused on the sound, listened for voices, the scrape of steel against a leather scabbard, anything to alert him to another's presence.

Long moments passed.

Naught.

With the foxglove still dulling his senses, he'd taken extra precautions, set extra wards. If anyone had tried to come near during the night, he would have known.

Over the hours past most of his weakness had diminished, his fast recovery due to Rowan's being fey. Known for its ability to heal, the powerful fey blood was restoring his health faster than he had believed possible.

"Aedan?"

At Rowan's sleepy voice, images of the hours they'd made love tangled within his mind. The way she'd responded to his every touch, her creative passion as she'd caressed him as well.

With a tender smile, he returned and knelt beside her. He nudged a swath of wheat blond hair away from her cheek, where her skin was dusted with a star-edged glow. "You are beautiful when you awaken."

A tinge of red stained her cheeks. "I look awful."

"Nay." He gave her a gentle smile, amazed at the feelings Rowan stirred. "You look like a woman sated, a woman whom I adore, and a woman whom I will cherish always."

Hope flickered in her eyes and then faded. "You know little of me."

"I know your presence is a gift," he replied, needing her to understand the magnitude of her presence within his life.

She opened her mouth to speak, shook her head.

Aedan lifted her chin with his finger, caught the questions haunting her mind. "What is it?" At her hesitation, he stroked his thumb along the soft curve of her jaw. "Rowan, you can trust me."

She drew a slow breath, exhaled. "You said I was your mate."

"A fact you find difficult to accept."

"Difficult?" She gave a shaky laugh. "Until yesterday, vampires were but a legend, terrifying creatures of the night. Now, not only have I met one, but I have made love to one."

She turned away, but he caught the distress in her eyes. By

the sword's blade, she loved him! Emotions stormed him: need, desperation, happiness.

In their meager time together, she'd given him a glimpse of their future. Except, with her humanness, her life would end too soon.

At the thought of losing her, an ache ripped through him. Sweat beaded his brow, and his fangs lengthened; he fought the urge to turn her so she could be with him forever. An act forbidden. Slamming his eyes shut, he struggled against his body's demand and the inherent need to claim Rowan with his every breath.

Within the quiet of the night, Aedan's lungs labored.

Concerned, Rowan turned. "Are you well?

Silence.

He lifted his lids. Under the sheen of moonlight, Aedan's scrutiny turned cold. A shudder wracked his muscled frame, and his fangs lengthened.

Tugging on her garb, she shoved to her feet, stumbled back. "No!" Regardless of what he made her feel, want, he was dangerous. She bolted for the entry.

"Rowan!"

Stones jabbed her feet as she ran faster. Without warning, strong hands caught her, turned her to face him.

"You will not leave me!"

Tears blurred her eyes as she pulled, twisted to break free.

Fingers tightened on her wrist.

Terror slammed her chest. "What do you *want* from me?!"

On a muttered curse, his hold gentled. "Rowan, never will I harm you."

Never would he harm her? He was a vampire. How could she have believed a relationship between them could exist?

Because they'd made love?

Merciful Mary, she'd made love with a vampire!

A violent shiver wracked her body. Her knees trembled, because she wanted him still.

"Rowan, listen to me."

Ashamed, she struggled to break free. "Let me go!"

"There is nothing to be ashamed of, nor to fear. Aye, I am dangerous, but never to you." He exhaled. His face relaxed, and his fangs withdrew.

Before Rowan stood the man she'd first seen, a stunning warrior who would make any woman want.

"Let me explain," Aedan said. Desperation trembled within his request, a raw plea that had her hesitating. Unsure, Rowan nodded.

On an exhale, he scanned their surroundings and then faced her. The strain across his forehead eased, but she caught the lines near his eyes, proof he wasn't as calm as he appeared.

" 'Tis normal for vampires to draw blood from our mates, but you are not a vampire. Neither will I convert you." He exhaled. "Our pairing is unique. More than your blood melding with mine, more than your wanting and being drawn to me. 'Twas destiny that we came together. A fate neither of us could expect . . . nor understand." He paused. "I struggle with the acceptance of such a pairing as much as you."

"Because you are a . . . vampire?"

His gaze grew intense. "Rowan, I am more than a common vampire."

"More?"

"Aye." His voice rumbled with authority. "I am the laird of the Highland Vampire Coven."

Astonished, she stared. "Their laird?"

"Aye. You found me naked, my garb and pendant with the clan seal stolen."

Nay, could not be true. 'Twas a poor joke. She'd watched his teeth lengthen, witnessed Aedan change into a ruthless killer.

He gave her a gentle shake. "Enough of those foolish thoughts! I am nae a killer, nor is this a joke. You are overwhelmed; how can you not be? But, hear my words, I speak the truth."

"I . . ." Fighting for calm, she studied the strong lines of his face, remembered the confident way he held himself as he spoke, his regal bearing. A day ago she'd believed him a braggart, or a thief on the run.

Not . . . a laird betrayed.

But, he'd promised to protect her from harm. He'd said she was his destiny. Yet she was but a commoner and he a laird, a man of tremendous responsibility and power. How was this conceivable? And if 'twas possible, did she want to live her life with him forever?

"You are my mate."

The calmness of his delivery changed naught. "People do not mate."

"I agree, but vampires are not human. Like wolves, when we find our life partner, we join forever."

"I am neither a vampire, nor a wolf."

"I am as confused as you," he agreed. "Such a bond should be impossible, yet you exist, and the moment I tasted your blood, I recognized you as my mate."

Torn, Rowan hesitated. Could she find happiness with this vampire, a fulfillment she'd believed unattainable because she'd been an outcast to the Highland clans? She could not forget the way they'd made love, the intensity, the passion, as if they were truly meant to be together.

But mates?

"If I accept there can be such a bond between a human and a vampire, what does this mean for us?" Us. She loved the sound of belonging, of being with Aedan forever.

Black eyes glowed. "A life together forever."

"Aedan . . ." Emotion swelled in her chest at the love she felt for him, at the dreams he made her dare to believe.

"Trust me."

"I do. Incredibly I do." She swallowed hard. "And I want you . . . for always." Tears spilled onto her cheeks, and he wiped them away.

"What is wrong?"

The tenderness of his voice left her aching. "Do you not think we wish for the impossible?"

"Nay." With infinite gentleness Aedan claimed her mouth. As Rowan's taste poured through him, pressure built, and his fangs lengthened. For a moment he allowed himself the pleasure of sliding them along the velvet curve of her throat. She stiffened, and then slowly relaxed. At her sigh, the way her body pressed against his in an intimate plea, he hardened to a painful ache.

Humbled by her acceptance of him, however much he wanted to sink his teeth deep and convert her, he would not do so. But, with each hour the urge to change her was growing. Would there come a time when he couldn't resist? Nay, whatever it took, he would leave her untouched. To remain human.

And half fairy.

"What of your people?" she asked, breaking into his troubled musings. "As I am human, how can they accept me?"

"They will."

Amusement danced in her eyes. "Because you will demand it?"

"Because when they meet you they will be charmed."

Her throaty laugh slid through him like warm mead, and he longed to take her again, but having lost her virginity hours ago, she needed to heal. The oncoming night would be soon enough, and then, he still must be gentle.

"Aedan," she said, her voice serious, "your people may demand you claim a life partner of your own kind."

"You are my destiny."

She arched a doubtful brow. "And that is all they will need to hear to convince them?"

"There are challenges to face." An understatement. Never had a vampire discovered his mate was a human, much less one half fey. The uproar at exposing her grim and murky heritage to his clan would be formidable indeed, but his people would learn to accept Rowan. He would demand it of them for, above all, he refused to lose her.

"Challenges indeed." She hesitated. "And what of the person you await this night? If he does not return to make sure you are dead, how will you find him?"

A question he'd pondered. "If no one returns to check the stone circle this night, I must return to my coven under disguise so as not to alert them that I live."

"Why not put the ashes from a fire within the circle?" Rowan asked. "Then, if anyone comes once we are gone, he will believe the remains are you."

"Nay, my scent would not be among the ashes . . ." Why had he not thought of it before? "But you are right. If I tossed a small length of my hair within the flames, whoever returns would detect my scent and be convinced I am dead." He touched her shoulder. "Wait here. I am going to retrieve wood."

A sudden mist swirled around him, and Rowan found herself staring into the night.

She scanned the sweep of trees beneath the moonlight.

Like a soft whisper, music flowed upon the breeze as if a person played upon a lute.

Impossible. And the song appeared to come from within the stone ring. Could this night become any stranger? Intrigued, she stepped forward.

With each step the music grew. Several paces before the massive pillars, a gust swirled around her.

A chill swept her, and Rowan stopped. Nay, she must return—

A deep tremor shook the ground. The earth inside the ring darkened. Like bony fingers, cracks split the turf, spiraling out from the center. Without warning, the wind rose, pulling her toward the gap between the stones.

Terrified, she fought to break free, but the force strengthened, dragging her body toward the towering pillars. *No!* Rowan opened her mouth to scream.

Then blackness.

Chapter Four

"Rowan?" Another shiver of fear ran through Aedan as he stared at Rowan's limp form in his arms. Her face was pale, her breath but a flutter against his skin. She lived. Barely. Had he taken a moment longer to return, she would have been drawn into the stone circle.

And would have died.

Before, he'd believed the circle sensed their connection, but after learning she was part fey, he'd dismissed any threat to her. The stone circle was the entry to the Otherworld, her home. But now, danger pulsed through the air, a malignancy that foretold ill.

For her.

Why? Rowan had no vampire blood within her. If she had—

A hum of energy like a breath vibrated through the air.

He stilled. Nay, 'twas impossible. Such was—

Whispers of light brushed against Rowan's skin, shimmered around her in a whimsical dance. His breath left him in a rush.

She carried their child.

Overwhelmed, humbled by such a gift, Aedan pressed a kiss upon her brow. Never had he believed he would find a woman who loved him. Now, Rowan had given him that and more.

"Rowan?" he whispered.

A soft moan fell from her lips.

He brushed her damp locks from her brow, the sheen of moisture revealing the subtle trauma upon her system, that indeed her body had begun to change. Would her fey blood protect her human side from the intense changes to come? How long would it take for their child to grow within her? Seven months as was the norm for a vampire child? Due to the strength of her fairy blood, would the time she carried their child be less?

And what of her human side? Would her body accept the presence of a vampire child, or would it rebel? By making love with her, had he endangered her life? Bedamned! Why had he not considered the chance of her becoming pregnant, or the ramifications? He'd been so caught up in wanting her, he'd thought of naught else.

Aedan blew out a rough breath. Now he understood. The power within the stone circle had detected the child and sensed that within its body pulsed vampire blood. A natural enemy of the vampire, the protective energy within the stones had sought to rid Rowan's body of the invader.

Had the power of the stones alerted the fairy queen? Nay, if so, Ysenda, Queen of the Otherworld, would have appeared. Though he'd planned to remain near the circle to try to catch his betrayer, for Rowan's safety he must take them far away.

"Aedan?"

At Rowan's feeble whisper he gave her a tender smile. "I am here." He gently laid her upon the soft grass, knelt by her side. "How do you feel?"

"I—I . . . am dizzy."

A mild symptom of her pregnancy. How long before she would feel the first kick of their babe? "I asked that you remain hidden. Why did you leave the cave before my return?"

A frown crowded her brow. "I heard the song of a lute coming from the stone circle. Curious, I went to find the source."

Anger sparked. The fey's passion for music was well known, though not to Rowan. It had been a trap set to lure her.

She started to sit, and Aedan helped her. "As I walked closer the ground began to tremble; cracks opened within the circle. I tried to leave"—a shiver wracked her body as she glanced toward the circle—"but it pulled me. I-I must have passed out."

Bedamned. And he'd caught her a second before she'd fallen inside. "Rowan," he said, keeping his voice calm, "I am taking you away from here."

Lines furrowed her brow. "I thought you needed to wait here another night to see if anyone returned to the circle?"

"Things have changed."

Shrewd eyes studied his. "What things?"

The waver in her voice had him damning the entire situation. "Rowan . . ." How did he explain the magnitude of what he'd discovered? Blast it, how could he not? "You are carrying my child."

"Your child?" A smile tugged at her mouth. He but teased her. Rowan waited for his answering glint of laughter, anything to assure her Aedan was merely jesting to lighten the moment. But, his expression remained intense.

She tried to pull back; he held her firm.

"It cannot be," she whispered, as if to speak the words would ensure their truth.

"Never would I lie about something of such import."

The seriousness of his voice shook her further. "How is such a thing possible?"

The faintest smile touched the corner of his mouth, faded. "You are a healer, you know how a child is created."

Frustration swelled. "That is not what I meant."

His face softened, and he took her hand, cradled it within his own. "My belief is that when we made love, our bodies recognized that we are mates and—"

"Created a child?" Her fragmented whisper echoed her shock. "I find it difficult to believe."

"Aye, there is much to accept."

"Except you have," she said, her mind overwhelmed, "completely, without any question."

" 'Tis nature's decision, and not my place to question her wisdom." Aedan glanced toward the circle, then turned back to her, his expression grim. "You are not safe here."

Reasons why she was unsafe poured through her mind, the foremost one being that she was in love with a vampire.

Black eyes narrowed. "Never would I hurt you.

"Nay," she whispered. With Aedan she found strength, a calmness she'd never before experienced, and a belief that, come what may, he would protect her.

A far-off yell echoed from the south.

Against the merest hint of morning, torchlight wavered in the distance.

A low growl erupted from Aedan. He released her, shoved to his feet. "The men who search for you."

She stood, caught his hand. "What are you going to do?"

Furious eyes met hers. "Kill them."

Heart pounding, she shook her head. "Their deaths will but incite more people to join in the search for me."

"Then I will wipe the men's minds, and they will remember naught."

If only 'twas so simple. "Should the men return to their village with no remembrance, 'twill convince any who hold doubts that I have cast a spell to erase their memories. Alas, they too will raise their swords and join in to try to catch and burn me at the stake."

His mouth tightened. "None will harm you!"

The determination within his voice left her shaken. "Aedan," she urged, "there must be another way."

He eyed her a long moment, his expression dark with anger; then his body relaxed a degree. "We will leave here. Before we go, we will convince them you are dead."

If they could, it would be an immense relief. "How?"

"The cliffs are but a few leagues to the west. We will travel there. Then, you will toss your clothes over the edge into the sea. Once we have hidden, you will scream, and the men in search of you will come running."

Simple, yet effective. "With my clothes floating atop the waves, they will believe that guilt-laden, I have jumped to my death."

"Aye. More important, they will end their search and report to the others that you have died."

"And what about the false evidence you were to leave to convince your betrayer you are dead?" Rowan asked.

"Once the men searching for you have departed, we will return, and I will finish the task."

A man's voice echoed nearby.

Aedan caught her hand. "Hurry." With keen night vision, he guided her through the forest. Soon, the rich sting of salt grew in the air, the ground soft with the moisture from the sea. He pushed aside the limb of a thick fir, and she gasped.

" 'Tis beautiful."

Cliffs, battered by wind and time, stood illuminated by the moonlight. Blasts of white erupted against the ragged stone where the surf pounded the sheer wall of rock below.

"Aye, 'tis a bonny sight, one I never tire of." He led her forward. Near the edge, he released her, nodded. "Go ahead and remove your garb."

However foolish, the thought of disrobing before Aedan left her shy.

Tenderness touched his face. "After the ways I have touched you, kissed you everywhere, there is no reason to be bashful."

Heat burned her cheeks. "Must you read my thoughts?"

He gave a soft chuckle. Always would she amaze him. Aedan lifted her chin with his thumb, bent to place a soft kiss upon her mouth. "I will not look."

Seconds later, the whisper of clothes sounded in the night, awakening images of her naked within his mind. His body ached to take her again, her sweet taste still warm upon his lips.

"I am done," Rowan said.

"Cast your clothes over the edge."

The flutter of clothes melded with the rush of waves.

His body hardened. Stealing but one glimpse of her lush body, he covered her nakedness with his cloak, then led her to the nearby bushes. "Now scream."

Rowan's yell pierced the night.

"Over there!" a distant voice called.

The thud of footsteps grew. Between the ripple of leaves, torchlight cast slashes of yellow upon the sway of grass and jagged rock.

"The tracks lead this way," a man snarled, his burr deep.

"Aye," replied another. "Toward the cliffs."

Fractured torchlight illuminated the men as they drew near, their faces mottled with anger.

Rage churned within Aedan as he struggled against the urge to kill those who would dare harm Rowan. Though he'd promised not to touch them, neither would he risk these men's catching sight of her. Within his mind he beckoned the air, thick with moisture from the sea.

Around them mist grew, thickening to a slow, subtle sweep of white.

The nearest Scot rubbed his arms, his scraggly beard accenting a weathered face lined with a grimace. "Blasted cold tonight."

"Aye," another man replied, shrewd eyes scanning his surroundings, "and looking as if 'twill be foggy as well."

Rowan stiffened.

Fury wrapped around Aedan. *These are the men who have been chasing you, aye?*

Surprise widened her eyes. *We can speak through our thoughts?*
He nodded.

The men, are they the ones after you?

Aye. *The bastards, 'twould sate many an urge to slay them.* He rubbed Rowan's arms, waited. Once the men saw the garments floating on the surf and departed for their clan, he would take her far away.

"Step with care, lads," called a man leading the group who had a deep scar slashed across his lower jaw. "I can hear the pounding of water. The cliffs are near."

A redheaded man close to the carved rock lifted his torch, the shudder of flames casting harsh shadows against his face. "The edge is over here." He took several cautious steps, paused and leaned forward.

"Do you see anything?" called a man farther to the back.

"Aye," the redheaded man answered. "A woman's gown floats upon the waves."

The man with the scraggly beard halted before the edge. He peered over, grunted. " 'Twas the lass's scream we heard when she jumped."

"Looks as if the witch killed herself," the man with the scar across his jaw grumbled. "Saves us the blasted trouble."

"Do you think she's dead?" a tall man asked as he moved to stand beside the others.

Silence descended upon the shoddy group, and Rowan tensed at Aedan's side. He covered her hand with his, gave a subtle mental push to the tall man holding doubt.

Gnarled fingers tugging at his scraggly beard, he shrugged. "Aye, the lass is dead; the clothes are proof. Besides, I see nay tracks leading away. Let us return to our clan. 'Tis good news we will bring."

"Aye," the redheaded man said as he stepped back.

Murmurs of agreement followed the group as they faded into the forest, broken torchlight spitting like evil whispers in their wake.

Rowan relaxed at Aedan's side. "Thank you."

"For?"

"The mist."

He lifted her hand, pressed a kiss upon her palm. "Only for you. Come, we must return to the cave. Once I am done, we will leave." The mist cloaked them as they walked, the coolness offering little relief from the heat of his need for her, which had been inflamed by his awareness of her nakedness beneath his cloak.

At the cave, Aedan halted. "Wait here." He entered the circle, sensing the immediate slow drain of his energy. Posthaste, he stacked kindling in an outline of where he'd lain and then used his dagger to cut a swath of his hair. He laid the strands atop the wood, then hurried outside the ring of ancient stones.

Focused on the branches, he gathered his power. Wisps of smoke curled, then burst into flame, the odor of burning hair strong. Within minutes, the roaring fire faded, leaving behind only ashes.

Soft footsteps echoed behind him, stilled. "Now, whoever has betrayed you will believe you are dead."

"Aye," he agreed. "As those searching for you at the cliffs believe you."

A tense silence fell between them, one laden with shadows. " 'Tis time to leave."

Rowan glanced up. "Where will we go?"

"To a place known only to lairds and members of high regard within the coven."

"A laird." Though soft, her words held tension.

"Aye," he said, "but I am a simple person, one who desperately needs you."

"Simple? Nay, Aedan, there is nothing simple about you." She stilled.

"What?"

Beneath the star-filled sky, her unsure eyes met his. "I will give birth to a princess."

"Or a prince."

Her brows arched. "Do you know?"

"Nay." Before she asked or said anything else, he wrapped her within his arms.

"What are you doing?"

"Taking you where you will be safe." He envisioned the sweep of mist, the cool moisture filling his pores, shattering his form in a violent rush. A whoosh exploded within his mind. Fragments of his body imploded, splintered into droplets. In a vaporous swirl, he cradled Rowan and flew north, her gasp lost to the echo of time, the frantic passage of air unbound.

A short while later Rowan fought the blur within her head.

"Steady, lass."

Strong hands held her, and Aedan's smile came into focus, full of pride and arrogance. She touched her temple. "What just happened?"

"I have brought you to my ancestral home."

They'd traveled?

"Aye," he said.

"Why did you not warn me that you would shift?"

" 'Twould have taken too long."

She blew out a frustrated sigh, turned to take in her surroundings. Darkness clung to the land. No, stars shimmered within the sky. The moonlight outlined wisps of battered clouds moving slowly in the night and the peaks jutting skyward around them with merciless care.

Rowan spun to face him. "We are atop a mountain!"

"We are." Pride coated his voice. " 'Tis the Cullinthe of Skye, land passed down through generations, a place shown to me in my youth."

Within the sheen of weakening night, the fading moonlight accented the approaching dawn. Like a painting of grandeur, the rugged mountains tumbled before her in an endless array.

Through a cut in the formidable stone, the ocean came into view. Waves surged ashore, washed over the lavish array of rocks as a layer of fog wove through the shoreline.

Touched, she met Aedan's gaze. "All my life, each night when I found my bed, I thought of the morrow, of the warmth of the sun upon the land and its rays upon my face." She exhaled, the magnificence sprawled before her stealing her breath. "Never did I think of the night as magical, but now, because of you, I shall think of it as no other." Pride honed his face, his expression that of a man born to guide his people, of a laird who ruled his land. He belonged in this regal, rugged landscape, his presence as necessary as the next beat of her heart.

Aedan lowered his mouth a breath above hers. "As is your presence to me. Soon, I must seek shelter from the sun's rays, but this moment is ours."

His deep burr rumbled through her as his mouth settled with delicate intimacy upon hers, as soft as the brush of a fairy's wings, as heated as the lick of flame. She melted, gave to him everything he asked for and more.

With infinite tenderness, he laid her upon a bed of grass, his body covering hers, his hands guiding her with each caress as he filled her.

"Aedan," she whispered. He made love to her slowly, exquisitely, until her body trembled out of control. His eyes held hers as he increased the pace, the intensity moving her higher, higher, until on a shudder she fell over the edge. Explosions of color swirled around her with vibrant appeal, reds, yellows, and blues on a background of radiant white as Aedan found his own release. Then she was floating, her mind warm with satisfaction, her body sated.

He rolled to the side and drew her with him.

Lulled by the steady beat of his heart, the haze of warmth within her body, she laid her head against his muscled chest. She could lie here forever.

A playful smile touched his lips. "Methinks you have forgotten your naked state."

Stunned, she lifted her head. "Yo—"

"Removed the cloak for your comfort."

Several replies came to mind. She wanted to scold him for his arrogance, for teasing her, but his genuine caring for her stole the words. No matter how he frustrated her, she found herself charmed.

He kissed the tip of her nose. "I knew you would be."

"What?" she asked, refusing to give him the satisfaction of acknowledging that he was right.

"Charmed."

She shot him a cool look. "Mayhap you misread my thoughts."

Laughter flickered in his eyes. "Nay, I heard you."

"A braggart you are."

"And you, my precious Rowan, are not only my mate, but the woman I love."

His simple words destroyed her, made her ache. All her life

she'd been an outcast. Men's only need for her was due to her expertise in healing, or to make a meal for children while a wife was ill. Now, Aedan wanted her for who she was.

Humbled, Rowan took in the man who moved her, touched her life like no other. Before, she'd feared becoming a vampire, but loving Aedan, carrying their child, she now embraced the change. Aedan was the man she loved, and she wanted to stay with him forever.

Forever.

Excitement built. A wish she could have. She opened her mouth, and Aedan pressed a finger against her lips.

"Enjoy this moment," he said, his words solemn, "the laughter shared. For now, let it be enough."

Unease filtered through her. "I would think my wanting to become a vam—"

"Rowan. There is much you do not know. Little either of us can change."

Reality shattered the dreams of her mind. "Because you are their laird, and I am naught but a commoner." Rowan sat up, stared out to where the sky to the east continued to brighten, announcing the birth of a new day.

"As I told you before, my people will accept you."

With a frown she met his watchful gaze, far from convinced. "Then what troubles you?"

Aedan closed his eyes, but not before she caught the look of pain. " 'Tis our child."

Panic swept her. "There is something wrong with our child?"

"Nay."

She fought for calm as she focused on a devastating thought. "Aedan, can a human give birth to a vampire child and live?"

His expression grew grim. On an exhale, he shook his head. "No one knows."

Chapter Five

Aedan stared up at the sky where sunlight began to outline the clouds. He damned the question of whether Rowan could give birth to a vampire child and live, damned the knowledge that in his desire to have her, he'd not weighed the fact. But standing here pondering her fate changed nothing.

" 'Tis time to sleep," he said, guiding her toward an interior cave, a place that would offer them shelter in its blackness and would allow him a deep, rejuvenating sleep. He waved his hand at a smooth slab of granite.

With a soft rumble, a hidden door opened.

Rowan gasped.

A smile touched his face at her stunned expression. "Go inside."

With hesitant steps, she entered. Eyes wide, Rowan spun to face him. "The rocks are glowing."

"Small animals live within the stone. When they sense a person's presence, they emit light."

Concern edged her brow as she studied the intriguing phenomena. "Has our presence upset them?"

He chuckled. "Mayhap." Aedan guided her through the tunnel deeper beneath the mountain, then into a large room supplied with garb made from linens, silks, and satins. He withdrew a dress. "Here."

Rowan accepted the beautiful white silk gown with hints of gold embroidered along the bodice like stardust tossed. " 'Tis beautiful." Humbled by the finely crafted garb, she shook her head. "I cannot accept such a splendid gift. This must belong to someone of importance."

"Indeed." He nodded. "To you."

Tears misted in her eyes. "Aedan."

He crossed to her, lifted her chin, and stroked his thumb across her lower lip. "You are the woman for whom I am destined, a woman who fills me with happiness, but more, the woman whom I will love forever."

She gave a shaky exhale. "How can you be so sure?"

Tender eyes studied her. "Are you not sure of what you feel for me?"

"I . . ."

"I can read your thoughts, Rowan." He brushed his lips gently over hers. "For me, 'tis the same."

"Aedan." Her voice trembled. "Less than two days have passed since we met. How can our feelings for each other be so strong?"

"Do we question the magnificence of a rainbow, the beauty crafted by the clash of sun and rain?"

"Nay, we accept what is given," she whispered as if tasting the words, savoring the possibility. "I wish to believe it, except . . ."

"Rowan, you are overwhelmed." He gave her a gentle hug. "How can you not be so with everything that has happened in so few hours? Men believing you are a witch, chasing you and wanting you dead, your meeting a vampire, one who is laird of his coven, becoming pregnant with his child, and falling in love."

"Aye, so much has happened. So much—"

"Go and change. 'Tis time for sleep. Did you not say so yourself?"

"I did." With a shy smile, she slipped inside the alcove.

Aedan rubbed the back of his neck. This night she could rest, but 'twould take many more to erase her doubts and allow him to overcome the challenges ahead. And there would be challenges, with his people, with the birth of their child, and with the fact that she held the blood of the fey, a fact he'd yet to explain to her. He dropped his hand.

Or should he?

Rowan still struggled with the terrors of the last two days. What good would come of adding more worries at this time? Her fey blood, her inherent strength, could indeed be her saving grace, could allow her to carry as well as bear his child. But, he wasn't sure.

Though she'd asked him to change her into a vampire, her bearing his child was enough of a risk to her life. He dared not provoke the fairy queen by turning one of her own into a vampire. If he did, Ysenda would surely demand his death. Without his presence to protect Rowan and their child, they would face a cold world, one where neither would ever truly belong.

However much he wished to believe his people would accept Rowan, he could not be sure they would. Neither could he forget that someone had left him to die. A traitor he must find.

And kill.

Enough of the worries to come. They had this day together and part of the oncoming night. Then, he must return to his people beneath some guise, find whoever wished him dead.

Moments later, Rowan reentered clad in the white gown. Had he not known her a commoner, with her regal bearing and majestic presence, none could have convinced him she was not a queen.

A wave of tiredness brought by the arrival of the dawn settled upon him. "Come." He took her hand, led her to the inner chamber where the scent of time and welcome sifted through the air.

Rowan's hand tightened within his. "I cannot see."

Of course, she lacked his sensitivities. Aedan lifted her in his arms, carried her into the next chamber deep within the earth, the power of the ancient lair warm upon his skin. With reverence, he laid with her upon a soft cushion of moss fragrant with herbs.

Rowan looked up at him, her wheat blond hair strewn about in luxurious disarray. "Though I can see naught, whatever I am lying on feels wonderful."

" 'Tis moss. From what I am told, it comes from a magical place."

"Magical?" Humor wove through her words.

"Aye." He lifted a lock of her hair, inhaled her scent. "I have missed my sojourns here. More than a year has passed since I have returned." He would not wait so long again. Easily he could envision his future visits here, his life ahead with Rowan and their child.

"Why have you been away so long?" she asked.

"The demands on a laird are endless, but proud I am to serve my people." Aedan lay beside her and caught her lips in a fierce kiss, then with reluctance, broke free. "Go to sleep, Rowan."

"What if I am not tired?"

At her teasing, he smiled. "Pretend."

She chuckled, and his heart warmed. "If 'tis your wish."

"It is." And so much more. "A caution: If you wake before I do, stay nearby."

"You speak of whoever tried to kill you?" Nervousness trembled within her voice.

However much he wished to avoid the discussion, it was reality, one they must face. "Aye," Aedan replied. "Until I find whoever is behind the attempt on my life, we must keep guard. Given the circumstances of how I was poisoned, I am confident it is a vampire, who must also seek sleep during the day. While you are with me, you will be safe. Now, close your eyes and rest."

On a deep sigh, Rowan snuggled against him. Within moments her breathing became even.

With her womanly scent infusing his every breath, Aedan slowed his heart. After one last sweep of the surroundings with his senses to ensure they were alone, he sent his body into a deep, much needed sleep.

The glow of the setting sun against the jagged peaks surrounding Rowan bathed the time-hewn stone in a wash of red. The color seemed so vivid. Mayhap the intense hue was a unique trait of the local stone. Or, had this special mountaintop been reserved for the laird of the clan?

Aedan's position as the Vampire Coven's laird gave her pause. They had enough challenges to overcome without adding that she was naught but a commoner.

Through the break within the stones, she scanned the land below, how the fading sun highlighted the beauty of the mountains, glowing on the roll of fog that embraced the upper peaks. Never before had she seen such wonder.

Leaves rustled behind her, and she turned. Another burst of wind sent the leaves twisting upon the limbs of a large tree growing from the ledge.

The tree's precarious placement should have been impossible.

But as if crafted by a spell, the massive trunk rose from the cliffs, its multiple gnarled limbs like desperate arms reaching for the sky, the fog surrounding its trunk bestowing upon the entire base an otherworldly glow.

"The tree is unique, is it not?"

At the deep male voice behind her, Rowan whirled. A striking man stood several paces away, his height intimidating, his eyes deep bronze as if sparks sent by a mighty stroke of a smith's hammer upon iron. Straight blond hair accented the sharp angle of his cheeks, his beard, and the hard line of his mouth.

Aedan's warning to remain nearby echoed in her mind. Why had she not remained beside him until he'd awoken?

"Wh—Who are you?" she asked.

The stranger lifted a curious brow. "As it is you who are trespassing within the private grounds of the Highland Coven, 'tis a question I should be asking."

Private grounds of the Highland Coven? Fear crawled through her. Aedan had told her this remote setting was known only to lairds and high members within his clan. This man was a vampire. From his presence, one high in rank within their clan.

On edge, she shifted to the balls of her feet in case she needed to run. "I am a friend of Aedan's."

His eyes widened in surprise. "You know the laird?"

The laird. Heat rushed through her cheeks. Of course, why had she not thought to address Aedan as his position demanded? "My apologies at my inappropriate reference. I but woke moments ago, and my mind is a muddle."

Curiosity spilled through the stranger's intense gaze. He strode toward her, his steps quiet, his stride graceful, that of a man comfortable with his power. Though he was a member of Aedan's clan, was she safe from an attack?

" 'Twould seem you know my cousin," he drawled. "Interesting, as never have I seen you within the walls of Caorann Castle."

"Your cousin?"

A pace away he halted. "Aye, I am Breac MacGregor."

Regardless of his relationship to Aedan, she still did not know whether he was someone she could trust.

A muscle worked in his jaw. "I asked if you knew the laird?"

"Aye, I . . ." How did she explain that his cousin was her lover?

That she carried his laird's child? Or, that Aedan wanted her to remain at his side despite the differences in their stations?

The vampire's nostrils flared as he circled her once. He halted a pace before her. "You are human." It wasn't a question.

Throat dry, she nodded and prayed, knowing Aedan would save her.

Shrewd eyes scoured the surroundings, where the last rays of the day faded against the horizon. "How many days have you been here alone?"

"Days? Aedan only brought me here this past night."

Shock on the vampire's face eroded to anger, a slow fury that erased any sign of kindness. "Aedan is alive?"

"Alive? Why would he not be al—" Alarm rolled through Rowan. The only reason Breac would believe she'd remained here alone for days was if he thought Aedan had brought her here expecting to return, then had died.

Nay, was murdered, an attempt that failed.

With sickening clarity she understood. Aedan's cousin was behind the attempt at his life. How many others were involved in his treacherous plan? *Aedan!*

"Where is he?!"

She shook her head. "I know not."

Lightning quick Breac's hand clasped her chin, angled her head from side to side. Understanding dawned within his eyes, then immense satisfaction. A slow, cruel smile settled upon his mouth.

"Mayhap you know not where he is," Aedan's cousin said, "but he will return."

"Why do you believe that?" she whispered, stunned he could discern such a truth.

"There is only one reason why you would be within the ancestral retreat and unconverted. You are of great importance to my cousin."

"I barely know him."

"Liar, I smell your pathetic human fear and his scent upon your skin." He jerked her forward, scraped his teeth across her flesh. Stilled. "You carry his child."

Her fear of moments before was nothing to this blast of terror. He could not harm her child. "You do not understand."

"As if I give a damn that my cousin is a fool."

"I—"

"The bastard you carry will nae live, of that I assure you."

Rowan tried to jerk free. "Nay—"

His hand shot out, connected with her jaw. The force sent her sprawling.

He stalked toward her, his face marred by bulging veins and fury. "Think you that a mere human holds any power against a vampire?"

"Nay," she whispered, her legs trembling as she shoved to her feet, pain throbbing through her skull. "Please, do not harm my child." Heart pounding, she focused on him, refused the urge to glance toward the cave's entry. Aedan would awaken any moment, and then he would save her. "Please, let me go," she said, keeping the vampire's attention diverted from the cave. "I will tell no one of this place."

He laughed, a cold brutal sound. "Nay, that you will not. When my cousin returns and finds you gone, he will come looking for you."

"He will not come after me," she said, her mind scrambling to buy precious time. *Aedan!*

The vampire's lip curled with disgust. "Enough. That I have wasted a word upon a human fills me with revulsion. Aedan will come, that we both know. And this time," he said with twisted pleasure in his voice, "he will die."

A fog shrouded Aedan's mind like a blanket. He mentally clawed his way to consciousness, his senses demanding he awaken. He gulped a deep breath, another. His heart kicked to life. He reached to his side.

Empty.

"Rowan?"

Silence.

A malignant unrest permeated the air, and Aedan shoved to his feet. "Rowan?"

The far off curl of wind echoed within the tunnels. Otherwise, all was morbid silence.

Mist swirled in his wake as he bolted outside. On edge, he scanned the chasm embraced by the mountains.

Naught.

He scoured the upper peaks. The moon's edge crept into the

sky, its eerie light warring with flickers of fading sunlight struggling in the wilting purple sky.

A wisp of residual anger tainted the air.

Anger? Heart pounding, he knew. Another vampire had been here, and since he'd known of this secret retreat, it had been a member of high regard within the clan. Whoever it was, he had Rowan.

Why? He dismissed the possibility that she'd been taken to feed upon. Once she explained his relation to her and that she was under his protection, any member of his clan would have left her untouched.

Or, he mused with growing dread, was whoever had taken her the same vampire who had plotted for him to die?

Aedan wanted to believe that after finding her here alone, the other vampire had taken her to his home to keep her safe until he found Aedan and discovered the truth. But a sinking feeling in his gut assured him her disappearance was due to foul play. That sixth sense had saved his life many times over; he would listen to it now.

While he'd slept, whoever had made an attempt on his life had arrived at the ancestral retreat and discovered Rowan outside. Somehow that vampire had gleaned that Aedan still lived, and had abducted her. But she'd not told her captor that Aedan slept deep inside the cave. If she had, no doubt he would now be dead.

Aedan battled the flood of rage, focused on the one who would dare to try to kill him, the same vampire who now held Rowan and their child.

Unless he'd already killed her?

Nay, if she had died, he would have sensed the loss. Their link, one that forever bound them, would have perished.

So she lived. But for how long?

Until whoever had abducted her tasted her blood, he wouldn't know of her fey heritage. Since it was forbidden to try to change a fairy into a vampire, if whoever held Rowan tried, the fairy queen would come, and he would die.

But, what of Rowan? What of their child? Would Ysenda, the fairy queen, allow them to live? Bedamned. He must find them before it was too late!

In a blur of mist, Aedan evaporated into the night.

Chapter Six

Rowan fought her growing panic as she took in the rocky coast, the weather-beaten mountains beyond.

"Do not think you can escape from me," Breac warned, the softness of his words, his complete control, terrifying. Judging by his actions, this vampire calculated his every move, left nothing to chance, except when it had come to killing Aedan.

In that he'd failed.

"Wh-Why do you hate Aedan?" she asked, needing to buy time to think up a plan to slip free.

"I owe you no explanation. But I find myself curious how a human has so entranced a vampire that he leaves her with child. Especially considering he is our Highland Coven's laird." He paused. "You have no marks on your neck. Why has my cousin not claimed you?"

"I know not."

Again his fist shot out.

Pain slammed through her cheek. Rowan stumbled back, caught herself as she fell against the rocks. *Please, let me not lose Aedan's child!*

The vampire stalked toward her. "Methinks you are a witch, a very dangerous one to have seduced a powerful laird and a vampire centuries old."

Chills swept through her at the damning label. "I am no witch."

"Nay?"

Tingles shivered inside her head.

He was trying to read her mind! Until Aedan had taken her blood, his powers had allowed him to mentally guide her. Naught more. But were all vampires' powers the same? Could his cousin read her thoughts?

Long seconds passed.

Deep bronze eyes smoldered. "Something is amiss," he said, his words slow, deliberate. "Regardless, you will serve my purpose well."

Purpose? Whatever his depraved intent, she knew it boded ill to Aedan. Her mental calls to him had remained unanswered. However powerful this vampire, she must somehow slip away and warn Aedan. Heart pounding, Rowan shifted to the closest rock.

In a burst of speed, the vampire caged her against the rough stone. Long, dangerous fingers clenched Rowan's wrist tightly. "Think not of escape." He jerked her to her feet.

Waves pounded the shore in her wake as he hauled her along the rock-cluttered beach, up a narrow, winding path edged by the time-hewn cliffs. With the steep incline, it should have been a difficult trek, but he ascended the near vertical slide of land with incredible ease.

The full moon on the horizon was just rising; hours remained this night before the vampire would seek the shelter of darkness against the sun, and who knew what he would do with that time.

Aedan!

Breac lifted her over the top of the cliffs, and an enormous castle came into view. Settled upon an immense cliff, its turrets spun skyward like a potent threat. Battlements severed the moonlight, spilling jagged shadows before her. Numerous windows were carved within the grand towers, the exquisite detail an exclamation of wealth. A sturdy wall surrounded the castle, the portcullis the first of many entries one would have to traverse before passing within the stronghold.

"Caorann Castle," Breac stated.

Aedan's home.

Why was Aedan's cousin bringing her here? How was he going to explain her presence? Did any of that really matter? His cousin wanted her dead.

A gatehouse rose within the scarred wall, the blackened entry foreboding, the iron gate securing the portal like jagged teeth.

He waved his hand. Metal creaked, and with slow menace, the forged iron lifted.

How strong were this vampire's powers? As laird of his coven, wouldn't Aedan be still more powerful?

"Move." Breac tugged her forward.

Eyes blurring with exhaustion, her legs threatening to give way, Rowan pushed forward.

With each step, she saw more of the immense castle, the sturdy building as formidable as their laird. She could envision Aedan within this powerful stronghold; his compassion and intelligence would make him a leader loved and revered. However much he believed otherwise, she did not fit in his world.

And never would.

Panic consumed her as she scanned the remainder of this intimidating fortress. Where was Aedan? With the moon ascending in the sky, he must be awake. And, with their blood bond, why hadn't he tracked her? Or, was there another unknown factor she hadn't considered?

They entered the bailey.

The vampires working inside stopped to stare.

A vampire with a long, white beard and bushy brows broke from a small group. With a nod, he strode toward them.

Pulse racing, Rowan watched the elder's approach. Was he part of Lord Breac's twisted plan to kill Aedan? Would she be handed over to him to die?

The elder vampire ignored her as he halted before them, an anxious expression on his face. "You have found The MacGregor?"

"Nay, Sir Wayrn," Breac replied, anger riding his voice, "but I have found the cause of our laird's disappearance."

The elder glanced toward her. Wizened eyes flickered with surprise. "This human?"

"Human mayhap, but also a witch," Breac stated.

Unsure what ill Breac was about, Rowan shook her head. "I am nae a witch, nor have I done anything to your laird. If there is any treachery about, 'tis by—"

Breac hauled her up before his face. "Do nae speak unless given permission."

Trembling, Rowan laid her hands over her stomach, where her child grew.

Bushy brows lifted. "The human lass carries a babe?"

"Aye," Breac hissed, his fingers unfurling from her garb. "Aedan's."

The elder's face paled. "It cannot be. Never would our laird leave a bastard child, especially not with a human."

"Aye, on that I agree. The lass must have bewitched him." Breac's fingers twisted in her hair, jerked her head back. "Tell Sir Wayrn."

Fear shot through Rowan, and her legs threatened to give. Lies, cast by the man who'd attempted to kill his cousin. But if she told the truth, she and her babe would die. She must stall.

At her silence, Breac's eyes darkened to a dangerous hue. Shaking, she nodded. " 'Tis the truth."

The elder stumbled back as if punched. "To place one's seed within a human is unthinkable for us. Never has such been done."

"Aye, which brings up a far greater concern." Grief slashed the anger on Breac's face. "Never would Aedan betray us unless the lass bewitched our laird with a spell of enormous strength." He paused. "I fear my cousin is no longer of sound mind."

The elder's face paled further.

"Sir Wayrn, gather the coven," Breac said. "I will explain everything then."

"Aye." With one last glare at her, Sir Wayrn spun on his heel and hurried off.

Never had a vampire slept with a human? Sir Wayrn's words echoed in Rowan's mind as Breac hauled her toward the massive steps of the keep. Aedan's belief that they were mates explained his actions. He was proud of his heritage and his people. Never would he betray them.

Fury built, blinding her to fear. " 'Twas you who drugged Aedan," she charged, "and then left him within the stone circle to die. Well you understood that the circle would drain a vampire's power and if he awoke, he would be unable to leave."

Violent lines slashed Breac's face. He caught her hands, jerked them behind her back.

Pain screamed up her arms.

"I see my cousin has done more than filled your belly with his spawn," he seethed. "He told a human what is forbidden."

"Mayhap," she replied, "but I saved his life, whereas you tried to murder him."

He grunted. "As if any will hear your claim." Breac withdrew a strip of cloth from a side pocket, secured it around her mouth with a hard yank. "Lass, if I were you, my worries would not be for Aedan, but for the few moments left of your pathetic life."

"Nay!" Rowan screamed, but the cloth muffled her cry.

"Enough." A crowd gathered as Breac hauled her up the steps to the keep. Curious stares mixed with excited whispers.

Her body trembling, she scanned the bailey, then looked toward the gatehouse where they'd entered a short time before. It was now blocked by the growing horde.

Breac raised his hand.

Expectant silence descended upon the throng.

"This night I bring disturbing news." Breac's voice boomed within the castle walls. "In my search for The MacGregor, I found this woman, who is responsible for our laird's disappearance."

"How can a human have any power over a vampire?" a vampire near the front yelled.

"Aye," several vampires grumbled in agreement. The doubts on the faces of those within the crowd showed they were far from convinced.

Breac scanned the throng, bronze eyes narrowing. "This lass is not a simple human, but a witch!"

"A witch powerful enough to bewitch our laird?" a wizened man near the front challenged. "The MacGregor is many centuries old, his power legendary."

Murmurs of agreement rippled through the crowd.

"How can a witch," the vampire continued, "however strong, cast a spell over Aedan?"

At their doubts, hope filled Rowan. Aedan's people loved him, respected him; they would not abandon him because of a few words cast by his cousin.

"Like you, I too held doubts, until I discovered an astonishing truth!" Breac placed his hand over her belly. "Aye," he roared as he glared at those before him, "she carries our laird's child!"

Outraged gasps echoed from the crowd.

"Nay," a woman rushed out, " 'tis an untruth!"

Breac shoved her before him, his hold cruel upon her wrist. "Lass, is it not true?" he called out. "Do you nae carry the child of our laird?" He leaned close to her hear and whispered, "Nod in agreement or die now!"

Tears burning her eyes, Rowan nodded, willing to do anything to buy time until Aedan could arrive.

" 'Tis truth," a woman near the back hissed.

"Aye," a man nearby choked out. "The blasted she-devil has enormous power."

Outrage exploded within the crowd, and satisfaction settled upon Breac's face.

Nauseous, Rowan turned away from Breac. Why would he not be pleased? He wanted to become their laird, would do whatever was necessary to become the clan's leader, including trying to kill his cousin.

Except, Aedan lived.

A fact he knew, a problem he was determined to extinguish by convincing his people Aedan was bewitched, not of sound mind. But when Aedan appeared, he would expose the truth, and Breac's treachery would fail.

"A witch," Breac continued, dragging her from her desperate thoughts, "one who believes herself cunning. Her personal goals must be lofty indeed."

"What would a witch be wanting with our laird or his child?" called an elder with a scarred face in the front.

Breac turned toward her. "To claim the power of being his wife. But never will she achieve her twisted goal."

A rugged-looking vampire in the back stepped forward. "Where is our laird?"

"I am still searching for him. Worry not, I will find him. But—" Breac gave a frustrated shake of his head. "—I dinnae know how to break the spell she has cast upon The MacGregor." He nodded toward several elders at the side of the crowd. "Oh, wise ones, 'tis guidance I seek."

Angry brows furrowed as the white-haired vampires huddled and whispered amongst themselves.

With a slight limp, a tall vampire stepped from the group, his face drawn. "My lord, we know of no way to break the witch's spell."

Breac blew a hard breath. "As I feared."

Feared? Anger slammed Rowan at the lies Breac had told, the gullibility of Aedan's people to condemn their laird without proof! Was their loyalty to their laird, a man who would sacrifice his life for them, shredded with fears of a powerful witch? She waited

for others to challenge Breac. She could see that many were far
from convinced, but they remained silent.

Eyes filled with tears, Breac scanned the crowd. " 'Tis with
great sadness and regret that I inform you, if our laird still lives,
his mind has been tainted by a spell that may be impossible to
remove. And," he said, his voice trembling, "if indeed my cousin
returns, he must be turned away. If he refuses . . ." He shook his
head as if he dredged the words from a battered soul. "Our laird
must die."

Chapter Seven

Aedan must die? Blackness threatened, but Rowan clung to consciousness—barely.

Grief ravaged the faces of the vampires below, as whispers rumbled amongst the crowd. But as the moments passed, Rowan could see their struggle with doubt fade. One by one, in unspoken agreement, they accepted Breac's lie that Aedan could no longer continue as their laird.

Sir Wayrn stepped forward, the weight of this grave matter lining his face. "Breac, will you lead us?"

Breac drew himself up to his full height, scanned the crowd, his face hewn in a somber cast. "Aye, 'tis my honor, one I take with a heavy heart."

Rowan fought to break free, glaring at Aedan's cousin when her every attempt failed. Damn him, somehow she had to stop him.

As the crowd's vile cures tainted the air, Breac shoved her before him. "The witch will pay for her treachery. Before the oncoming dawn, she will die!"

"There is no need to wait," a vampire with a scar across his jaw said, his fangs lengthening. "Toss her down. We will see to her death."

Cheers rose from the throng, and hunger burned in their eyes.

"She has made us suffer by cursing our laird and friend, and suffering will be her fate," Breac stated. "Have a fire built within the center of the bailey."

No! Rowan struggled against Breac's hold; one of his fingernails dug deep into the pulse at her neck. She stilled.

"Is it your wish to die now?" Breac hissed. "I assure you, if I slashed your neck and cast you into the crowd, my people would gladly feed upon you. I believe 'tis their wish."

Heart pounding, Rowan shook her head.

Wood clunked.

She glanced across the bailey. Vampires piled branches at the center. Small limbs were quickly covered with sturdy logs, which would burn for hours.

"You see your penance ahead, a death that will be painfully slow," Breac said with a laugh, the boom of his voice echoing out to the crowd. "Let me keep you waiting no longer." He shoved her down the steps.

The vampires parted before them, cursing her, yelling inventive tortures to add before her death.

The stacked wood grew as they closed in on her. Tremors rippled over her skin at the thought of flames scorching her.

Strong arms eagerly claimed her from Breac's hold. "Bewitching our laird," Sir Wayrn charged. "A fitting death for you." He slid ropes around her wrists, her legs, jerked tight.

Hemp bit into her flesh. Focus. *Aedan!*

Silence.

No, their blood connected them. He had to hear her! *Aedan, help, they are going to burn me!*

Where are you? Rage echoed within his voice as it burst into the mayhem swirling in her mind.

Caorann Castle!

Mist exploded a pace away. Aedan stood within the fade of white, his face carved in furious outrage. Striding forward, he tore off Rowan's gag.

Air, fresh, cool, slid down her throat.

Breac whirled, cursed. "Guards, light the fire!" He dove onto Aedan.

Pain tore through Aedan's body as his cousin drove him against the ground.

Straddled atop him, Breac reached toward his chest.

Outraged his cousin would dare attempt to tear out his heart, Aedan caught Breac's wrist. Bones cracked, shattering beneath his raw force. "Bedamned your betrayal!"

"Aedan!" Rowan screamed.

Aedan glanced over.

Vampires had cast torches at the base of the wood stacked below Rowan. It caught, roared to life. The stench of smoke filled the air.

By the sword's blade! He catapulted his cousin back, shoved to his feet, and lunged toward her.

In midair, Breac tackled him. With a powerful force, his cousin hurled him against the keep.

Shouts of warning echoed through the bailey as their clan encircled them, creating an arena for them to spar.

With a curse he glanced toward Rowan.

Her face paled against the growing flames, her eyes betraying the belief she would die.

Nay! Aedan shoved Breac away, bolted toward the flames, the crowd parting before him. Heat singed the air; smoke billowed around him, the stench of it thick. Aedan severed the ties holding Rowan and leapt with her well away from the dangerous spew of flames.

"You are safe," he whispered, cradling her against his chest.

"Aedan," she whispered, her body trembling, "I-I thought I was going to die."

Unease rippled through the throng as the vampires watched them.

Aware that until he'd dealt with his cousin, she was far from safe, Aedan set her down. "Stay here. I must—"

Feet plowed into his chest. Aedan stumbled back.

Breac's lengthened nails dug into Aedan's flesh as they rolled upon the earth. His blood and Breac's melded with dirt.

"You will nae save her!" his cousin yelled.

Using Breac's momentum, Aedan rolled him onto his back and pinned his arms. Chest heaving, he glared at him. "She has done naught!"

"Aye, she has tainted you," he spat, "left you crazed and unfit to be our laird."

Several vampires nearby watched Aedan with suspicion, and sadness poured through Aedan. In his lust to become laird, his cousin had become twisted, lost in his greed for power. Worse, Breac had poisoned the minds of their people, with lies he must dispel.

Regardless of their bond of blood, as long as Breac remained at Caorann Castle, he would seek to undermine Aedan's position if not attempt to kill both him and Rowan. Though they had spent their youth together, lads who had played tricks on others as they'd grown, then men who'd turned to each other for advice, it changed naught. However much he loved his cousin, Breac must leave.

"You are forbidden ever to return to the Highland Coven," Aedan commanded. "And fortunate that I have not killed you for your attempt on Rowan's life, or for the lies you have spoken."

Breac hesitated, then tears blurred his eyes. "God's teeth, Aedan. What have I done?" He looked away. "You are my blood, yet ... Shamed I am. More than you will ever know." Several tears fell. "Please, I beg you, give me one more chance."

Aedan remained silent. Before this day he would have. Nae any longer.

Breac's body grew limp as if he'd given up, as if he understood the travesty he'd committed. However much Aedan detested Breac's banishment, 'twas his cousin's actions that had made it imperative. He released his cousin, shoved to his feet. "Be gone."

Without comment, Breac dragged himself to his feet. After one last look of regret, he stumbled toward the portcullis.

Exhausted, tired of the treachery from his own kin, Aedan turned to Rowan. At her tired smile, his heart warmed. She would—

Air burst from his lungs. Breac's elongated nails sliced his back. Furious, Aedan turned.

The blur of his cousin flashed past.

Rowan screamed.

Aedan whirled.

Breac stood before the roar of flames, his body marred by cuts and bruises, a malignant smile deforming his face. At his feet, Rowan's body lay twisted, her neck slashed, her blood pumping upon the earth.

Aedan stared in disbelief at the woman he loved, the woman who moved him like no other, the woman his cousin was trying to kill. Anger so hot, so feral it held its own life, filled him. He lifted his eyes to Breac.

"For this you will die!" With a roar, Aedan attacked his cousin, each slash of his flesh satisfying, the burn of betrayal guiding his every swing.

"You are unfit to lead us," Breac seethed as his blow sent Aedan stumbling back.

"Nay," Aedan snarled as he sprang forward, damning each second lost before he could reach Rowan. "That honor belongs to you!" He slashed his cousin's chest, reached in, tore.

Shock fragmented Breac's face as he looked down. Blood, dark and ugly, spilled from the ragged flesh. Inside, an empty cavity gaped where once had lain his heart.

As if in slow motion, Breac lifted his head, stared at the pumping red mass upon Aedan's palm. "What have you done?"

"Killed a traitor."

A feral smile wavered upon his cousin's face. "I may die, but so will the lass and your child."

With a curse, Aedan threw his cousin's heart into the air. He focused. A swirl of mist enveloped the heart, and then it exploded in flames. The stench of blood permeated the air. Sickened, damning what must be done, he turned to the body of his cousin. Breac's eyes were now empty, staring at nothing.

Aedan focused.

Mist swirled over Breac's body, then flames ignited, the heat intense, the smoke thickening to a dense haze. The flutter of a cool breeze tumbled past, and the churn of white cleared. Where once his cousin had lain, only a blackened outline remained, all that was left of a man he had loved since they were young lads.

Rowan! Aedan ran to her, knelt at her side. Her wheat blond lashes flickered open.

A frown shimmered upon her face. "Ae-Aedan?"

Her pain-filled whisper cut deep. On a rough swallow, he took in the gash across her neck, her blood congealing upon the earth, her eyes growing pale as she struggled to breathe. His body shook as he drew her into his arms.

She was dying.

Nay, he could not lose her now! He stared at the sky bright with the pulse of stars, at the heavens so filled with life. Whoever he needed to beg to spare her life, he would.

He stroked his thumb across her brow. "I am here."

"I-I love you." Her lids wobbled as she struggled to keep them open. "If I do not—"

"Do nae speak. You must save your strength."

Rowan closed her eyes, fought the wash of agony, the lure of blackness that offered relief. It would be easy to give in, but to do so would be to embrace death.

Death?

Nay, immortality.

Hope spiraled. "Aedan, co—convert me into a vampire. It is the only way to save me, to save our child."

Strain etched his face as he took her hand, pressed a kiss upon its palm, his own shaking. "If I try," he whispered, his voice raw with self-condemnation, "you may die."

"What?"

"There might be another way," he said. " 'Tis possible you can heal yourself."

Heal herself? Another wash of pain rolled through her. Rowan rode the tide until it ebbed. "You ar-are making little sense."

"At the cave," Aedan explained, his words rushed, "when we made love, I discovered you are part fey."

"Part fey?"

"Aye. Your ancestors are from the Otherworld. Your ability to heal is more than a gift, but a consequence of your heritage. Fairy blood holds the ability to heal."

Her eyes widened. "I am a fairy?"

"Half."

"Ho-How . . ." She fought the meld of confusion and pain, but clung to his impossible claim. "How can one be half fairy?"

"Rowan, at this moment 'tis unimportant." He brought her hand to his cheek, pressed his own atop. "You must look within yourself, draw from your inherent strength, from your ability to heal and repair your wounds."

"I . . ." Her world blurred. She gasped, struggled to breathe. "Rowan!"

Aedan's voice echoed from a distance. She clung to his outrageous claim. Her lifetime of difficulties trying to fit in with her clansmen, her instinctive knowledge of where a person was wounded and the herb to heal all made sense now. 'Twas simple: How could she fit in when she was not of this world?

"Rowan!"

From far away, a desperate voice echoed. Hands rubbed over her skin, and then the coolness of a cloth swept across her neck.

Use the powers of the fey to heal yourself!

Murky blackness weighted her chest as she fought to breath.

Could she heal herself? Rowan focused on points within her body where the pain built, discerned what must be done.

Heat grew within her, a slow spiral that sent waves of tingling along her skin. The sensation of tissue weaving together filled her.

"Aedan?" she whispered.

At her feeble words, Aedan's heart stumbled. "Rowan?" Though she'd embraced her fey powers, had begun the healing process within, he sensed her body's struggles. She was bleeding out faster than she could repair the damage.

She could not die!

As if to mock his wishes, her skin grew deathly pale, and the heartbeat of their child became pathetically weak.

Regardless of her fey blood, she was not strong enough to repair her damaged body. In but moments, Rowan's and his child's lives would end.

The crowd edged closer, their whispers rising to an uneasy murmur.

Furious, Aedan glanced up, surveyed their belligerent eyes and scowling faces. His people held doubts of his lucidity, were unsure because of the lies spewed by his cousin suggesting that he was caught beneath Rowan's spell.

Why had he not suspected Breac from the start? He exhaled. Because he'd thought of him as a brother, had never believed his cousin capable of such treachery. And like those around him, he'd been wrong.

Aedan quelled his anger. His people had questions; How could they not? The laws under which they lived and their belief in their laird's sanity had been cast into doubt.

He clasped Rowan's hand within his own, scanned his people. "I am nae bewitched." He kept each word steady. His people needed a confident voice, to hear the laird they knew, one who had served them with all his heart. "Breac lied to you in his attempt to become laird of the Highland Coven. Several days past, he poisoned me with foxglove, then left me in a stone circle to die."

Whispers filtered through the crowd, and they glanced toward his cousin's charred remains.

At Rowan's rough breath, Aedan glanced down. "There is no time to explain. You must trust me in my decisions."

"The woman is nae a witch?" asked an elder vampire close by.

"Nay," he replied. "She saved my life. Now, I must save hers."

"But . . ." Sir Wayrn stepped forward, stroked his long, white beard. "You told the lass she was half fey."

Aedan nodded. "She is."

The elder paused. " 'Tis forbidden to try to convert a fairy into a vampire."

And no one knew whether trying would kill her, Aedan silently added. "Her human side will change. As for the rest, I am unsure." He held Sir Wayrn's gaze. "If the ancient law proves true, and my trying to change Rowan brings Ysenda, the Queen of the Otherworld, 'tis a risk I will take."

"You would give your life for a human woman?" Sir Wayrn asked.

Aedan nodded. "Aye."

Another gasp shuddered through his people.

When faced with losing the woman he loved, he did not give a damn about his own life. Aedan focused on Rowan. She was his world; without her his days meant naught. "Rowan will live and bear my son."

The pulse at the base of Rowan's neck grew erratic.

Stilled.

On a curse, Aedan sank his fangs deep within her neck. Her rich blood sang through his body, a force unlike any he'd ever known. Within the cave she'd dripped her life-giving essence upon his tongue. He'd experienced the power, the healing properties of her blood, but 'twas only a pittance compared to his drinking straight from her.

With each swallow, his body strengthened.

With each swallow, she and his child died.

Her heart, his son's, ceased.

His mind a maze of terror and determination, he slashed his fingernail across his chest, pressed her mouth against him and willed her to drink.

She lay unmoving.

Drink!

Her body shuddered.

He would not lose her! *Rowan, drink from me now!*

She gasped, the slightest sound, but to him it was a miracle.

Her lips, unsure in their innocence, drew unsteadily as they sought his lifesaving blood. Her throat worked. Swallowed. Seconds later, she took another drink.

Within the fragile quiet, her heart stumbled, then began to beat. A second later, their son's shuddered to life.

Hands shaking, Aedan cupped her head, guided her as she fed, continued to mentally encourage her. Soon her body would begin its change. Because his son already held vampire blood, odds were their child would live through the conversion.

Naught but time would tell if Rowan's body would endure the transition. Would her fey side reject the advance of the vampire blood?

If so, she would die.

Shaking, Aedan smoothed his hand through her rumpled hair. Rowan's feeble efforts shifted into a steady draw, but the paleness of her face exposed her struggle.

Confident she'd taken enough for the conversion, he lifted her mouth away, laid her gently back, then sealed the cut. Gently, he lifted her in his arms. "Rowan, I am—"

The air exploded around them with an angry boil. A pulse of energy, raw with fury, threw him. Hewn stones quaked as he slammed against the castle wall.

With a roar, he sprang to the ground in search of his attacker.

Another blast tossed him back. Cursing, he stood. Stilled.

Paces away, from within the vortex of power, stepped a woman, her alabaster skin flawless, her stature regal. The air around her churned with luminescent shimmers like diamonds.

Ysenda, the fairy queen.

The ancient law was true!

Outraged violet eyes narrowed, focused on Aedan. Her every movement carved with fury, the Queen of the Otherworld strode forward. A pace away, she halted. "Aedan MacGregor, Laird of the Highland Vampire Coven, you dare try to convert one the fey!"

Frustration mixed with anger as Aedan held the queen's gaze. He gave a slight nod. "Ysenda, Fairy Queen of the Otherworld. 'Twas never my intent to bring harm to one within your care, nor to challenge ancient laws."

Rowan's body shuddered within Aedan's arms, and her breathing grew weak. By the sword's blade, her conversion had begun!

"Rowan was dying," he said, his voice rough with emotion. "'Twas the only way to save her."

"Save her?" Disbelief took over Ysenda's expression as she examined Rowan. Her gaze riveted on him. "Well is it known such an act is forbidden by ancient law, that such an attempt could lead to the fairy's death. And"—she raised her arms, her eyes as stormy as the swirl of night—"it is an act that will now lead to yours!"

Chapter Eight

Against the haze of agony, Rowan struggled to remain conscious. She heard the echo of a woman's voice declaring that Aedan had broken an ancient law, and heard her threat to kill him.

Nay, he could not die!

On a trembling breath, Rowan fought to open her eyes, to make her mouth form the words within her mind. "Wait! Do nae kill him!"

At her pain-roughened words, the regal woman hesitated. A shudder whipped through Rowan as she battled to remain conscious, to remember how Aedan had addressed this regal woman. Ysenda, Fairy Queen of the Otherworld.

Against the full moon, the fairy queen frowned, her perfection outlined in a silvery glow as if of diamonds cast, her golden gown bright against the dark backdrop of vampires crowded within the bailey.

Disbelieving eyes met hers. "You of the fairy world," Ysenda boomed, "who have been condemned to nocturnal life and savagery, you would save a vampire?"

"They are not savages," Rowan replied. Despite her fear, Aedan's claim that she was half fey echoed within her mind. Her heart ached. In his attempt to save her, he'd broken an ancient law, a fact he'd ignored at the risk of his own life.

Humbled by his selfless act, loving him with her every breath, Rowan felt tears fill her eyes. "Before I met Aedan, I believed the same, ex-except he is a fair man, one who cares for his people, who harms none unless he must to protect his own. Savagery?" She shook her head. "Nay, vampires take only what is necessary to live, and leave those who sustain them well and ignorant of the event."

A well-manicured royal brow lifted. "Now you champion our natural enemy?"

"Our enemy?" Rowan battled a wave of weakness. "Wo-Would an enemy risk his life to save a fo-foe?"

The queen's mouth thinned. "Why else would a coven's laird dare transform one of the fey if not out of a desire to control her powers?"

"For love," Aedan stated.

The fairy queen whirled, the outrage in her eyes striking Aedan. "Love?"

"Aye," he said. "I love Rowan with all my heart." The vampires crowding the bailey gasped, but he ignored them. "She is but an innocent caught up in my cousin's twisted attempt to become our coven's laird."

"How did she ever become involved in a power struggle for lairdship of the Highland Vampire Coven?" the queen demanded.

"My cousin poisoned me and left me for dead. Rowan found me and saved my life. When my cousin discovered her and learned of our bond, he abducted Rowan. In an attempt to place doubt upon my ability to be laird, he brought her to my home, Caorann Castle. For proof, he labeled her a witch and claimed she'd cast a spell upon me."

Skepticism was plain in the queen's eyes. "This does nae explain the need to challenge ancient law by attempting to convert her into a vampire."

"When I found Rowan, my cousin had her tied to the stake to burn."

Ysenda took in the roar of flames within the bailey. The fire popped and cracked as burning branches collapsed.

"I saved her," Aedan said, "but not before my cousin slashed her neck. Had I not tried to save her, she would be dead."

"You have nae saved her." Scorn layered the fury within the fairy queen's voice. "All you have given her is more pain. In the end she will die."

His entire world stilled. "I was told the outcome of converting a fairy to a vampire is unknown. And therein lies the potential for hope."

"Mayhap," Ysenda replied. "But the blood of the vampire is a natural enemy of the fey. How can the outcome nae be death?"

"Because," Aedan replied, emotion roughening his words, "Rowan is only half fey. Her other half is human."

The queen's face paled. "Half human? Such a bond is forbidden."

He held her gaze, allowing his anger free reign. Could Ysenda not see Rowan was suffering? "I know not the details, but my hope is that with the diluting of Rowan's fairy blood, there is a chance she will survive."

"You overstep your boundaries, Laird."

"Mayhap," he stated, his voice hard, "but to save Rowan's life, it is a step I would take again." People exchanged uneasy glances within the crowd. Questions, aye they would have them. Another issue to attend to in a mounting pile, ones he would take care of once he knew Rowan's fate.

Rowan trembled within his arms, gasped, her garb clinging to her sweat-soaked skin.

"Regardless of the broken law, Rowan has begun to change. Unless you strike me dead, I am taking her to my chamber. And if it is within my power, I will save her life." Furious, half expecting a bolt of lightning to strike him dead, Aedan envisioned the swirl of fog.

"Laird MacGregor," the fairy queen called.

"Queen Ysenda, Sir Wayrn will escort you to my chamber to supervise if you wish." Aedan's body shattered into mist, bringing Rowan's with it. He flew, then rematerialized inside his chamber.

Oblivious to the luxury of silk and velvets gracing the walls and the thick woven rugs crafted with intricate detail, he laid Rowan upon his bed. With a wave of his hand, he slammed the windows shut, severing the moonlight, extinguishing the flicker of torchlight, banishing any illumination that might increase Rowan's sensitivity to pain.

"Aedan!" she gasped.

He knelt beside her, brushed away the sweat-laden hair clinging to her brow. "I am here."

"Ev . . ." She panted, gave a soft groan. "Everything aches."

"Aye, 'tis your body purging your human traits." He damned her agony, knowing the torment to come would be worse, much worse, before he knew whether her fey blood would reject the vampire and end her life.

The whoosh of the door had him glaring over his shoulder.

The fairy queen entered. Her gaze collided with his. "You dare much."

"For Rowan," he said with a deadly whisper, "I dare anything."

A soft cry escaped Rowan's lips. "Aedan?"

He turned. Paleness washed Rowan's skin, a translucence so sheer the whisper blue veins beneath her skin lay exposed. "I am here." Hand trembling, he picked up a damp cloth from a nearby bowl, then wiped it over her brow. "You are beginning the conversion."

Her mouth worked, then she swallowed. "Ho—How long will it take?"

Agony cut through her whisper and tore him in two. "No one knows."

"No one knows," Ysenda stated, "as no one has been foolish enough to dare try to change one of the fey."

At the coolness within the fairy queen's voice, Aedan leveled his gaze upon her.

"But," the fairy queen continued, "your fairy blood will speed the process. A day, two at most."

Unless Rowan died.

The fairy queen did not need to say the words. The reality haunted him like a curse.

Rowan arched upon the sprawl of blankets. "Ae-Aedan, 'tis like my body is on fire!"

Again he wiped the square of sodden cloth over her brow. "Aye, 'twill pass."

On a moan, Rowan twisted upon his massive bed.

Never had Aedan felt so helpless. Watching her suffer, her body raw with agony, he understood fear for the first time.

With a scream, Rowan collapsed upon the bed.

Queen Ysenda walked over, sighed. "She has passed out. A blessing."

Aedan glanced up. The fairy queen's compassion seemed at odds with the woman he'd first met. "Aye." Now there was nothing to do but wait to see if Rowan would live.

Angst stormed him as the long seconds passed. He willed the passage of time, damned the same.

He pressed a soft kiss upon her brow and wished for a miracle. "I love you, Rowan."

"I find your sentiment interesting," Ysenda said.

Frustration at the situation spilled through him, and he shoved to his feet. "Why did you not kill me?"

"It was Rowan's wish to allow you to live. A request I am unsure I can grant."

He arched a brow. "I am surprised you would consider her request."

"As am I."

Silence stumbled between them as they watched Rowan.

Unsure what to say, if the right words could even be found, he rubbed the back of his neck. Aedan shot Ysenda a cool look. "I am amazed Rowan was allowed to live among the humans, considering she is only half of their blood."

Silence.

He glanced over.

Sadness touched Ysenda's face as she stared at Rowan's limp form upon the bed. " 'Tis because I did not know of her existence before this night."

She had not known? "I thought you knew all within your realm of the Otherworld."

"I believed so as well." She paused, her eyes dark with struggle and questions. "Did Rowan say naught of her mother or father?"

Unsure why Ysenda asked, he nodded. "She explained that as a babe, a man claiming to be her father dropped her off at the healer's home. He'd said Rowan's mother had died giving birth."

"Did the healer know the mother as well?"

"Nay, naught except she was not from the Highlands."

Understanding dawned on Ysenda's face, then shifted to sadness. "Of course. That explains everything."

"Everything?"

Queen Ysenda nodded. "When Rowan's mother learned she was with child, she fled the Otherworld."

"Because the father of the babe was human?"

"Aye," Queen Ysenda replied. "Because he was a human, I forbid her ever to see him again."

"Why did you not seek their child—Rowan—out?" Aedan asked.

"I could not sense the child's existence, because her fey blood was weakened by her human side. But, when you changed Rowan, the natural repelling action of our blood against yours sent ripples through the heavens which I picked up, however faint."

He nodded. "Aye, that makes sense. A mess indeed."

"More so than you understand," she said. "But my daughter, as well as her child, 'twould seem, walked outside the lines of convention when they chose the men they would love."

He stilled. "Your daughter?"

"Aye." Violet eyes leveled on him. " 'Twas my daughter that ran away."

Chapter Nine

Aedan stared at the fairy queen in shock. "Rowan is your grand-daughter?"

"Indeed she is," Ysenda said with quiet regard, "and a princess."

"I—I know not what to say."

"I assure you," Ysenda replied, "this day has offered enough confusion for us all."

"Aye, it has." Aedan now saw the similarities between Ysenda and her granddaughter. Both had strong features. The pure white hair of the queen was a luxurious mass, the same texture as Rowan's wheat blond locks.

There were so many questions to ask. From the bewilderment on the fairy queen's face, she wished answers as well. Except, with the approach of dawn, questions would have to wait.

"Dawn approaches, and I must sleep. It will be alongside Rowan." The queen's mouth tightened, but on this point he refused to yield. "With my bond to Rowan," Aedan continued before she could speak, "I will be able to provide her protection even in sleep."

Ysenda arched a doubtful brow. "A guarantee of nothing."

" 'Tis a guarantee that I will give my life to protect hers."

Tense silence echoed through the room.

"Rowan may not live through the conversion." Ysenda's voice trembled at the last.

"She will." He swallowed hard. "I love her and cannot lose her!"

"We do not always receive what we wish."

"You think I do not understand that?" He raised his hand at

his outburst. "My apologies. I love Rowan. If there is anything I can do to save her, I will."

Ysenda remained silent.

He had not really expected a reply. He might as well say the rest of it. "If Rowan survives, I request her hand in marriage. With your permission."

"Permission?" she scoffed. "We are natural enemies. A union between you and Rowan is forbidden."

"Laws of the fey. Rowan is but half fairy. She carries my child. And, she is my mate."

Ysenda's face hardened. "Mate?" She waved away his reply when he started to speak. "Regardless of what I believe, your reasons change naught."

"Love is nae fair in whom it chooses. For whatever reason, I have been gifted with Rowan's. I ask for your permission out of courtesy, in hopes that peace can be found between our worlds." He paused. " 'Tis your choice to end the strife or allow an age-old animosity to continue."

"I do nae know if I can allow such."

Frustration coupled with tiredness. "You have lost one daughter who sought but to follow her heart. Would you risk a grand-daughter newly found?"

Anger flared in the queen's eyes and then faded. "The decision is not an easy one."

"As Laird of the Highland Coven, I will win many an enemy by choosing Rowan to be my wife."

Ysenda studied him long and hard. "If I allow my grand-daughter to wed you, many will be furious in the Otherworld as well."

"For Rowan, I shall risk the outrage of my people," Aedan replied. "What of you?"

She gave a weary sigh. "I have much to consider."

He nodded, pleased Ysenda would contemplate his marriage to Rowan. "For now our thoughts must be on Rowan."

The fairy queen nodded. "Indeed. Sleep. I will be outside."

"You will stay within Caorann Castle?"

"Aye." Violet eyes narrowed. "If Rowan dies, so shall you." With a sweep of her hand, iridescent smoke whirled around her, and she vanished.

Aedan sagged against his chamber wall, stunned by the events of the last few hours, amazed Rowan's grandmother had not killed him outright.

He studied Rowan.

Her chest remained still. After passing out from the torment of the conversion, she'd succumbed to the deep sleep of a vampire, and all her internal systems had shut down. He refused to believe her body was giving up, that instead of moving through the conversion process, she was dying.

Heart aching at Rowan's desperate state, he lay beside her and drew her into his arms. "Sleep deeply. When you awaken, your transformation will be complete." Aedan closed his eyes and prayed he'd spoken the truth.

Agony pummeled Rowan's body, torturous lashes that stung her over and over, only to begin again. Aedan! His name echoed through her mind, but she couldn't see him or hear him within the blanket of misery. She struggled to push through the hurt, only to lose herself where naught existed but pain.

The fey within her recognized the truth—she was dying.

Rowan worked to hear the sound of her child's heart. Failed. He could not die!

She fought for calm, to retain her grip on sanity. *Aedan!*

Silence.

Panic overwhelmed her as she tried to push through the foggy confusion to somehow reach Aedan. A rush of sound filled her mind like bubbles. Without warning, coolness tumbled over her. Exhausted, Rowan sagged back and found herself standing within a mist.

Framed between breaks of white, fields of potent green unfolded before her.

She frowned. Where was she?

In the distance, a light grew, and a soft hum began, beckoning her.

Curious, Rowan took a step forward. Stunned, she stopped. The pain had disappeared.

"Nor will you ever hurt again."

She shielded her eyes against the bright light where a voice echoed. "Who is there?"

"Your destiny."

Peace radiated from the voice, so soft, so luxurious, it lured her to relax. "My destiny?" None of this made sense. She struggled to remember why she'd hurt so much, but found naught except for the image of Aedan.

"His life is elsewhere."

Rowan walked toward the brightness. "Who are you?"

"You know."

With a frown Rowan glanced around, took in the soft hues, the scent of lavender mixed with that of the wildflowers of her youth. Memories stumbled through her mind, beautiful images she'd seen during her life, the rush of a waterfall as it cascaded into a deep pool, the waves of the ocean as they surged up the beach, the gentle fall of rain upon the grass.

Confused, she studied the glow of light before her, a diffused, welcoming pulse. And understood.

She'd died.

A tremor shook her. Nay, let her be wrong.

"Aye, my child, your new life has begun. Here you will be pain free and will find naught but happiness."

"Nay, I cannot be happy without Aedan."

Rowan! His voice echoed from the distance.

She whirled, secluded in the shroud of white. "Aedan?"

"He cannot hear you."

She turned. "Please, I wish to go back."

Silence. "None has ever requested to leave."

"A fact I can understand. Never before have I felt such welcome, such acceptance, but never before have I felt the love that Aedan has given me."

Silence hummed within the cocoon of warmth. "If you go back, you will step into your life as before, into agony so intense you will wish for this peace."

She hesitated. "If I go back, will my child and I live through the conversion?"

The light pulsed. "Aye."

"Then, 'tis my wish to return."

"You are certain?"

Rowan nodded.

"So be it."

The light dulled.

Pain rushed into Rowan like a mace driven into unprotected flesh. Her body throbbed, hurt more than she believed possible.

"She is awake."

Aedan's distant voice reached her. Rowan fought against the pain, fought not to slip beneath consciousness. "Ae-Aedan?"

A hand as soft as it was strong lifted hers. "I am here."

She forced open her eyes, found him watching her, his fear easy to read.

"She is a vampire?"

At the dazed yet melodic voice, Rowan shifted her head, winced against the slash of agony. The fairy queen stood but a pace away.

"Only half," Aedan replied, his voice thick with wonder. "My blood has melded with hers, and incredibly, as I'd hoped, she has retained her fey aspects, and lost only her human side."

Beads of sweat slid down Rowan's body as she struggled to concentrate, to understand the full impact of his words.

"Impossible," the fairy queen whispered.

" 'Twould seem not," Aedan replied.

The regal woman rubbed her brow. "This is all such a muddle." She gave Rowan a gentle smile. "There is much I wish to ask you, but later, once you have recovered."

"Incredibly, I am feeling stronger," Rowan replied, finding with each passing second her words were true.

Aedan gave her hand a gentle squeeze. " 'Tis the mix of vampire and fey blood. Both hold enormous strength and ensure you will quickly heal."

She touched the curve of her stomach, surprised to feel the kick of her child against her palm.

"Your child will grow at an accelerated rate due to the mix of fey and vampire blood," Ysenda explained.

Rowan nodded, understanding there was so much more she would learn. From the puzzlement on the queen's face, she was not alone. "You have questions."

Ysenda studied her a long moment. "Laird MacGregor said you were left upon a healer's doorstep."

"Aye," Rowan replied. "After my mother died giving birth, my father struggled to raise me. He felt it a prudent choice."

"Since you were half fey, he would." The fairy queen's hands trembled. "How many summers are you?"

Confused by such a question, Rowan frowned. "Eighteen, Your Highness."

Tears shimmered in Ysenda's eyes. " 'Tis true."

"True?" Rowan asked.

"You, child," the fairy queen whispered, "are my granddaughter, Princess Rowan Campbell of the Otherworld."

Epilogue

Rowan leaned against Aedan's arms as she stared down at the sleeping babies nestled in their beds. "They are so small," she whispered, aware that, part fey and part vampire, they would be ultrasensitive and easily awakened.

"They will grow fast," he replied.

"Three." She shook her head. "Who knew I carried triplets."

Aedan smiled, his expression filled with pride. "Magic indeed."

"I am thankful my grandmother has accepted you." She lifted her gaze, smiled. "Has accepted us."

" 'Twas that or lose contact with a granddaughter and her great grandchildren."

"More, I think it was your insisting we name one of our daughters after my mother."

"Guinevere is a regal-sounding name."

"Aye," she agreed, "but a token of peace all the same."

"Aye." He winked. "One that worked well, might I add."

With a smile, she took in their children, and her heart filled with pride. "Elspeth and Seòras have your eyes."

"And your smile." Aedan drew her into a slow kiss, lifted his head. "Our children. A miracle."

"They are." She shook her head. " 'Tis hard to believe so much has happened in such a brief amount of time."

He brushed a sweep of hair from the curve of her cheek with his thumb. "Aye."

Sadness touched Rowan. "I am sorry your cousin is dead."

"Do not be. Breac's greed sealed his fate."

"I know. Still, I wish it could have ended otherwise."

"As do I, but 'tis done." Aedan took her hand in his, gave it a gentle squeeze. "Never must we forget that our joining, though for us a miracle, will be frowned upon by many vampires as well as many fey."

Like an ominous foreboding, a chill raced through her as she studied the innocent faces of their sleeping children. "Never would I wish them harm."

"Nor I, but 'tis a consequence of our love."

"Aye." She lifted the tiny hand of her closest daughter, pressed a kiss upon miniature fingers, and then tucked Elspeth's hand beneath the coverlet. She turned to Aedan. "But my wish is to focus on the joys of this day. The challenges ahead will come."

"Indeed."

He claimed her mouth in a long, passionate kiss, and Rowan's worries fell away. This moment she would savor the man she loved, their beautiful children, and the gift of family found. And if she and Aedan's meeting and falling in love seemed like magic, it was only fitting, with her being part fey. 'Twould seem a perfect ending indeed.

Never Been Bitten

Erica Ridley

For Frank Stout,
a born romantic

Chapter One

October 1830
Lincolnshire, England

To some, the Wedgeworth soirée might appear a splendid crush of debutantes, dandies, and music, but to Miss Elspeth Ramsay—inveterate bluestocking, indifferent spinster, and, most damning of all, *tradeswoman*—the evening's crush was simply her latest assignment. As planned, she'd been commissioned to enter the world of the ton.

If Ellie were a fidgeter, she might have been nervously smoothing nonexistent wrinkles from the nicest of her outdated gowns. She did not fidget. If she were a coquette, perhaps she would be twining one of her wayward curls about her finger whilst simpering at the eligible bachelors. Ellie did not simper. If she were socially ambitious, she might be near to a swoon at having arrived at a High Society fête as the particular guest of the youngest daughter of a duke. She did not swoon. Instead, Ellie stood in the farthest corner from the orchestra, surreptitiously surveying the crowd and hoping none of them would notice her in the shadows. After mentally cataloguing and discarding each of the revelers as harmless, she turned to her benefactress with a raised brow.

"Well?" she said, impatient to calm her client's irrational fears and escape the oppressive splendor. "Where is he?"

Rather than being affronted by this impertinence, Miss Lydia Breckenridge beamed with self-satisfaction. "He has not yet arrived." Miss Breckenridge nearly bounced on her satin-slippered feet. "I knew you'd be able to discern human from inhuman upon sight, you being an authority on the paranormal—"

"I am no such thing!" Ellie was unable to bear this speech with continued calm. "I am a woman of science, Miss Breckenridge. If anything, I am a 'professional skeptic.' To date, every such claim I've investigated has been quickly proven false, and I don't doubt this one shall unfold in the same way." As much as she and her mother desperately needed the coin, Ellie couldn't help but give a slight shake of her head. "Vampires, indeed."

"But don't you see?" Miss Breckenridge insisted, eyes shining. "That's what makes your involvement perfect. When even *you* are forced to admit true evil walks amongst us, the rest will be obliged to take heed."

"And do what?" Ellie asked sensibly. "Drive a stake through his waistcoat?"

"What a horrid image." Miss Breckenridge's brow creased. "To be honest, I had not thought so far in advance."

Ellie forbore mentioning she doubted her client had thought over any portion of her preposterous belief. Rudeness was never warranted, and besides, she planned to earn the promised ten-pound note. "At what point did you first suspect the new earl in town to be a vampire?"

"No, no," gasped Miss Breckenridge. "You've got it all wrong."

Ellie blinked. "He's not a vampire?"

"He's not a *lord*." Miss Breckenridge sniffed. "Despite his so-briquet. He's a younger son of a family in the Scottish Highlands, distantly related to the head of some forgotten medieval clan. He's not a member of the peerage whatsoever. How could he be, if he's an undead immortal?"

"How indeed," Ellie said faintly. "How, then, did he cut such a swath?"

For a moment, Miss Breckenridge's eyes turned dreamy. "Mártainn Macane may be penniless and a cursed bloodsucker, but he's devilishly handsome."

"Penniless!" Ellie exclaimed, forming a much sharper impression of her quarry. His motive might not be much different than hers, but his method stood in stark relief. *She* had never feigned bloodlust for gain. "I deduce he puts himself forward in order to take advantage of innocent debutantes."

Miss Breckenridge gestured at the swirling crowd. "No need for such, when young and old alike throw themselves and their purses in his path at every opportunity."

Ellie's lip curled at the very idea. "I'm sure he cannot refuse such marvelous gifts. The women are aware of his . . . nature?"

"Aware? He's nigh irresistible," Miss Breckenridge confessed in a whisper. "Undoubtedly part of his dark magic. The competition to be the devil's chosen has eclipsed the judgment of every otherwise sensible woman who finds herself caught in his gaze."

Ellie's client clearly thought herself the heroine of a gothic novel. Either the higher the social rank, the lower the intelligence, or this Mr. Macane was an extremely skillful magician indeed. She'd bet he was nothing more than a two-bit actor who had changed his venue from the streets to soirées. "How can he be so successful and also so terrible?"

"How?" Miss Breckenridge blushed prettily. "Because he's bad in a very, very good way. They've gone so far as to dub him Lord Lovenip, and my brothers tell me the betting books overflow with wagers as to which female he shall claim next." Her eyes widened in horror. "Oh, I do hope you yourself do not fall prey to his wicked charms!"

"Oh, for the love of—" Ellie coughed daintily into her gloved hand, reminding herself that money earned for a fool's errand was still money earned, and she'd be wise not to let her mouth get in the way of the Breckenridge coffers. "Have no fear on that front, Miss Breckenridge. I have yet to find the man capable of turning my head."

Her benefactress cast a discerning eye at Ellie's drooping curls and woefully out-of-fashion gown, managing to convey without a single word that Ellie's spinsterhood was far more likely due to Ellie's own inability to turn heads, rather than any fault inherent in the eligible gentlemen.

Be that as it may, Ellie's distinct lack of position in Society afforded her the perfect disguise: insignificant wallflower. Unlike third-daughter-of-a-duke Miss Breckenridge, Ellie had the ability to stay both in sight and unnoticed at gatherings such as this. Granted, this was the first time she'd been commissioned to investigate a vampiric Scotsman, but she held complete confidence that she would put paid to such nonsense in short order.

Her spine straightened as a wave of whispers rippled through the ballroom like froth chasing the tide. An unnatural hush immediately followed.

Although the orchestra kept playing, the music now had a tinny, street-corner quality, as if the melody were being strained through a battered ear horn. The dancers did not falter, but their steps became disjointed and mechanical, as if they were marionettes painted to resemble aristocracy, rather than the pleasure-seeking lords and ladies they'd been just moments ago.

Ellie's senses became overwhelmingly acute. Miss Breckenridge's breathing seemed to echo about the chamber, her perfume suddenly noxious. Ellie's pulse thundered with such force, she fancied she felt the heat of her blood coursing recklessly through her veins. For the first time in her life, she had the inexplicable desire to flee the premises while her heart still beat.

Then there he was.

A leather thong tied thick chestnut hair at the nape of his neck. Eighteen stone of solid muscle sculpted effortlessly into ebony breeches and bone-white muslin. His skin was just as pale, yet managed to convey the strength of marble rather than the fragility of ivory. Impossibly bright sea-green eyes gazed knowingly from beneath dark lashes. Blunt cheekbones accentuated a wide, firm mouth set in a mocking smirk above a strong jaw.

He was too big, too pale, too predatory. He should not have been beautiful, but he was.

The music bobbled in his wake, losing its rhythm, then tumbled forth at twice the tempo. The sharp-edged lords and ladies loosened their joints until they too were fluid and careening about the ballroom once again. Widows and debutantes alike spun in and out of his path, inventing steps where there should be none, dipping to expose both cleavage and bared necks, twirling ever closer even when the music was done.

A giddy countess lost her equilibrium when she could not keep her eyes from him. Without even facing in her direction, he righted her with a mere touch of his palm against the small of her back. She fainted into her husband's arms. The remaining ladies were too entranced by Mártainn Macane to take notice.

Ellie swallowed hard.

Lord Lovenip, indeed. For there could be no other man capable of stirring a stately crowd into such a frenzy with nothing more than a moment of his presence.

With what was surely superhuman strength, Ellie cut her gaze from the man sucking all the air out of the previously well-ventilated ballroom and forced her eyes to her benefactress. Perhaps it was the act of severing the inexplicable connection to the rakish Highlander or perhaps the unreality of the moment had been entirely in Ellie's mind, but once the arresting Scotsman no longer filled her vision, the rest of her senses shifted back to normal. Her pulse no longer clogged her ears, her blood no longer simmered beneath her flesh, and Miss Breckenridge was no longer breathing like—

All right, yes. Miss Breckenridge was still breathing like a broodmare in labor. If her bosoms heaved any more vehemently, they'd heave themselves right out of their fashionably low bodice. Ellie uncurled fingers she didn't recall clenching and pressed a trembling hand to her own bosom to assure herself she was in no danger of exposing any womanly curves.

None of the other ladies seemed afflicted with such spinsterish sensibilities.

Everywhere Macane stepped, widows and debutantes swarmed. They taunted him with their long slender necks and bared décolletage, angling for a dance and hoping to tempt him with the naked flesh displayed above the lace of their gowns. The married ladies were coyer, fluttering glazed eyes at him from over their husbands' shoulders.

He could have his pick of anyone in the room, Ellie realized with a start. Could and, most likely, did. Young, old, married, widowed—they were all shamelessly, shockingly available if he but wished it. The well-favored Scot seemed blind to the tiny dramas of gentlemen clinging desperately to their negligent wives and turned instead to the buffet of virginal misses fairly leaping from their duennas' custody and into his arms.

The steps of country-dances led him to one, then another, then yet another, leaving them all flushed and breathless and smitten, panting and clawing for the chance to tumble into his embrace once again, as if addicted to his scent.

It was horrifying and appalling and . . . more than a little exciting. Every time he chose a pastel angel from the adoring crowd,

Ellie's flesh tingled as if it had been her hand he had touched. Every time he spun an enraptured young miss out of his arms for a beat or two, Ellie felt the loss of contact down to her very bones. It was as if she could feel what they felt, both the delicious sense of vulnerability as one wide-eyed innocent after another let herself be trapped in his arms, as well as the darker thrill of possession, of mastery, of control over everyone who fell within his line of vision.

If the dukes and dandies felt threatened by the relentless power exuding from the dashing Mr. Macane, they disdained any instinct for confrontation. The married gentlemen clutched their wives to their chests as best they could. The unattached bucks melted into the wainscoting like wolf pups cowering before the leader of the pack.

Macane spared a glance at neither set, as if none of the gentlemen present posed the slightest threat to him having his way with whomever he wished. No matter what that might entail. Although Ellie had, as expected, seen no signs whatsoever of the handsome Lord Lovenip's being tempted by blood rather than by the ladies themselves, he was certainly dangerous in his own right, and a volatile addition to any throng. Not to mention provocative.

"Miss Breckenridge—" Ellie sucked in a breath, shocked to have heard a stammer in her voice. One would think this man had cast a spell over the room. "Miss Breckenridge," she began again, once she had regained her command over both voice and body. "Presumably, the man who has enraptured the entire party without uttering a single word is the infamous Lord Lovenip. I see him dancing with those he should and those he should not, but nothing more untoward than that. I thought you said he . . . bites?"

"Not all of them." With obvious difficulty, Miss Breckenridge tore her eyes from the man in question. She turned toward Ellie, her movements sluggish, as if she yearned to tilt her face to him. "And not all the time. That's what makes him harder to catch." Her shoulders lifted with a sigh. "And it's why nobody believes me." Miss Breckenridge's voice lowered. "He's not playacting, Miss Ramsay. He's a predator."

Unconvinced of dark magic afoot, Ellie pursed her lips and considered. "What is he waiting for, then? A solicitation?"

"A temptation, rather." Miss Breckenridge lifted one of her slender arms and gave a flick of the wrist at the teeming crush. "He's bored. He's danced with these women before, many times. Such is the burden of the Upper Ten Thousand—there are a limited set of us at any given party."

"A trial, to be sure," Ellie murmured.

"I have had a devil of a time catching him in the act," Miss Breckenridge continued. "My own sister doesn't acknowledge the truth, which is what prompted me to hire a professional. Nothing short of impartial corroboration will gain me her ear." She gave a sharp nod. "I shall now step aside and allow you your head."

"Very well." Ellie returned her gaze to the riveting Highlander who somehow made six-plus feet of controlled muscle seem elegant and graceful. She strongly suspected the virginal misses swarming about were in danger of losing something far more irreplaceable than a ration of blood, but how on earth could Ellie prove it?

"Dance," she suggested to her client. "Dance with him, and I promise to watch very closely. I shan't even blink."

Miss Breckenridge recoiled as if Ellie had suggested eating spiders with tea. "Are you mad? I've no wish to be nibbled upon by Lord Lovenip, no matter how handsome the devil's spawn might be. Dance with him yourself if you'd like to tempt him into action."

Nibbled upon. Yes. That did sound—Ellie gave her head a violent shake. *No*, rather. What bug was in her brain today? She had no wish to be nibbled upon, by him or anyone else. Furthermore, while Mr. Macane might be a rake of the first order, that hardly made him an undead creature bent on draining the blue blood from London's finest. Should she risk a dance to prove it? Why, certainly. Miss Elspeth Ramsay was more than willing to get *her* hands dirty in the name of science.

But how?

No one knew her. She was a dowdy spinster in outdated attire, hidden in a shadowy corner of the ballroom. Anonymity was the crux of any covert investigation. That's why every time she infiltrated a crowd, she spent the first quarter hour mentally chanting, *Don't look at me, Don't remember me,* at everyone who passed her by. Her wish was always granted. Or perhaps someone of her station would never suffer particular attention. It went well against the grain to wish for the opposite. And even if the unthinkable happened and Lord Lovenip *did* happen to notice an unremarkable old maid flanking the third daughter of a duke, he'd suppose her Miss Breckenridge's chaperone before he thought her a viable dance partner.

Besides, did she even know how? Ellie frowned, realizing for the first time that her ability to perform dance steps—or not— was one of the many maddening holes in her memory. Her mother had cautioned against taking this assignment, as if Ellie might forget herself and never return home. Utter nonsense. What Ellie could not forget was how badly their pockets were to let. They could ill afford to turn down money, and it was just a simple ball. Ellie would stick to the shadows, as always, and hopefully return home overlooked but a few pounds richer. And life would go on as always.

But she couldn't stop the traitorous voice inside her head from whispering, *Look at me; notice me* as she stared at Mr. Macane's devastatingly handsome form.

Unsurprisingly, nothing happened. His focus was on his simpering dance partner.

Chest tight with resentment and envy, Ellie shifted her gaze to the insipid debutante in his arms. Beautiful and probably brainless. *I hope you fall.*

The girl's legs collapsed beneath her.

Ellie gasped in shock at the coincidence, unconsciously pressing her back against the uneven wall.

Macane extended a graceful hand to the trembling girl at his feet, but his dark gaze focused over her head, as if he could see through the throng and through the shadows, to the young lady trying desperately to melt into the wainscoting.

"You can't see me. You can't see me," Ellie whispered, suddenly and unreasonably terrified.

"He can," Miss Breckenridge corrected, her voice faint. "I fear you've been marked."

Ellie's body fought to free itself from the wall, as if pulled toward him by a force more powerful than her self-control. At the same time, every sense, every pore, screamed danger. Her breathing faltered and her heartbeat sped until her only reality was herself . . . and him.

The melody ended, and a new one began. Without breaking eye contact with Ellie, Macane handed the young girl off to her mother and strode forward, his step purposeful, his eyes determined. Despite the crowd, despite the music, despite her own breath rasping loudly in her ears, from across the ballroom she could clearly hear him speak his first word of the evening.

"*You.*"

And then he pounced.

Without seeing him cross the dance floor, without any memory of peeling herself from the far wall, their shadows intertwined and those eerily beautiful green eyes were piercing her to her soul.

"I—" Ellie faltered, unsure what she'd meant to say, or if there truly was anything *to* say.

He frowned, which only served to unnerve her even more. "You're not—"

"I forgot to make introductions," gasped Miss Breckenridge, at Ellie's shoulder. "Of course. Mr. Macane, allow me the honor of presenting Miss Elspeth Ramsay. Miss Ramsay, *this* is Mr. Mártainn Macane."

Yes. Obviously. But all Ellie could do was stare up at him, mesmerized by the tiny crease between his brows, as if he were as puzzled as she was to find herself the object of his attention. Who had he thought she was? And would he leave, now that his hopes had been disappointed?

Mr. Macane's brow smoothed, and his chiseled features relaxed into a mask of perfect ennui. He inclined his head and favored her with a close-lipped smile.

Miss Breckenridge would no doubt assume he did so to hide unsightly fangs. Ellie knew better. Close-lipped smiles were what one did when one was only pretending. Her mastery of the art enabled her to mask her own humiliation at not being worthy of a true smile. His unexpected interest had been nothing more than a case of mistaken identity. More than understandable, given the crowd and the distance they'd had between them. Now that the dancing shadows thrown by the glass chandeliers no longer masked her features, he could finally see her for who she really was: nobody.

Never had she felt her lack of status so keenly.

He gazed at her a moment longer than was proper, undoubtedly determining the best way to extricate himself from an un-desirable situation. To Ellie's surprise, he extended his hand. "Shall we?"

She blinked at him until her addled brain deciphered his mean-ing, then she croaked, "Dance?"

"Certainly." The edge of his mouth lifted as if he found her amusing.

Ellie was not amused. She was mortified. And determined not to let it show.

"Go," her client hissed, sotto voce. "I shan't even blink."

Head held high—given that this dance would secure her place in infamy, and she'd no longer be able to cavort unnoticed amongst the ton, and how was she to earn a living without her anonymity?—she allowed him to lead her onto the parquet. Then she re-membered that perhaps she'd better not hold her head *too* high, as it tended to elongate one's neck, and she had no wish to em-ulate the brainless ninnies exposing their bare skin to him at every turn. She would be different. She would be . . . immune.

And if not, well, at least she would act like it.

When he led her about the perimeter of the floor, keeping time with the music, she was delighted to discover her feet did in fact know the right steps, even if her head didn't. Unfortu-nately, that meant she needed something else to concentrate on.

Macane.

The dark-haired Scotsman perfectly embodied London fash-ion—except for one detail. Ellie's gaze settled upon his bare neck. Strong, pale, and all the more striking due to an inexplicably ab-sent cravat. Miss Breckenridge had mentioned that as one of his affectations. While the dandies struggled to keep their heads afloat above clouds of starched linen cascading from beneath their chins, Mr. Macane was shockingly unique. He did as he wished. He danced with whomever he wished. And, if Miss Breckenridge was to be believed, he drank from whomever he wished.

Ellie's eyes widened as she realized the thought of his lips at her throat quickened her pulse more from excitement than fear. What was wrong with her? Why did her blood thrum faster, as if calling out to him?

She focused on the curve of muscle between his neck and his shoulder, attempting to shame herself into behaving properly by proving his heartbeat was steadier than hers.

Except . . . she couldn't find a pulse point.

Frowning, she tilted her head and listened for the sound of his breathing. She couldn't hear that, either. Strange, for her senses tended toward the extraordinary. She could see the individual fibers in the fine linen stretched across the expanse of his chest, but could not detect the pulse at the base of his neck. She could discern the fine leather of his shoes and the worn satin of her own, but could not detect the merest breath exhaling from his nose.

She leaned into him a bit more than she ought, certain that she was missing the obvious while sharing the thrall of the mindless fancy gripping the ton. But even with her face close enough for her breath to send a stray curl brushing against his powerful chest, all she could hear was the pounding of her own heart, and all she could see was herself acting a proper ninny.

Ellie pulled back and glanced up at him in embarrassment.

His eyes were not on hers. His gaze was locked on the base of her neck, where her own pulse point fluttered like a butterfly struggling to break free from its cocoon.

A slow smile curved his lips, gapping just long enough to flash a sliver of white teeth. Not fangs, Ellie told herself. Just teeth. As normal as hers. She took a deep breath and shivered as she inhaled the scent of cologne and clean linen.

Everything had an explanation. Macane was an accomplished rake, not a vampire. He happened to be brilliant at the art of illusion. With his absent cravat and his close-lipped smiles, he lent just the right touch of mystery and illicit adventure to woo the golden flock. Genius, actually. If she'd thought of it first, perhaps she'd be the celebrated Original of the ton, rather than the spinster who investigated frivolous claims for the rich.

She glanced up at him again. His mouth was no longer curved in a smile, but it was still wide and firm. The swooning ladies could keep their macabre fantasies. She'd much rather have that sensual mouth kissing her than biting her. If there weren't such a crush of people . . .

As if they shared one mind, his next artful spin took them from the sparkling dance floor to a spot behind a hand-painted Chinese folding screen—which hid the entrance to the gardens. Before she could object (presuming she would have objected)

Ellie was out the door and beneath the moonlit sky, still cradled in Macane's arms.

A frisson of trepidation caused her to catch her breath. She stared up at him in a panic. Might he actually kiss her? As far as she could remember, no one had ever tried. No gentleman had ever noticed her long enough to think of it. And now—what if she did it wrong? What if she did it *right?* What would be expected of her then?

"You're beautiful," he murmured. "You dazzled me even as you tried to hide."

Well, that was laying it on a bit thick. Ellie wasn't ugly, but nor were artists dueling for the honor of painting her portrait. She was plain. Worse than plain: She was *nondescript*. Wracking her brain for an appropriate setdown to such ridiculous flattery, she narrowed her eyes at him . . . and nearly swooned at his expression.

He was sincere. Or if not, he gave a bloody good impression of it.

His eyes were rapt on her face, as if he had been searching for her all his life. His gaze had softened, making his features less harsh and more open. His arms cradled her gently, his hands splayed at the curve between waist and hips. He was being far more familiar than anyone of her acquaintance—far more familiar than any right-minded young lady should allow—but Ellie was so enamored by the idea of having entranced *him* that she couldn't bring herself to pull away.

His lips parted. Hers did too, mostly because she was having trouble remembering to breathe. Her lips suddenly felt too dry. She edged out the tip of her tongue to lick them and gasped when his hold tightened painfully. She felt strangely powerful, as if she truly were beautiful.

He lowered his face to hers. His eyes were no longer the crystal green of the sea, but rather a shimmering black. Rather than try to process the transformation, Ellie cleared her mind and let her own eyes flutter closed. She was going to be kissed for the first time. And she was going to enjoy it.

Her brow creased when the delicious pressure of his parted lips brushed the base of her throat rather than her waiting mouth. The sharp edge of bared teeth grazed the tender skin at the curve of her neck. He wasn't going to kiss her—he was going to bite her!

Instinct forced her to react at lightning speed. But instead of shoving him away as she could've sworn she had instructed her limbs to do, Ellie returned the favor and sank her own teeth into his cravat-free neck.

Mutual shock held them immobile for an interminable moment. Realizing the ignominy of what she'd just done, Ellie pulled away in horror before he could thrust her from him bodily. To label him thunderstruck would be the understatement of the century.

He touched his neck with the tip of a finger. The pad of his white glove came away pink with blood.

"Good Lord," he growled, his expression fierce. "Did you just *bite* me?"

Chapter Two

For the first time in centuries, seasoned warrior Mártainn Macane was nothing short of gobsmacked.

From across the ballroom, he'd been certain the ethereal creature with the wispy red-blond curls was the runaway bride he'd blood-sworn two centuries before to capture and return to his laird, uniting the most powerful clans.

After a closer look, he'd been even more certain that this lass was not his laird's betrothed. First, she was too young. Granted, vampire bodies ceased aging at the hour of their deaths, but the Deserter had been in her late twenties when she'd succumbed, and this waif wasn't a day over eighteen. Even in the dark, she was the picture of youthful innocence. But the most inarguable evidence was the girl's panicked breathing and rapid heartbeat. If vampires' hearts continued to beat, they wouldn't need to consume blood.

Yet—the lass had *bitten* him. What the devil was he supposed to make of that? He would force an answer from her, if necessary.

Possessed of preternatural vision, Cain could clearly make out the uncommon beauty disguised in commoners' clothing before him. For maximum intimidation, however, he needed to be certain she could see him just as clearly.

He swung her back through the open doorway and into the ballroom. The Chinese folding screen still hid them from the masses, but the candles flickering on the chandeliers overhead mottled them both in shifting patches of light. Either the Deserter had donned a human guise capable of fooling the most celebrated hunter of Clan Mac Eoin (which was impossible on all counts) or the redoubtable Miss Elspeth Ramsay had a wee bit of explaining to do.

"Speak," he commanded.

Miss Ramsay's crystal blue eyes stared up at him, her expression nothing short of horrified. Slender, petal-pink lips parted, but nary a word escaped. Just visible was a row of clean, white teeth. A single drop of crimson stained the blunt point of her left incisor. The sight of his own blood held him spellbound.

In spite of himself, Cain was almost painfully aroused. Even though her inexplicable assault was more mystifying than maddening, he could not tamp down the sharp yearning in his soul. No human had ever dreamt of biting him. That mating ritual was for vampire clans alone. And he hadn't set foot in his homeland for over two hundred years. Oh, how he longed for Scotland, even now.

Were Miss Ramsay a vampire, her incisors would have been much longer, much sharper. Were she a vampire, he could have her. Och, were she a vampire, she would not be staring up at him with her face full of fear and a drop of her victim's blood still glistening on her teeth.

He, a victim! The incongruity nearly incited him to throttle her. He was a warrior first, a vampire second, a victim never. And to have been surprised by a living girl, of all creatures. The humanity fairly steamed from her.

"Speak," he repeated hoarsely.

She remained frozen in silence.

Even more confounding was the undeniable fact that she'd twice ignored his command. As far as Cain knew, resistance was impossible. Human minds were unable to withstand the will of a powerful vampire. Even more potent was a vampire's spoken word. In centuries of history, he'd never heard of a human failing to obey vampiric Compulsion. Was it possible the girl was in too much shock to process her environment?

"Speak," he said again, but this time gently, so as not to startle her overmuch.

The tip of her tongue nudged between the parted edges of her (very normal, very human) teeth.

Rapt, his entire body tensed in fascination.

The tip curled over her incisor, trapping the sole drop of blood between her tooth and tongue. Her pupils contracted, giving her iris the unsettling appearance of a solid disc of icy blue. Her chest stopped moving and no breath escaped her pink mouth. Her heart slowed—or perhaps time itself stopped as Miss Ramsay's tongue disappeared once again, taking that single drop of his blood with it.

Music crashed down around them, and the moment was gone.

Leather boots and satin slippers slapped methodically across the floor as the brainless hive trampled about the parquet on the other side of the folding screen. Perhaps it was simply acute homesickness that was making him uncharacteristically torpid, imagining significance where there was none.

With a strangled gasp, Miss Ramsay clasped a white-gloved hand to her face as if holding back bile. Her eyes were normal, if a bit glassy and over-wide. Her breathing was shallow. She looked as if she might bolt at any second.

Cain bit back a frustrated sigh. She was clearly not the vampire he'd been seeking for centuries . . . but she was troublesome nonetheless.

Before Miss Ramsay's arrival into his life, he had been on his single longest run of successful love nips (as the ton was wont to call them) in ballrooms across England. A slight sting where the curve of his neck met the muscle of his shoulder proved a reminder that the skin there had been broken. He could scarcely credit that the chit had succeeded where he had not.

He gentled his hold on Miss Ramsay and whirled her around the folding screen and back into the tide of dancers. Part of his carefully crafted mystique was never to abscond with fair maidens for a second longer than it took to take a sip of ambrosia and turn the memory into a half-remembered dream. He would not allow Miss Ramsay's unprecedented counterattack to ruin his acceptance in Society. The more invitations extended to "Lord Lovenip," the better chance he had of locating the Deserter.

Meanwhile, he would solve the puzzle of Miss Ramsay.

She released her lower lip from between her teeth and finally met his eyes. "I—I didn't mean to bite you."

Unquestionably. He gave her a half smile. "Then why did you?"

Miss Ramsay blushed. The blood rising to kiss the pale softness of her cheeks was nearly Cain's undoing.

"I don't know," she muttered.

He believed her. Miss Ramsay was hardly one of his kind. She was far stranger. "I believe it's safe to say that you're not like the other ladies."

"Certainly not." Her chin rose defiantly. "I'm smarter."

His amusement was overshadowed only by his interest in her choice of adjectives. She hadn't said she was prettier, or wealthier, or better connected. She'd chosen an attribute for which no one in the room cared one whit. Well, except for him. A warrior prized intelligence above all other traits.

"You're certainly less predictable," he agreed, pleased to see the blood rise to her cheeks anew at the reminder. He leaned closer. She smelled so fresh, so fragile, so *alive*. He should have kissed her when they were hidden in the gardens. "Are you from this part of the country? Or are you a city miss, barely surviving until the Season is upon us again?"

If he hadn't been watching her so closely, he might have missed the tiny frown that flickered between her brows.

"Neither." She broke eye contact, shifting her gaze over his shoulder. "And you?"

A pretty evasion . . . Cain wondered why she felt it necessary. "I was born on the Isle of Mull, but I've now been in England more years than I lived in Scotland."

Her focus returned to his face. "Is it beautiful? Your homeland, I mean?"

He smiled despite the pain in his heart. "Very. Have you never had the opportunity to visit?"

She shook her head.

"You ought, if you get the chance." It occurred to him she might not have the means for extensive travel; then he discarded the thought as nonsense. Country ball or not, one was not invited to rub noses with this set of people if they did not believe their guest to be of means. "Have you traveled much?"

"More than I prefer to have done." An expression flashed across her face too quickly to decipher. Anger? Distaste? Regret? "Are you afflicted with wanderlust, my lord?"

"To lust," he said with a wicked smile, "and not the slightest inclination to wander."

As hoped, the blush once again rose to her porcelain cheeks. Miss Ramsay was by far the most fetching female in the entire region. No doubt their dancing together after having stepped behind the Oriental folding screen would add a new page to the betting books on the morrow. After having treated himself to a pretty neck, he refrained from further dalliance—meaning Lord Lovenip had never continued to dance attendance upon anyone he'd sequestered for a quick bite. And here he was—swirling a young lady about the room long after, with not a hope of disguising his enjoyment of the flirtation.

"You're shameless," she admonished.

He grinned. "Guilty as charged."

"And highly inappropriate," she added.

He pulled her closer and dipped his head to whisper in her ear. "You wound my sensibilities, madam."

She shook her head in consternation and amusement. Not the reaction he usually effected, but then, nor was Miss Ramsay the usual sort of female. He was having far more fun than he'd had on his previous dances added together.

"I doubt you *have* any sensibilities," she said tartly.

Rather than reply, he allowed his gaze to settle on her lips. Ninety-nine times he'd whisked an English rose into a garden for a quick nip at her neck, and for the first time, he'd rather kiss one senseless. Miss Ramsay gazed at him with sharp intelligence, rather than mindless flirtation. She kept her secrets to herself and turned his questions back upon him rather than prattle endlessly about nonsense. And after centuries of witnessing human interaction, this was the first time he honestly couldn't guess what a mortal would say or do next.

He only hoped it involved kissing.

The melody closed on a crescendo. The musicians set down their instruments for a brief intermission. Propriety demanded he release Miss Ramsay from his embrace. Cain did so, blaming his distraction for not having Compelled the orchestra to keep playing. He bowed. She dipped in the briefest of curtseys and slipped away amongst the milling nobility.

The moment the musicians returned, he would secure her hand for another dance. He would purloin her at first opportunity, abduct her back out to the gardens, and tempt a hunger that had nothing to do with blood. He yearned to taste *her*, to feel her breath on his skin, the warmth of her flesh, the flutter of her heart beating against his chest.

But when the music resumed, she was gone.

Cain searched the ballroom, then the peripheral rooms, then the entire grounds. Nothing. She had disappeared without a word. Without even letting him know how to reach her, should he wish to do so.

He wished for much more than that.

Luckily, a woman like that could hardly escape notice. Her being the recipient of an invitation meant *someone* had to know her well enough to invite her. Besides, the upper circles were woven so close that he was undoubtedly the only person present who hadn't had the pleasure of receiving her card. He would have her direction in a trice.

"My apologies." He paused before a clump of florid peacocks. "Could any of you tell me Miss Ramsay's direction?"

The gentlemen screwed up their faces at him as if he'd spoken Gaelic. "Who?"

"Miss Elspeth Ramsay. Red-blond hair, dimple in her left cheek, impertinent but undeniably bonny . . ." Cain trailed off as he realized both his words and the accompanying hand gestures were most likely ill-advised in polite society. "That is to say, the lovely young woman I was just dancing with."

A passing viscountess came to a sharp halt upon overhearing this last. There! He knew finding a simple direction wouldn't be that difficult.

"Did you dance the last waltz?" she asked, blinking as if just having awoken from a deep sleep. She rapped his shoulder with a painted fan. "Horrid, horrid beast. You well know I would love to be your . . . partner."

Cain made the expected flirtatious replies and circled about the room, growing more and more incredulous after each frustrating encounter. Not a soul could help him. For the first time since he'd entered Society, the lords and ladies had taken their eyes from him—just long enough to have missed his waltz partner (and the detour into the gardens) entirely.

Even more baffling: No one had ever heard of Miss Elspeth Ramsay.

Chapter Three

If the perturbed expression on her client's stony face was any indication, Ellie would not be earning a single penny for her fruitless investigation into Mr. Macane. If anything, Miss Breckenridge's continued silence indicated Ellie should count herself lucky to have been granted a ride home in the Breckenridge carriage. She had been hired to prove Lord Lovenip either monster or fraud, and instead she had first assaulted the suspect, then flirted shamelessly with him, followed most ignominiously by fleeing the scene altogether. Ellie could well acknowledge how such behavior might be perceived as a breach of contract.

"Do forgive me," she blurted when she could no longer stand staring into her erstwhile client's icy countenance. "I am all apologies. I should not have—"

"It's not what you should not have done," Miss Breckenridge snapped, "but what you *should* have done, yet failed to do. I brought you to the ball specifically so you could scientifically evaluate Mártainn Macane, not so you could—"

"Don't say it," Ellie begged, blushing furiously at the realization her client might have witnessed the role reversal in the gardens. She'd gone and ruined an opportunity for easy money by losing her mind. "I know it was not at all well done of me, but when I realized what he was about, my only thought was that the best defense is a quick offense, and the next thing I knew—"

"—was that you'd disappeared entirely," Miss Breckenridge interrupted coldly. "And once I *did* come across you, nothing would do but to leave. Leave! A mere hour and a half after arriving! Regardless of your contract with me, one does *not* depart a Wedgeworth soirée a moment before three, and it isn't even half one. I'll be gossip fodder for days. And here we are, without an iota more information than when we began. What have you to say for yourself?"

"Very little, Miss Breckenridge." Despite the luxury of the carriage, the sumptuous squab beneath Ellie's bustle felt as though it were filled with rocks rather than down. Despite the latest technology in joints and shocks, every time the wheels rolled over the slightest pebble, Ellie's body was so tense, she felt each bump all the way to her bones. She needed Miss Breckenridge's patronage far more than Miss Breckenridge needed her. For the daughter of a duke, the soirée had been nothing more than an evening's lark. But for Ellie, it had meant food and shelter. She and her mother needed those ten pounds to survive. "All I can say is that I would not have assaulted him had he not tried to attack me first. When I realized he wished to bite me—"

"*What?*" Miss Breckenridge's jaw dropped. When Ellie failed to elucidate quickly enough, Miss Breckenridge trapped Ellie's shaking knee in a surprisingly strong grip. "Are you talking about Mártainn Macane?"

"Yes," Ellie said with a slight frown. "Er . . . aren't you?"

"You spoke with him? And he tried to *bite* you?"

"Yes," she repeated, blinking slowly. The thread of the conversation seemed to be unraveling in opposite directions.

Miss Breckenridge clasped Ellie's knees even tighter. "Where?"

"In the gardens," she stammered. "There was a Chinese folding screen near the exit, and he—"

"No, no, you ninny, where did he try to bite you?"

"Er . . . on the neck?" Ellie answered, deciding now was not the moment to take offense at being called a ninny. She certainly deserved the appellation for overreacting thusly to a perceived attack.

"On the *neck*," Miss Breckenridge crowed. "What did I tell you? I knew he was evil!" A panicked expression quickly replaced joy, and Miss Breckenridge's stupendous grip transferred from Ellie's knees to her shoulders, jerking her forward. Miss Breckenridge pulled Ellie's curls from her nape, twisting her head first one way then another as she inspected all angles of Ellie's neck. "Are you certain he didn't bite you? You won't make any kind of witness if you become a monster yourself or succumb to his unholy hypnotism. Dear heavens, what would I do then?"

"He didn't bite me. I swear it." Ellie wrenched out of her client's grasp and flattened her shoulders against the thick wall separating them from the driver's perch. "And there's no such thing as monsters."

Miss Breckenridge sputtered, "No such—my dear girl, you were nearly bitten by the spawn of the devil himself, and you wish to quibble over the *existence* of vampires?" She waved a silk-gloved hand in Ellie's direction and sat back with a pleased nod. "Certainly now you *must* believe."

"We have proven he bites," Ellie admitted begrudgingly. "We have not proven that he drinks blood."

Even as she said the words, she recalled the taste of that single drop of blood on her tongue, and her body thrilled with a sensation she could only liken to arousal. Her petticoats seemed simultaneously too tight, too heavy, too thick, the carriage too quick and too confining, and the oxygen altogether too insignificant to fulfill the quantity needed by her gasping lungs.

For a moment, a very brief, very intense moment, she had wanted him with terrible acuteness. Her vision had closed to only his face, his neck, and she'd longed to bite him, kiss him, tear his clothes from his limbs and demand he do the same to her.

Even now, she could taste his blood in her mouth, feel his strength beneath her palms, smell his scent and his own arousal, sense the danger exuding from his every pore. It was the disturbing sensation that she, too, was just as dangerous that had snapped her out of her trance long enough for her to gather her wits. Some of them, anyway. At least she'd managed to finish the waltz without attacking him again.

"Even if we'd proven he has a taste for blood," she said, grateful the dark interior of the carriage would mask her telltale blush, "that would not prove him a vampire. It would just make him . . . an extremely eccentric Scot. One must have empirical evidence before making sweeping claims."

Miss Breckenridge smiled as if, shadows or no, she detected the lie of Ellie's forced confidence. As if she saw through the careful façade of bluestocking scientist to the very rattled young woman underneath.

"See? You just presumed it possible—if not *probable*—that we will in fact prove your eccentric Scot boasts a taste for blood." Miss Breckenridge gave a pleased nod. "Whether you admit it or not, you are already starting to believe."

Peevishly, Ellie returned her client's gaze and refused to respond.

Miss Breckenridge carried on nonetheless. "Besides, drinking blood isn't the only sign of demonic vampirism."

One of Ellie's brows lifted despite herself. "No?"

At this query, Miss Breckenridge shook her head triumphantly. "What else is there, then? Empirically, that is."

"For one, vampires cannot abide sunlight." Miss Breckenridge's voice dropped to a whisper. "And no one has ever see Mártainn Macane during the day."

Ellie's shoulder twitched, but she refrained from indulging in a shrug. "With all due respect, that simply proves he dislikes the sun. Given that pale complexions are de rigueur, avoiding the sun hardly makes him suspicious. I'm a night person myself. I cannot remember the last time I gadded about during the day, if I ever have, and I'm certainly not a vampire. My own mother rarely leaves her bedchamber before dusk—surely you don't accuse her of vampirism, too?"

"No, no, of course not," Miss Breckenridge said with a wave of her lace-gloved hand. "But then, your mother hasn't been running about biting nobility, as Lord Lovenip does." Miss Breckenridge gasped dramatically and pressed her hand to her throat in obvious consternation. "Oh dear Lord, I've gone and used that ridiculous moniker myself." She screwed up her face and glared at Ellie as if the slip were somehow Ellie's fault instead of her own. With a sigh, she collapsed back against her seat. "What can I do to convince you vampires exist and that the dashing Mr. Macane is living—or rather undead—proof? Is it money you wish? Here . . ." She opened a satin, monogrammed reticule and dug through its contents before brandishing a crumpled five-pound note. "I'll double the amount. This now, and fifteen more once you conclude the investigation. What do you say?"

Ellie stared at the wrinkled banknote in her client's elegant outstretched palm. The money would mean everything to her and nothing at all to Miss Breckenridge. Her client hadn't been about to sack her out of disappointment over her behavior, but rather due to a belief that she wasn't taking the situation seriously. Given that Ellie had felt herself under her mother's ultra-conservative thumb her entire life, and had begun scientific investigations as much out of rebellion as industriousness, she could certainly empathize with a desire to be taken seriously. To know her own mind. Regardless of whether her beliefs matched everyone else's.

"Very well." Ellie plucked the crumpled paper from her client's palm and slowly, methodically, flattened it across one knee before folding it carefully and consigning it to the darkness of her own, otherwise vacant purse. Then she returned her gaze to her client and tried to apply her most scientific perspective to the topic at hand. "Are there any characteristics shared by supposed vampires that are not also plausibly explained by eccentric, but wholly human, actions of man?"

Miss Breckenridge bit her lip in consideration. "Well, I've never seen him eat a morsel of food, or drink a single drop of punch...."

"No one with any brains drinks the ratafia," Ellie countered logically. "It's horrid."

"Fine." Miss Breckenridge's eyes narrowed at a spot just above Ellie's shoulder for a long moment. Her sudden victory squeal nearly knocked Ellie out of her skin. "A mirror!" she exclaimed, rapping Ellie's knee for emphasis. "Vampires have no reflections, and no one has *ever* seen Macane anywhere near a looking glass. I will double—nay, *treble*—your fee if you but maneuver him before a glass!"

Ellie hesitated. There was little she wouldn't (honorably) do to earn such a sum, but what was the likelihood of success? She leveled her gaze at her client and infused her voice with as much calm rationality as possible. "If Mr. Macane has a visible reflection, you will agree that I've disproved your theory?"

Miss Breckenridge's blinding grin bespoke utter confidence. "I will, indeed—because he will not have one. And I know just how to find out. My birthday is but a fortnight from now, and I've already planned a three-day party. I shall invite Macane—and you shall attend as well, of course—and we will have done with this investigation once and for all."

The five-pound note in Ellie's purse weighed as much as a five-ton anchor. Her family desperately needed the income, but there was no hope of Ellie attending a three-day party. She'd had to misrepresent quite a few details of tonight's festivities to garner her mother's permission for the outing.

"I apologize," she said quietly, "but there is no chance at all of my attendance. My mother is quite protective and will never allow me out of her sight for so long. She doesn't even know where we were tonight."

Miss Breckenridge's eyes widened. "Where on earth does she think you are?"

"At a local estate . . . helping you find a lost kitten," Ellie admitted with another furious blush. "If Mama for one moment suspected I attended a soirée, I should never be allowed out of her sight again."

The young lady across from her merely laughed in response. "I am a Breckenridge," she said matter-of-factly, "and no one tells a Breckenridge no. I will call upon you on the morrow to extend the invitation in person. There will be no chance of refusal."

Ellie gulped. Miss Breckenridge might consider herself a royal flush, but Ellie's mother was a wild card more likely to be repulsed than impressed by Quality lineage.

Chapter Four

The next morning, Ellie jerked the steel tip of her dip pen out of her mouth for what was surely the hundredth time. She might not damage the dip pen's metal exterior, but she was certainly flirting with cracked teeth or a splatter-ink moustache.

She'd woken up with a hunger like never before, and when an entire tray of kippers had failed to dampen the cravings, she'd developed a disturbing oral fixation on anything and everything she could put in her mouth. The sudden desire to chew on household miscellany was just as strong as the unladylike stomach rumblings that propelled her into the kitchen a mere hour after she broke her fast.

Luckily, her mother's predilection for staying abed until after noontime meant Ellie was unlikely to be discovered face-first in the larder.

"Toast? No . . ." Ellie murmured to herself. "Clotted cream? No . . . Boiled vegetables? Definitely not . . . Hrrgmmph?"

She jerked to a stop as she realized she now had an entire carrot protruding from her mouth. She removed the vegetable and glared at the many tooth marks now marring its surface. She had *never* liked carrots, and here she was gnawing at one as if compelled to do so. What she really wanted was meat. Surely there must be—aha! An entire slab of . . . Well, Ellie had never been in a kitchen during the actual cooking process, so she wasn't exactly certain what it was she was staring at, but it was meat, and therefore, food.

Ellie was thrilled with her find and dying to partake, but how on earth was she to prepare it? Blast. Either she would have to suffer her hunger pangs until lunchtime, or she would be forced to make do with what she had. Biting at her lower lip, Ellie gave in to temptation and reached for the platter.

"Elspeth!"

"Aaagh!"

Ellie whirled around, simultaneously trying to hide the heavy platter behind her back whilst preventing its gravitational slide toward the stone floor. She failed on both counts. Silver clanged to the floor. Pink droplets sprayed the hem of her butter-yellow morning dress. The ill-used carrot rolled to a stop when it collided with the toe of her mother's slipper.

"Er . . . good morning, Mama." Ellie did her best at a sunny, innocent smile and hoped she didn't have bits of carrot—or ink stains—upon her teeth. "Did you sleep well?"

Her mother closed her eyes and scrunched up her face as if wishing very hard that she did not have a daughter who skulked about the pantry at half eleven, gnawing on root vegetables and dropping trays of raw meat. This was, of course, a wish destined to remain ungranted, but Ellie sank to her knees anyway and did her best to gather up what had most likely been meant for tonight's supper. Her mother unscrunched her porcelain face and opened her long-suffering blue eyes.

"Elspeth, darling," Mama began in her softest voice. The one Ellie dreaded above all others.

Being called "Elspeth darling" was never a good sign, nor was the sight of her mother awake before noon. All indications were for Ellie to flee, and flee now. If she weren't already on her knees grappling for the fallen carrot, she would have obeyed the impulse.

"What the devil are you about, girl?" Mama demanded in much put-out tones.

"I was hungry," Ellie murmured without looking up. "Just looking for a light repast."

Mama's incredulity was palpable. "A light repast of whole carrots and a pound of venison?"

"You're awake a few hours before schedule," Ellie interjected, hoping some quick misdirection would save her from having to invent an explanation. "What could have possibly dared to disturb your slumber?"

"The howling of the wind." Mama pulled her shawl tighter

and glared over her shoulder at the frost-specked windows. With luck, she had forgotten about the carrot.

Having gathered the foodstuffs, Ellie rose to her feet and returned the tray to the larder. The majority of the venison could be salvaged. Ellie had hoped to be a breadwinner, not exacerbate their poverty.

She shook out her skirts, rolled back her shoulders, and met her mother's gaze bravely. A wasted effort, of course, since even if Ellie had been decked in finery fit for a queen, she would still be a pale shadow of her mother. Mama awoke from slumber with golden ringlets, big blue eyes, and a perfect cupid's-bow smile. Ellie awoke from slumber with a lopsided mane of red-blond tangles, bloodshot eyes, and a crick in her shoulder from falling asleep curled up on the library sofa. And an inexplicable yen for raw vegetables.

"I've been thinking . . ." Mama said. Another bad omen. Mama tended to think things like *you would look lovely in orange damask*, or *why don't you read the original text in ancient Latin*, or *if you don't stop complaining about your hair, I'll cut it off and have done.*

Ellie braced herself. "Say your piece."

"I've been thinking," Mama repeated more firmly but without meeting Ellie's eyes, "that it's time."

"No." Ellie's heart began to gallop. The pantry was suddenly too small to comfortably breathe. "Mother, no. *Please.*"

"Elspeth, you knew when we moved here it would not last forever." Mama's voice was calm, steady, and vexingly reasonable. "This cannot be a shock."

"But why now?" Ellie hated her own powerlessness, despised her inability to keep the panic out of her voice every time she found herself participating in these dreaded conversations. "I truly like it here."

Her mother sighed. "You always do. And we cannot stay."

"But—but—" Miss Breckenridge flashed into Ellie's mind, followed quickly by the promise of ten-pound notes and another glimpse of Mártainn Macane. "I've made a friend," Ellie blurted, not certain whom exactly she referred to, and for the moment uncaring. She would employ as much hyperbole as necessary. "How can you ask me to leave when I finally belong for the first time?"

"I told you not to make friends," Mama replied, intractably calm in the face of Ellie's growing desperation. "If you had listened to sound advice, there wouldn't be anyone to fit in with. End of discussion. Prepare whatever you'd like to bring. We leave by the end of the week."

"To go where?"

"You'll find out when we get there."

"I shan't go." Ellie took a deep breath. "You can leave if you like, and post me a letter when you get there. I'm an adult. And I'm happy here."

It was more than that, actually. More important than mere happiness. For the first time in her life, Ellie felt useful.

No—Ellie *was* useful.

She investigated specious claims of the idle rich. While her acts were neither heroic nor exciting, she had earned money for her family and was shaping her own life. She enjoyed disproving folktales of werewolves and vampires, and she had absolutely savored the singular experience of dancing in a Society ballroom.

If she listened to Mama, she'd do nothing but sleep her life away, muddling through depressing bouts of wakefulness encaged in the library with brandy-laden tea and endless stacks of spine-creased books. Ellie knew every printed word in their library by rote, could read them all in their original tongues and discuss them in almost any language, but what was the point of any of it if there was no one to discuss anything with and no chance of experiencing an adventure of her own?

"You can make all the mulish expressions you want, young lady, but we are leaving. Pack, or don't pack. If you wish to leave with nothing but the clothes on your back, that's up to you. But we're going, and that's final." Mama's perfect brow creased as she gave Ellie a small smile. "Darling, I'm doing this for *you*."

"You always say that."

"It's always true."

"And yet, just when I'm comfortable with a place, it's suddenly time to leave. Why must we flee in dead of night? Why must I keep to myself and never make friends? Would it be so terrible if I were to have a bosom acquaintance? Or attend an opera? Or—or—fall in love?"

Mama's vise-like fingers closed around Ellie's wrist before she registered her mother had even moved. "The opera is overrated," Mama's soft, steely voice whispered into Ellie's ear, "and you will *not* fall in love."

Ellie jerked her arm back. She squeaked in surprise when she actually wrenched it free. Even Mama was visibly shocked. She had always been stronger, in every possible meaning. She won every argument, triumphed in every battle, whether of wits or strength or will. But here they were, toe-to-toe, chin to chin. Ellie's wrist was sore, but it was free. *She* was still free.

For the moment.

Ellie well knew that she could refuse to leave as much as she'd like, but in the end, if Mama went, she would, too. Partly because she couldn't afford an overnight in an inn, much less an entire life of independence. But mostly because she loved her mother.

If Mama would just stay put somewhere, Ellie would be blissfully content. It was the bouncing about she couldn't stand. Just when a place became comfortable, just when faces started to seem familiar, just when she began to feel at *home* . . . the next moment she was tossing trunks into a carriage at midnight and racing through a starless countryside to a place even stranger than the last.

When Ellie had been younger, she'd actually believed her mother when she'd claimed they relocated at random intervals simply because Mama suffered ennui if she stayed overlong in one spot. Recently, however, Ellie had begun to notice a glassiness just at the edges of her mother's eyes during their inevitable fights. *Panic.* Whatever the true reasons were, Mama did not force Ellie to pick up roots out of idle cruelty. She was truly as desperate to leave as Ellie was to stay. Mama was just better at hiding it.

She might not have a grand purpose to life, but Ellie was in possession of an invitation to a house party, and she'd be damned if she would give that up as well without a fight. If she couldn't have the kind of life she'd always dreamed of, at the very least she wanted to experience the upcoming weekend. And when she left, she would carry the memory with her.

Mama was staring at Ellie with narrowed eyes and a brow creased with concentration, as if she was hoping to force her daughter to acquiesce with the mere force of her will. It almost worked. Every other time, it *had* worked. But not today. Today, Ellie stood tall, with her messy hair, her juice-stained hems, and her bruised-but-unfettered arm akimbo on her hips. They both knew she would end up living wherever her mother wished. But Ellie did not have to pack her things right now.

"My best friend's birthday is coming up," she began, toeing the fine line between exaggeration and outright lies. "If you are asking me to abandon her without so much as a word, the least you can do is allow me to accept her invitation to visit first. I may never have the opportunity again. And we can leave the following week just as easily as this one."

Mama's frown increased. "Elspeth, darling. Please listen. We are not leaving for me. I do this for *you*."

"Then wait for me." Ellie relaxed her stance and softened her voice. "Let me call on my friend for the weekend. I will only be gone a few days."

"But why would you wish to? You've never spent a single night from home."

"You've never allowed it."

"And why should I do so now?"

"Mother, you don't have a choice. I'm old enough to mind my manners and not embarrass myself. I'm also old enough to have a little fun. Look at it this way: We will leave soon. If you allow me one small freedom, this will be our last word on the subject. When I return, I will pack peaceably and immediately, and we can set off as soon as you'd like."

Her mother's lips pursed. "And if I cannot agree?"

Ellie lifted a shoulder. "Then it will be a battle every step of the way."

Mama was silent for a long moment. Perhaps she could not fathom why her daughter had lost her habitual obedience.

For her part, Ellie wasn't certain when Miss Breckenridge's invitation had gained such importance, but there was no denying that it had now become the brass ring dangling just out of reach, and she was determined to make one last leap.

And earn the promised fee. Running away cost more than staying put, and they had enough trouble making it through each day.

Mama shook her head. "Elspeth darling..."

Ellie longed to collapse her shoulders in defeat. She forced her spine even straighter rather than give the impression of sub-missiveness.

"Ladies?" The deep voice came from beyond the pantry, where their sole manservant stood in the shadows bearing a single white card upon a small silver tray. "It appears Miss Ramsay has a visitor."

"*Who?*" Mama demanded, wild-eyed.

"The card says Miss Lydia Breckenridge." The manservant proffered the tray.

If Ellie thought her mother had been blindsided by her daughter's recent strength of will, Mama was downright apoplectic over the shock of impending company.

"Show her to the sitting room, if you please," Ellie commanded before her mother could catch her breath. "I'll be there posthaste."

With that, she edged past her mother and raced to her bed-chamber for a fresh gown.

Although she changed as rapidly as she was able, she fully expected to discover Miss Breckenridge half-mad from one of Mama's brutal interrogations. Instead, Ellie found her benefactress to be unattended, drifting about the sitting room with what could only be described as an air of befuddlement.

"Good afternoon." Ellie glanced about the simple room in search of whatever might have discomfited Miss Breckenridge so. "Is something amiss?"

"Amiss?" the young woman echoed, her brow clearing. "That's precisely it. Nothing at all is amiss!"

"I'm afraid I do not follow." Ellie motioned her guest onto a sofa and took the seat opposite.

"The Breckenridge estates are a positive museum, every inch filled with antiquities fighting for space with the latest Parisian baubles. Your domicile—while quite serviceable, Miss Ramsay, I mean no insult—hasn't a single gewgaw on display. It gives your home quite a refreshing, timeless appeal." Miss Breckenridge shook her head and laughed. "I daresay your staff is the more content, not having to spend every minute dusting the same tired gimcracks."

Ellie forced a smile, unsure whether her home had just been complimented or slighted. She tried to see her plain surroundings through a stranger's eyes.

While everything was tasteful and tidy, the "everything" in

question did in fact consist of no more than the bare necessities. Aside from a few pieces of furniture and a handful of candelabra, the sitting room contained nothing else. Ellie could scarce imagine living in the chaotic opulence Miss Breckenridge described. Not only were antiquities and Parisian baubles quite above the Ramsays' means, their inevitable midnight flights from one corner of England to another inherently prohibited attachment to any given item.

It was therefore a happy accident indeed if their inability to own any belongings had produced an ambiance of—what had Miss Breckenridge called it?—timeless appeal.

Ellie frowned slightly upon the realization that her benefactress might have been using the term in a more literal sense than originally interpreted. The Ramsay home contained no clocks, no newspapers, no correspondence, no diaries, no family portraits. . . . It looked exactly as it always did, with nothing in vogue and nothing to mark the passage of time. Viewing her home from such a perspective, Ellie began to suspect she had been quite cleverly insulted, and could not help but take affront on behalf of her family's simple lifestyle.

"Miss Breckenridge, I hardly think—"

"Do I interrupt?" came a smooth voice from the doorway.

"Mama!" Ellie rose to her feet, an attack of nervousness overwhelming her momentary pique. She had stood her ground against her mother, and there was no telling how Mama would react in consequence. "Miss Breckenridge, this is my mother, Mrs. Ramsay. Mama, this is my—this is Miss Breckenridge, whom I've told you so much about."

Mama arched a slender brow. "The one with the birthday, I suppose."

Miss Breckenridge could not suppress a startled blink at that rejoinder. Wordlessly, she, too, rose to her feet.

"Just so, Mama." Ellie tamped down a grin at the idea of Miss Breckenridge's being on the receiving end of an uninterpretable comment, unsure whether she had just been subtly insulted.

"How do you do," Miss Breckenridge said at last. "I do have an impending birthday, and I've come to call for just that reason. I'll be two-and-twenty next Saturday, and nothing will do but to have your daughter at the celebrations."

Ellie cringed as her mother's smooth expression quickly changed

to disapproval. "Celebrations" did not sound like two young girls roaming a country estate far removed from the public eye. "Celebrations" sounded like the sort of thing Mama would forbid out of hand. Ellie fixed her gaze on Miss Breckenridge, willing her not to say anything else that might give Mama more ammunition for a refusal.

"Mrs. Ramsay, it would be my honor and pleasure to have your daughter's presence at this weekend's house p—"

No, no, it's not a party, Ellie thought desperately, wishing she'd taken advantage of the brief privacy in order to coach Miss Breckenridge on subjects to avoid. *Remember, we're just two friends. No High Society. No grand crush. Just us. And your pretend kitten.*

"—for an overnight stay," Miss Breckenridge corrected, apparently recalling Ellie's words the previous night. Her voice took on a far-off, wistful tone. "I am not one for big gatherings, so nothing will do but a long, quiet weekend with my dear friend and my darling cat."

Ellie jerked her gaze to her mother, who was still eyeing the two young ladies beneath raised brows.

"Elspeth found the lost kitten?"

"Yes, Mama." Ellie schooled her features into the most angelic of expressions. "She's the most cunning little creature, and I would so enjoy the opportunity to play with her again. Do say I can go."

When the resulting silence began to overwhelm the small sitting room, Miss Breckenridge put in earnestly, "I live far enough away that nothing less than the full weekend will do. I would be happy to send a carriage for Miss Ramsay as well."

"We have our own carriage, thank you very much," Mama snapped.

Rather than being taken aback, Miss Breckenridge seemed delighted by this response. She turned to Ellie with an air of satisfaction. "Then I shall see you on my birthday, dear friend. Good day to you both."

And with that, Miss Breckenridge took her leave.

Ellie, however, knew better than to assume capitulation on her mother's behalf. Until the word "yes" audibly crossed her mother's lips, the battle had not been won.

"A lovely girl, isn't she, Mama?"

"Don't try my patience, Elspeth."

"Just let me do this one last thing. Let me have a small taste of freedom, of friendship. Of belonging. Then I'll go wherever you wish."

Ellie stepped forward until she was but an arm's length from her mother. Miss Breckenridge's birthday party had become the most imperative engagement of her life.

They desperately needed the money—now more than ever, if another infernal cross-country trip loomed scant days hence. But even more than that, Ellie *wanted* to go. She wanted to see the estate so smothered with messy riches, to hear the music of an orchestra swell around her. And, if she was being honest, she really wanted to lay eyes on Mr. Macane once more. Not because she gave Miss Breckenridge's fear of Lord Lovenip any credence, but because Ellie rather liked him.

He'd *danced* with her. Perhaps he'd do so again.

"Please, Mama." Following her mother's example, Ellie kept her voice calm and reasonable. "I don't wish to fight. I would just like to spend a few days with a friend before we run off yet again to some remote place where we won't know a single soul."

Mama's eyes narrowed. "A girls' weekend, she said. Just the two of you and a kitten?"

"And her parents, of course," Ellie put in quickly, lest her mother denounce the plan due to a lack of proper supervision.

"Very well," her mother said with an appraising once-over and a sigh. "But do not make me regret this."

"Truly?" Ellie's stomach dipped in a swirl of glee and apprehension. "I can go?"

"*We* can go," Mama corrected with a sharp nod. "I'm coming with you."

Chapter Five

Cain cursed whatever demon had incited him to descend upon the Breckenridge country estate perched atop a whip of a curricle.

Vampires might be immortal, but immortality did not exempt one from the discomfort of foul weather. Thunderclouds enshrouded the sky, echoing Cain's darkening mood. Where he had once been hopeful that tonight was the night he would encounter his elusive prey, now he was simply hopeful he'd encounter a roof, and with luck, a fire. He was shivering and soaking wet and miserable.

So were his horses.

The beasts no longer believed him when he promised their destination must be around the next bend. The ragged lightning coursing across the sky terrified the grays as much as the roaring thunder that followed. Yet the intermittent flashes of bright white shooting across the thick woods were the only source of light along the serpentine trail. His favorite mount had thrown a shoe over one of the many patches of fist-sized rocks atop unstable mud. But the smartest choice was to continue on. His lodgings were already an hour past, and his home a forgotten memory until he, as hunter, returned with the prize.

Rain-blurred lights flickered around the next bend. In his excitement, he scarce discerned a small, dark shape huddled directly in the path. His horses reared. Cain barely wrangled them under control in time to avert their course. He might have missed the trembling ball of mange altogether, had it not whined

plaintively upon the realization it was about to be trampled to death.

Cain leaped from his rain-soaked perch, barely vaulting over his skittish horses. He landed hard on his left shoulder, but did his best to ignore the sickening snap and the sharp flash of pain. There was no time. He scooped up the shivering pile of wet fur and rolled out of the way seconds ere they both would've had the full weight of a pair-and-carriage squelching them into the mud.

If his horses had been alarmed before, now they were altogether panicked. They shot off along the pitch-black trail at a suicidal pace, the phaeton clattering perilously behind. Unsteadily, Cain hauled himself to his feet. He tipped his face into the driving rain and let the pelting drops clear the dirt from his eyes before bending his head to inspect the bundle quaking in his arms.

A puppy.

It licked his face, and Cain laughed despite himself. He'd lost his curricle, lost his horses, and broken his collarbone, but he'd managed to save the life of a half-drowned puppy.

"Stupid creature," he scolded under his breath, but scratched its ears anyway.

He knew better than to stop for animals. He definitely knew better than to pick them up and cuddle them to his chest. But he loved animals and couldn't resist rubbing the puppy's belly and scratching behind its ears.

Wincing, Cain set off after his horses, puppy in hand and mud dripping from his face. When he'd accepted the Breckenridge invitation, he had wished to make an Appearance—and damn his arrogance, now he certainly would.

His clothes were ruined, his hair a fright, and his shoulder... Och, at least the snapped bone wasn't protruding from his skin.

Had he been in Scotland, he would've already procured the sustenance necessary for rapid healing. But he was in godforsaken England trying to pass for human. Regardless, no maiden in her right mind would offer a nip to a mud-stained rogue in such abominable condition. He would simply have to give his best careless-rake smile and feign nothing was amiss. The usual.

"Well," he murmured to the shivering puppy. "If we're to be stuck with each other, we might as well introduce ourselves. You can call me Cain. And I'll call you . . ." He studied the puppy in his arms. Light brown fur, dark brown eyes, a quick, wet tongue, and a whip of a tail that managed to slap Cain's tender shoulder and spray dog-scented rainwater into his eyes with every swipe. "The more I think on it, the more I come to believe *you're* the one who should be called Cain," he informed the recalcitrant puppy, and was rewarded with exuberant face-licking. "As that's already taken, you'll have to settle for . . . Moch-éirigh."

Closing his eyes, Cain shook his head in self-disgust. He'd lost his mind and *named* the damn thing. Hadn't he sworn to himself a thousand times over that his puppy-adopting days were done? And hadn't he triply sworn that he was done torturing himself by giving animals names that reminded him of home, and of things he could never, would never, see again? He'd named his grays Sunrise and Sunset, and now he'd gone and named the puppy Early Riser. As he had been, once. Back when it was a joy to greet the dawn and spend the day awash in sunshine.

A regular glutton for punishment, he was. He deserved the bittersweet reminder of who and what he was.

He took a deep breath—which only served to unbalance both dog and collarbone, and was unnecessary for survival in any case—and tramped forward into the night, his eyes squinting against the onslaught of rain. The puppy snuggled tight against his unbeating heart. They both desperately needed a bite to eat, so the sooner they descended upon the festivities, the better.

After what felt like miles but was likely no more than ten minutes of cursing and stumbling, Cain could fully make out the Breckenridge estate looming up from the darkness. Unlike Cain, his horses were apparently in no rush to make themselves known. Instead, the grays stood perpendicular on the muddy path, their faces buried in a thatch of rain-battered grass.

He managed to fetch the ribbons without dropping the puppy and hauled himself back onto his perch. With a tug, his horses abandoned their meal and resumed the miserable trudge to the Breckenridge stables. The ceaseless rain managed to cleanse nearly all the mud from both Cain and puppy, but had no ameliorating effect whatever on tangled fur or ripped linen.

The swarm of liverymen who rushed to greet the carriage had enough breeding to hide any shock at Cain's appearance—or perhaps he was not the only guest to have arrived worse for wear from the vicious downpour. A stroke of fortune, since he was scarcely in any condition to Compel the minds of a dozen servants at once.

Nonetheless, brown and bedraggled was not at all the impression Cain hoped to make upon the weekend revelers, and his sole request of the obsequious footmen was to be granted admittance through a side door, so as not to cause a stir. This petition caused startled blinks all around, but in short order Cain found himself welcomed to Breckenridge via the connected conservatory, and ushered to sumptuous guest quarters featuring both a crackling fire and a large bath.

Heaven, Cain decided the instant he sank into clean, warm water. Hell, he amended, upon the unexpected accompaniment of his new puppy.

By the time the dinner bell sounded, Cain felt . . . well, if not like a new man, then at least like a reinvigorated Scottish warrior disguised as a harmless—and shameless—Society flirt. He had played this role for so long that sometimes he almost forgot he was acting. Both personas were men of single mind. The real Cain just wanted to return to his homeland with the missing vampire securely in hand. The false Cain just wanted the mysterious Miss Ramsay in hand. Rather, his hands on her bonny face, the fragile curve of her neck, the ample swell of her—

He groaned and considered dumping himself back into the oversize tub, dinner clothes and all. He *meant* the false Cain just wanted *women*. All women. Any women. The sillier the better, so as to afford greater access to the sweet nectar flowing hot beneath their perfect skin.

Why, then, had Miss Ramsay sprung to mind? She was far from silly, more warrior-like than waiflike, and she had no business whatever strong-arming his thought processes. Given that he was apparently the only one to have registered her presence at the Wedgeworth rout, they were unlikely to cross paths amongst the high-nosed Breckenridge set. And he was unlikely to cross paths with anyone at all, if the only thing he intended to do all weekend was kneel on the floor getting dog hair all over his gloves and breeches.

With a final pat for the puppy, Cain pushed to his feet and

slipped out the door. Or he would have, had Moch-éirigh not been of a mind to follow along between her new master's boots. Thus began a ten-minute farce wherein Cain and the puppy chased each other in and out of the doorway as they attempted to settle their difference of opinion. Cain won the battle, but only just. After securing the door, he leaned against the thick mahogany to pluck one-handedly at the stubborn puppy hairs clinging to his lawn and buckskin. He was thus engaged—though he pretended to be merely catching his breath—when the youngest daughter of his hosts entered the corridor bearing a lit candle.

"Miss Breckenridge." He bent in a deep bow. "Felicitations on your birthday."

The girl in question nearly jumped out of her skin. She apparently had not noticed his presence in the sunken shadows of his closed doorway. Now that he had made himself known, the horror in her visage seemed to indicate she rather suspected him of wishing to celebrate by ravishing her right there in the hallway. He wasn't sure whether it was good manners or panicked indecision that held her frozen stiff, just ten paces away.

Presumably having decided between abandoning whatever mission set her in this direction and continuing on her path, she inched forward, albeit keeping comically close to the far wall.

"How do you do, Mr. Macane." She inclined her head, but did not offer her hand. Instead, she lifted a gloved finger to her neckline and tugged a slender chain into view. A moment later, the chain's pendant was revealed to be a delicate silver cross.

Cain cut his sharp gaze to her face, where Miss Breckenridge's previous panic had been replaced by a highly suspect expression of wide-eyed innocence. She knew! No—how could she know? Besides, if she *knew*, she would hardly have admitted him for a weekend house party. And yet, his hunter instincts reminded him that nothing was ever coincidence. Particularly as his hostess continued to finger the silver cross and search his face for clues as to his reaction.

Moch-éirigh took that moment to ram into the other side of the bedchamber door. Cain whirled around to verify the security of the latch that, for the moment, appeared to hold. The puppy's plaintive cries, however, were far from muffled. Nor were the unmistakable scratching noises of her tiny claws rending against the antique wood. Blast. Cain was not so foolish as to open the door and risk whatever wild behavior his new puppy longed to enact. Nor was he so foolish as to imagine his hostess would be remotely pleased at what were bound to be permanent scratch marks marring the interior panel of the door.

But when he turned around, to his surprise Moch-éirigh had succeeded where Cain had not—Miss Breckenridge was disarmed completely.

The silver cross was still visible, but lay forgotten against the lace fichu of her gown. Her candle listed precariously in her outstretched hand, and she was goggling at him with nothing short of wonder. Incredulous wonder, perhaps, but wonder nonetheless.

"You have a *dog?*" she demanded, her voice pitched high with the same level of shock in which another person might have asked, *You have fangs?*

"A cursed puppy," he admitted with another bow. "You have found me out."

Miss Breckenridge stared at him openmouthed, apparently content to stand there gaping at him until the small flame melted her taper to a nub.

"May I escort you to dinner?" he asked.

Suspicion returned to her features full-force, but Miss Breckenridge was astute enough to realize she had but two options: Give an invited guest the cut direct en route to the planned festivities, or place her palm on his proffered arm.

A well-timed whine by Moch-éirigh decided the matter.

She relinquished the taper to Cain's free hand and settled the barest tip of her fingers on the crook of his evening jacket.

When they reached the intersection leading to the opposite wing, Cain's muscles tensed. There had been no telltale sound, no scent, no flicker of flame or shadow, no hint at all that they were not alone—yet his every sense was prickling. He jerked his head around just in time to glimpse a slender woman at the far end of the corridor slip into the furthest chamber and disappear. For a moment, he'd thought it might be Miss Ramsay, but the movement had been too quick, too soundless. The only audible heartbeat had been that of the woman on his arm. And most damning of all: He'd recognized her.

"What is it?" Miss Breckenridge stammered, alarmed. "Did you see something?"

"A woman," Cain answered. "Do you know her? Medium height, golden hair, very beautiful . . ."

"Of course I know her." Miss Breckenridge's lips pursed, as if she interpreted his interest to be of the licentious variety. "She is not to be disturbed. She's a guest, just like yourself, and the reason I was in this wing to begin with. She has the headache and shall not be attending dinner, but I assured her anything she desired from the kitchens was hers for the asking, should she be hungry later."

Cain's eyes narrowed. If his instinct was correct, the woman's hunger could not be quenched with anything present in the Breckenridge larders, short of partaking of the servants themselves. "Tell me—is she from the family Munro?"

"No." Miss Breckenridge's raised brow indicated she now perceived him as more of a dunce than a deviant.

He made no further comment. Perhaps his leap from the carriage had addled his brain as well as broken his shoulder. First he had thought his hostess suspected him of bloodlust, and then he imagined glimpsing an infamous runaway vampire under the same roof. What he needed was a nice, warm sip of fresh blood to clear his head and put his shoulder to rights.

"Come to think of it," Miss Breckenridge said presently, "I'm not rightly acquainted with her given name. We simply addressed the invitations to Mrs. and Miss Ramsay."

He came to a dead stop. *"Ramsay?"*

Miss Breckenridge nodded abstractedly. "She'll feel worlds better after a good night's rest. I'm sure you'll meet her on the morrow, when we break our fast."

"Is this woman any relation to the Miss Elspeth Ramsay you introduced to me at the Wedgeworth soirée?" he asked, careful to keep his tone light and disinterested.

"Her mother, of course," Miss Breckenridge replied with a little laugh. "Although she looks more like an elder sister. A bit melodramatic that way, too—reminds me of my own sisters. She was in a perfectly pleasant mood until she realized there were meant to be other guests, and then suddenly it's *oh dear, I must retire from the shock*, and off she floats. Her daughter is turned out excellently, though. She's clever enough to—"

But here Miss Breckenridge broke off her speech, with a snap to her teeth and a blush to her cheeks. She stared resolutely forward, as if determined not to meet Cain's gaze.

For his part, silence was just the thing, as his mind was reeling with implications and calculations. If "Mrs. Ramsay" was in actuality Aggie Munro, then of course she'd appear more like a sister than a mother, as her looks had been frozen at six-and-twenty . . . three hundred years earlier. Perhaps young Miss Ramsay was a great-great-great-descendant thrice removed or some such, but more likely she was simply a human lass, chosen for her superficial resemblance rather than any convoluted blood relation.

Because his glimpse had been from a distance and his quarry awash in shadows, the cynical side of Cain's personality prepared for the possibility of mistaken identity. The elder Ramsay might well be human, and Cain not the slightest bit closer to his goals.

His heart was hopeful, however. Too many signs pointed otherwise. That *was* Aggie. He was sure of it. But what about Miss Ramsay? Since no vampire parents had ever beget a human child, some deeper game must be afoot. Servitude? Coercion? The very thought made his flesh run cold.

His castle had plenty of human servants, but all of them were perfectly aware of who they served, and how. Any of them were welcome to leave at any time—although they would be psychically Compelled not to breathe a word of the truth and to forget everything they had seen.

So, what was Elspeth Ramsay doing pretending to be Aggie Munro's daughter? Either young Miss Ramsay had known all along whom Cain was and why he was so far from home, or else she was an innocent being dishonorably used by an unscrupulous vampire, either as an alibi, a distraction, or a slave. What if Miss Ramsay was an involuntary companion, forced into servitude by vampiric Compulsion? Aggie could have abducted her as a child, changed her name, forced her to forget her parents, her past life, her identity. Being human, Miss Ramsay would have been powerless to resist. She could also have been a food source for as long as she'd been an unwitting prisoner. Cain's fingers clenched. A harmless nip here and there was one thing, but using thought control to enslave an innocent girl was quite beyond the pale.

If only there were some way to broach the topic without, well, broaching the topic. Cain frowned and quickened his pace. His desire to taste and touch Miss Ramsay had now been eclipsed by a desire to see her safe and well protected.

He glanced down at Miss Breckenridge. Although she seemed more discomfited than delighted in his presence, she, too, was an innocent and not to be exploited. Or was Miss Ramsay perhaps a willing participant in whatever scheme Aggie Munro was about? Cain shook his head. Even were that the case, a human girl clearly had origins outside of a vampire clan, which meant she came from *somewhere*, and whatever complicity Aggie had engendered in her young charge had undoubtedly arisen from machinations rather than fair play. Nonetheless, it was paramount to discover just how closely Miss Ramsay knew her "mother."

Upon reaching the dining hall, Miss Breckenridge shot from his arm to join a gentleman undoubtedly leagues more eligible. Grouped in ranked pairs, the guests filed into the dining room to take their seats. The placard bearing Cain's name was just far enough away from Miss Ramsay that there was no hope of private conversation, although his removed position on the opposite side of the table did afford him an unobstructed view of her profile.

She was lovely. Easily as comely as the infamous Aggie Munro. But unlike his quarry, whose beauty was legendary, Miss Ramsay seemed wholly unaware of her extraordinary looks. Her soft, red-gold curls framed large blue eyes and a lush rosebud of a mouth. Her gown, although not the first stare of fashion, boasted high-quality tailoring. The aquamarine confection complemented that lustrous hair and the creamy perfection of her skin. How she could believe anyone immune to her charms was beyond his ken.

Cain frowned to realize that the other guests were, in fact, incomprehensibly unaffected. No one glanced in Miss Ramsay's direction, much less engaged her in conversation. Despite her being seated between two easygoing lads and directly across from a notorious flirt, none of the three seemed aware of her presence . . . nor did she attempt to engage their attentions.

Instead, she kept her eyes focused on her plate, where she spent the entirety of the meal nudging each course with the tip of her fork without consuming any of it. Did she seem paler than last he saw her, or was it a mere trick of the light? Perhaps she had taken ill. Bending his head to concentrate, Cain isolated the sound of each guest's heartbeat until he recognized hers. Faint, but steady.

He lifted his gaze and considered her down-turned profile. She seemed to be having an absolutely miserable time. If she were not here of her own free will, such enslavement would drive another nail into Aggie Munro's (figurative) coffin. But first, he needed to be certain. *Look at me*, he commanded her with his mind.

As before, his order went unheeded.

He gradually became aware of the conversation around him and was alarmed to discover a picnic had been planned for luncheon the next day. He would need a full feeding to be able to withstand the rays of the sun. Since that didn't seem likely, he would be forced to remain indoors.

The moment the meal drew to a close, the gentlemen rejected the habit of retiring for port in favor of immediately joining the ladies for card playing. Cain would have preferred to stalk his prey. But as this was the last time the company would be together this evening, and he would necessarily be indoors much of the morrow, he would take advantage of the game play in order to steal a moment of Miss Ramsay's time.

His opportunity came before the players had settled at the tables. Miss Breckenridge had been standing near Miss Ramsay until being borne away to determine which guests would partner at which tables. Cain positioned himself just behind Miss Ramsay. Close enough to whisper into her ear. Or to feather kisses beneath the curls at her neck.

"Miss Ramsay," he murmured. She started, but did not increase the distance between them as she turned to face him.

"Mr. Macane," she responded composedly, although her pulse pounded louder in Cain's ears. He would have liked to attribute the phenomenon to mutual desire, but her expression gave nothing away. She nodded in the direction of his broken collarbone. "I trust you don't suffer unduly?"

He very nearly gaped at her uncanny comprehension, then realized she was not referring to his swan dive at all, but rather to their previous encounter. "Nary a mark remains," he assured her with a playful smile, "and you are welcome to bite me anytime you please."

The sweet scent of blood teased his nostrils as a touch of pink feathered across Miss Ramsay's cheeks as she lowered her eyes and glanced away. She was so easy to embarrass, so lovely, so... human.

Never before had the chasm between what he was and what she was seemed so insurmountable. He was a vampire. She was human. It would never do. As much as she intrigued him, he longed to experience the biting ritual shared by a vampire couple in love. There was no greater sensation in this world. And while Miss Ramsay would undoubtedly make a very bonny bedmate indeed, vampiric mating rituals were not something they would be able to share. Particularly since her humanity was one of the qualities he liked best about her.

Miss Ramsay's humanity—and implicit mortality—brought the specter of Aggie Munro back to mind. He needed to find out what, if anything, Miss Ramsay knew... and then decide what to do about it.

He lowered his voice. "Have you been to Scotland?"

"I told you last time I had not." She raised a brow at him in a mock-disgruntled expression. "Were you not attending?"

"I was undoubtedly preoccupied with my baser instincts at the time." He gave an exaggerated leer and startled an involuntary giggle from her. He smiled back to distract her from the import of his next question. "How about your mother? Has she been to Scotland?"

"*Mama?*" Miss Ramsay repeated with choked laughter, as if she had not heard a more preposterous idea in her lifetime. "She won't even visit the milliner, much less go on holiday."

Cain carefully monitored her heartbeat and breathing pattern, but could discern no deception. Whatever Aggie Munro was about, Miss Ramsay was not privy to the wherefores. But perhaps there was still something to be learned.

"Ah," he said sorrowfully. "Then you'll not know about Foulis."

Her brow furrowed. "Who's Foulis?"

"Not a who, a what. Foulis was one of the most enchanting castles in Scotland... until it burned down yesteryear."

Miss Ramsay's eyes widened in sudden understanding. "Oh... is that why you're spending time abroad? Foulis was your home?"

Cain shook his head. "Mine still stands. Foulis was home to clan Munro."

The confusion creasing Miss Ramsay's brow was genuine. "Then what does it have to do with me? Or my mother?"

He lifted a shoulder. "Perhaps nothing."

And perhaps everything. When he rounded up Aggie Munro and dragged her back to Scotland to face the tribunal, where was Miss Ramsay meant to go?

Chapter Six

Well before dawn, Ellie awoke to hunger pangs so acute she had to clench her teeth so as not to cry out with pain. She must have been clenching them all through the night, because even her gums were aching terribly.

She couldn't recall having consumed a single bite of last night's meal. The inevitable row once Mama realized she'd been tricked into attending a house party had soured Ellie's appetite completely. This morning there was no ignoring the biting pangs twisting her insides into painful knots. Ringing for service would only awaken Mama, however, and there was no sense starting the day with another terrible row.

Ellie dressed as silently and quickly as she could, but caught herself gnawing on everything within grasp—the nub of a pencil, the handle to a comb, even the knuckle of her own finger. If she didn't find the Breckenridge kitchens soon, she'd be down on her knees chewing holes in the carpets.

The drowsy hall boy at the end of the corridor pointed the way to the kitchen before snuggling back into a large wingback chair. A stroke of luck. Ellie would just as soon pillage the pantry unaccompanied.

She had just finished off a leg of meat and was halfway through sucking the marrow from the bone when the distant creaking of a door snapped her back into the present.

Ellie jerked the tooth-marked bone from her mouth and stared at her red-tinged fingers in horror. Had she just eaten raw meat in a blind stupor? What the devil was wrong with her?

She dropped the bone into a waste bucket and slid the now-empty platter onto another. Desperate to rinse the bloody evidence from her hands and face before the kitchen staff came upon her, she hurried to the water pitcher—only to find it empty.

"Blast."

Ellie scrambled to a rag bin and rubbed her mouth and fingers with a cloth that smelled strongly of brandy. No matter. She would far rather stink of wine at six o'clock in the morning than have her face smeared with the juice of . . . whatever she'd just consumed. Good Lord. She snatched a mint leaf from a nearby jar to cleanse both her breath and mind of the memory.

She tossed the rag back into the bin and swallowed the mint just as a small tornado of fur shot through the kitchen door and launched itself directly at her. Any remaining trace of foodstuff would have disappeared under the ministrations of an excited, lapping puppy.

Ellie's pent-up breath dissolved in a burst of nervous laughter. Had she known her only witness would be a little tea-colored puppy, she wouldn't have been so hasty in getting rid of the bone. In fact . . . why deprive the adorable creature? With the licking, wriggling puppy balanced in the crook of her arm, she picked her way back to the scrap bucket in search of the dropped bone.

Her success in this mission was rewarded with instant abandonment as the puppy snatched the bone from her grasp and shot into the shadows to noisily consume its prize. Ellie shook her head and smiled at the wagging tail just visible in the darkness. How marvelous it would be to have a pet! If only she and Mama didn't spend so much time running from nothing to nowhere, perhaps Ellie would've been able to have a dog or a kitten or anything at all to call her own.

She was so entranced by the puppy's overzealous tail-wagging and bone-chewing that she scarcely registered the kitchen door's opening once more, until a familiar masculine voice spoke wryly from the corner.

"I see you've met my dog."

She whirled around to find Mr. Macane lounging against the closed door, one hand hooked at his waist and the other lazily massaging his shoulder. Perhaps he hadn't slept well. As she'd also been unable to settle into sleep, she'd spent hours at the window, gazing up at the moon.

"Good morning," was all she said aloud, however. Being alone with a notorious scoundrel was scandalous enough without adding the topic of how he spent his nights to the mix. "I see you're both early risers."

Amusement flickered across Mr. Macane's handsome features. "I don't think she sleeps at all."

"It's a girl?" She grinned at the puppy's wagging tail with renewed delight. "What's her name?"

He gazed at the shadows as if debating whether to divulge a dark secret. After a long moment, he gave a one-shoulder shrug and replied, "I call her Moch-éirigh."

"Mac Eric?" Ellie repeated doubtfully. "What a horrible name for a puppy."

Mr. Macane blinked at her, then laughed. "Not Mac Eric. *Moch-éirigh*. It's . . . Scottish."

"What does it mean?"

A hint of a smile still played about the edges of his lips. "It means 'early riser.' "

"Oh, it does not." Ellie shook her finger at him in mock chastisement. "It probably means, 'I love calling attention to myself.' "

"You too?" he answered innocently. "Why then, we have something in common."

She laughed. "Unlikely. People who've never met you know all about your exploits, whereas those who've met me dozens of times recall neither my name nor my face."

Mr. Macane's raised brows indicated his skepticism. "I find that hard to conceive."

"Believe as you will." Annoyed with herself for having voiced such a private hurt, Ellie feigned an irreverent smile as if she'd been bamming him all along. "In any case, Mac Eric is certainly adorable."

"*Moch-éirigh*, wench," Mr. Macane growled good-naturedly. "And if you must know, it's *you* I find captivating."

"Did you just compare me to your dog?" Ellie gave her head an exaggerated shake. "And to think the gossips pegged you as an accomplished rake."

His sea-green eyes focused so intently on her face that Ellie didn't even register any movement in the room until she realized there was now a mere hairsbreadth between them.

"Do not belittle your own worth or underestimate the power of your beauty." His voice was low, his gaze seductively honest.

"While it's true many so-called ladies are both interchangeable and forgettable, you are not one of them. The others may remember me, but they do not want me. They seek the *idea* of me. A moment, a night, a dance . . . something to talk about over tea. You are a mystery."

Ellie gazed up at him, captivated as much by his intoxicating proximity as by his words. There was little ambient light in the small kitchen, but somehow she could see him clearly. Pale skin, high cheekbones, dark eyelashes framing light-green eyes. Even more striking were the bare neck at six o'clock in the morning and the contrasting chestnut mane caught in a leather band at the nape.

The most disconcerting of all, however, was how he smelled— or, rather, how he didn't smell. Ellie had always been uncomfortably aware of the odor of others—dust, sweat, too much perfume. Mr. Macane's scent was almost too light to be detected, pleasing to the senses but impossible to place, even for Ellie's nose. She felt herself leaning into him, face upturned and mouth parted, trying to inhale his very essence.

His gaze dropped to her lips, as if he thought her angling for a kiss. Perhaps she was. He was so strong, so charming, so larger-than-life. And if his words could be believed, he was just as tempted as she was.

He dipped his head until their mouths were but a few inches apart.

"A few years from now," he murmured quietly, "some other buck will be cutting a new swath, and my name will be forgotten. What makes me who I am is what *I* think about who I am. You must prize your own values above those that are forced upon you by Society." The corners of his eyes crinkled. "And when a bedazzled swain foolishly compares your beauty to that of his dog, just say thank you."

"Thank you, foolish swain." She returned his smile without retreating to a safer distance.

One of his hands lifted, coming ever so close to her face, but hesitating before going so far as to touch. Ellie's body tingled, her every muscle tense with expectation and want. His fingers trembled. Longing to know how his ungloved hand would feel pressed against her cheek, she tilted her head just a fraction— but that's all it took.

His hand cradled her face; his thumb gently caressed her cheek. The heat of his gaze never left hers. He lifted his other hand to the back of her neck to tangle in the mass of curls she hadn't bothered to tame. He splayed his fingers against her nape as if meaning to pull her to him, but there was no need, because she was already falling forward, eager for his kiss.

His lower lip brushed hers, sending shivers of delight down her spine. She gripped his upper arms for balance, and because she'd been dying to feel the hard muscle beneath his jacket from the first moment she saw him. Impossibly, he felt even bigger than he looked, as if he could lift an entire carriage if he had a mind to. At the moment, Ellie seemed to be the only thing on his mind.

Lips parted, he rubbed his mouth softly against hers, once, twice. The third time, he traced the path with the tip of his tongue, as if yearning to know the taste of her skin, of her mouth. He pressed his body against hers, and this time when their lips touched, she felt—teeth.

On her *ankle*.

Loud barking filled the small kitchen as the puppy used claws and teeth to drive them apart, attempting to scale them both, as an adventurer would climb a mountain.

Startled, Ellie took a step out of harm's way just as the puppy all but launched herself into her master's arms—where Ellie herself had been, just seconds ago. For a precious, incredible moment.

"My apologies," he managed to get out between dodging effusive puppy kisses. "It would seem Moch-éirigh is a bit jealous. You know how Scottish women can be."

Ellie shook her head. "What would I know about Scottish women?"

" 'Elspeth' is as Scottish as Moch-éirigh." Twisting, he wrangled the puppy out of his hair. "An Elspeth by any other name—"

"Call me Ellie," she interrupted before he could mangle Shakespeare further. "Only my mother calls me Elspeth."

"As you wish, Ellie. You may call me Cain. Not even my mother calls me Mártainn." He winked, as if waiting for her to catch on to a private joke. When she realized he'd used the puppy's antics to distract her into first-naming each other, she burst out laughing.

"You're shameless."

"And more."

The kitchen door burst open and a half dozen scullery maids rushed in. Their wide eyes went from the puppy, to Mr. Macane, to Ellie . . . and there they stayed. Probably they'd like an explanation for what an unchaperoned young miss was doing alone with one of the dashing male guests. Undoubtedly they hoped for an indication of why this clandestine rendezvous was in the kitchen. With a dog.

Since she hadn't an explanation for any of it, Ellie simply smiled at the staff, dipped a half curtsey at Cain, and escaped without acknowledging the questioning stares.

When she reached her bedchamber, Ellie crawled back atop the mattress with her stomach full and her mind relentlessly reliving the feel of Cain's mouth rubbing against hers and the sensation of his tongue tasting her lips. She dozed and awoke feeling strangely flushed.

The sound of her mother moving about the adjoining room indicated Ellie had overslept—and was likely in danger of missing the picnic.

She scrambled out of bed and rang for a maid. Last night, the thought of a picnic had seemed deathly boring, but now she couldn't wait. She was eager to see how Cain would comport himself in the light of day. Would he be the consummate rake, flirting shamelessly with the other ladies as if no stolen moments had passed between them? Or would things be . . . *different* somehow? Ellie wasn't so silly as to believe a single kiss would convert him from hedonist to lovesick suitor, but she couldn't stifle the sudden wish that her wardrobe wasn't so plain and her jewels nonexistent. A moment's dalliance with Ellie Ramsay was all well and good when otherwise unengaged in the kitchens, but even in her finest gown, she would look a proper dowd when she stood amongst all the other young ladies.

Ellie groaned. Miss Breckenridge would certainly be present and in her rights to demand news of progress regarding her claim. Ellie had been so busy casting sheep's eyes at Mr. Macane, she'd completely forgotten she was meant to be investigating his potential undeadness. There had probably been any number of reflective surfaces in the kitchen, and if she'd had her mind on her pocketbook rather than the taste of his lips, she could've proven the myth false in a trice.

In the meantime, however, Ellie meant to make the most of the weekend. Mama might be content to spend every moment sequestered in her bedchamber, but a ton house party was a rare opportunity for actual fun, and Ellie was damned if she'd let it pass by unenjoyed.

As soon as she put her hair to rights, Ellie headed straight for the hall ... only to be waylaid by a voice from her mother's shadowy bedchamber.

"Elspeth, where are you going at this ungodly hour?" Mama emerged from her chamber, somehow able to pull off an aura of regal hauteur despite being enshrouded in a flowing caftan.

"It's half two, Mama." Ellie gestured at the crack of light streaming from the bottom of the still-closed curtains. "There's to be a picnic and perhaps riding."

"But you can't go out there!" Her mother's strong hand once again grasped Ellie by the wrist. "You could get ... sun fatigue."

"I'll be fine, Mama. I won't forget my parasol." Ellie tugged her wrist free and strode toward the door, then paused as she recollected an earlier concern. "Speaking of remembering things ... All the furor over birthdays made me realize I can't precisely recall my own age. I know this sounds ridiculous, but ... How old am I, again?" She laughed lightly to cover her embarrassment.

Mama wandered away, as if just now noticing the small landscapes dotting the walls. "You'll be two-and-twenty," she answered distractedly. "The same as your friend. Don't ask such silly questions."

Frowning, Ellie watched her mother straighten the already straight frames, then turned and left the chamber before another argument erupted. But as she walked to join the others, Ellie couldn't shake the suspicion that her eternally self-controlled mother had been unaccountably fidgety. It was unsettling to think Mama might have been hiding something, but Ellie couldn't possibly imagine what there could be to lie about. Except for the niggling suspicion that Ellie had already turned two-and-twenty. *Last* year.

Before Ellie could consider the topic further, Miss Breckenridge spied her approaching and motioned her over to the small crowd. The marble antechamber smelled strongly of soaps and colognes. Lord Lovenip was nowhere in sight.

"I hope you're hungry." Miss Breckenridge fairly skipped across the entranceway to the front doors. "Cook has outdone herself!"

The butler flung open the doors. A passel of footmen bearing large baskets lined the pathway curving down the hillside. Beaming, Miss Breckenridge stepped across the threshold to lead the way, her guests filing out behind her.

Bringing up the rear, Ellie overheard one gentleman murmur to another, "Got yours?"

"It's the only method of survival," his companion replied with an irreverent grin. "Cheers!"

Laughing and jostling, they removed metal flasks from their waistcoats, clinked them together, then took turns downing healthy swigs.

Spirits of some kind, no doubt, but whatever it was had to be better than warm ratafia. After the events of this morning, Ellie couldn't help but wish they'd offer some to her, too.

In unison, the two men swiveled to face her, flasks in hand. "Fancy a nip?"

Surprised at their apparent ability to read her mind, Ellie was startled into accepting one of the flasks. Although the gentlemen were watching her more vacantly than expectantly, they were now the only three left dawdling in the house. She might as well take a courtesy sip and have done, so they could catch up with the others.

Having successfully rationalized astoundingly unladylike behavior, Ellie gingerly tipped the flask just enough to taste its contents. Liquid fire scalded her throat and scorched her nostrils. Flask outstretched, she doubled over, coughing. Whatever it was, it was even worse than ratafia.

She hastened from the two gentlemen lest they offer her more spirits, only to freeze on the front steps when the sun's rays hit her full on. The conversation with her mother had discomfited her so much that she'd forgotten her parasol after all. She'd been a child the last time she'd strolled in the sun unprotected, and all she could remember of that outing was ending up in bed for a week. But she was older now. Stronger. Besides, if she went back for a parasol, she'd lose the group completely and, like as not, end up arguing with her mother again.

Sighing, she curved a hand over her eyes to shield them from the blinding glare and hurried across the lawn.

Whether as a result of the sun's heat or the effects of the devil's own whiskey, she was dizzy and thickheaded by the time she rejoined the group. Not only were the guests' individual scents overpowering to Ellie's nose, she fancied she could hear their breaths, even their heartbeats, and was oddly distracted by every glimpse of a bare throat or ungloved wrist. It seemed all the ladies had been hoping for Mr. Macane's accompaniment.

A steadying arm circled about Ellie's waist. Who . . . ? Ah. Miss Breckenridge.

"Are you quite all right?" Her client's brow knit, her voice low with concern. "You don't look at all the thing."

"All your fault," Ellie managed uncharitably. "Can't stop thinking about vamp—"

"*Shhh.*" Miss Breckenridge spun her away from the others. "Your breath smells like spirits." She clapped a hand to her forehead as if she, too, had a devil of a headache. "Never say my brothers offered you drinks from their flasks."

Ellie blinked slowly. "Those were your brothers?'

"Of course those audacious pups are my brothers—hence their humiliating stories today at breakfast. Oh! Of course. You didn't come down." Miss Breckenridge tsked. "You should know better than to imbibe spirits on an empty stomach, Miss Ramsay, and you oughtn't sample anything my brothers offer, no matter how full your stomach. Why don't you return to your chamber and lie down? Ring Cook for some soup. It's miraculous, I promise."

"All right," Ellie mumbled, disappointed to be returning indoors a mere fifteen minutes into the day's adventure but seeing no other recourse. With her head spinning so, she would never manage a long hike in the sun.

"You do look deathly pale." Miss Breckenridge placed her hand on Ellie's arm. "I shall have to accompany you."

"No, no, it's your birthday." Embarrassment flooded Ellie's cheeks. "I'll be fine in time for dinner; don't you worry."

Miss Breckenridge's pursed lips exposed her skepticism, but already her name was being called by various members of the party. "I'll have my brothers take you. They did this; the least they can do is escort you inside."

"I'm fine," Ellie lied, willing her spine to steady. The last thing she wanted was more witnesses to this humiliation. "Go ahead. Truly."

Without waiting for a response, she headed toward the house. She concentrated so hard on not tumbling insensate into the grass that at first she failed to notice she'd walked slightly off-target and was rapidly approaching the side of the manor, rather than the front door. Just as she turned to correct her mistake, the sound of rapid panting caught her attention. She lurched forward. With one hand splayed against the bricks for balance, Ellie leaned her head around the corner.

A large greenhouse protruded from rear of the manor. And there, frolicking in the conservatory's long shadow, was Cain's puppy.

Chapter Seven

Cain wandered restlessly amongst the dense greenery in the darkest nook of the conservatory, hoping to avoid both servants and revelers whilst his puppy cavorted out-of-doors.

His fractured shoulder was healing, although not as quickly as he would have liked. If he had been thinking about his injury, he would've spirited away one of the party's insipid coquettes for a drop or two during last night's card-playing. Instead, he had been thinking about the bonny Miss Ramsay. That is, when he was capable of rational thought at all.

After centuries of fruitless searching and prolonged homesickness, he had crossed paths with renegade vampire Aggie Munro. At long last, he could see an end to decade upon decade of solitary hunting, peppered by the occasional wild pup that invariably grew old and died, leaving Cain to walk his path alone. No more. If he could not talk the deserter into accompanying him peaceably, he would return her forcibly. He had not gotten close to his quarry just to fail now.

Then there was the question of returning Miss Ramsay—Ellie—to her real family. Whomever they might be. Depending on how much detail Aggie had Compelled her human companion to forget, Ellie might never recall her true life . . . or even her true name. "Elspeth Ramsay" was much too Scottish for a modern English rose. Aggie might have stolen her as a child, might have used enough Compulsion on the parents so that they even forgot they *were* parents, violating virtually every sacred tenet of the rigid Code at once. Unforgivable, as far as Cain was concerned, but the Elders valued his brawn, not his opinions. He was simply required to deliver Aggie to their mercy.

Victory was finally at hand ... if unexpectedly bittersweet. Cain had no desire to turn Ellie's world upside down and then abandon her in the wilds of England to fend for herself, but what choice did he have? He certainly couldn't drag a human girl into the heart of vampire territory. Not without her becoming just another servant.

Without freedom, she would not be allowed to leave the keep, much less to return to England. Cain could never consign another person to the same desolate homesickness he himself had suffered. And he would never forgive himself if Ellie were Compelled to spend the rest of her life serving the Elders.

So why did he feel like he was losing something important?

Cain leaned his good shoulder against the conservatory wall. He bloody well knew why he regretted leaving Ellie. Because he *liked* her, dammit.

She was bonny, clever, delightfully skeptical. . . . He'd actually had to work to charm her and was not at all confident as to the extent of his success. She, for her part, had managed to charm *him* quite effortlessly, with her arch wit and unpredictability. Yet her very mortality ensured he could never have her. His clan only accepted fellow vampires as mates, and he would not turn her. Conversion had been banned for centuries, for good reason: Only one in a hundred survived the process. Even were it legal, it would still not be worth the risk. Besides, what he liked best about Ellie was her humanness. He'd damn near sprained his cheek muscles keeping his smiles at bay so as not to flash his fangs on accident. Being in her company was simply good fun.

Even if she could accept him for who and what he was, he still could not have her. Regardless of his clan's laws against mating with a human, Cain wouldn't be able to bear falling in love with someone who would grow old when he would not, who would die when he would not, who would leave this world—and him—forever.

The slight squeak of a hinge set his muscles on edge. If the sound heralded the arrival of servants or a groundskeeper, his gift of thought compulsion would keep unwanted questions at bay. But if the entire party had decided to take a turn amongst the exotic flowers, his blood-weakened state might not afford him the energy needed to Compel a multitude of people at once. He would be forced to . . . mingle.

With a sigh, he straightened to his full height and prepared for the worst. The thick rows of tangled flora offered plenty of shadowy nooks, but if Cain had never sought to hide from immortal warriors, he certainly would not cower from a gaggle of ladies and lordlings. Let them do their worst.

"Cain?" called a warm, familiar voice. "Are you here?"

From the first sultry syllable, Cain's entire body stood at attention. *Ellie*. Bloody hell. He might have faced less danger with the picnic-goers after all.

"Here," he managed, inanely pleased his voice hadn't cracked like that of some green youth.

"Where?" she called, her footsteps falling faster.

Cain didn't answer, couldn't answer, because even as his addled brain sought to form a reply, she stepped into view. If he'd still had breath, she would certainly have stolen it away. He swallowed hard.

Although she stood at the opposite end of a long row of hothouse flowers, just enough dappled sunlight filtered through the tropical blooms to give her silhouette an angelic glow. Not that he needed the reminder. Stray curls danced alongside elegant cheekbones. A simple gown highlighted a perfectly curved figure that required no ruffles or flounces to distract the eye. The faint, but irresistibly sweet scent of her blood blended with the perfume of the flowers, pricking both his nostrils and his nethers.

"You look . . . dashing." Blood infused her cheeks at the apparently unintentional compliment, but she boldly took another step in his direction.

Dashing? Cain glanced down at himself abstractedly. His costume was Corinthian out of necessity rather than personal style. After so many decades of ever-changing styles, the vagaries of vogue blended into incomprehensibility. Cain followed fashion in order to avoid looking like a centuries-old relic. He donned the sheep's clothing du jour to better stalk his prey. Except for those ridiculous cravats. He'd never worn one as a warrior or as a Scotsman, so he'd be damned before he noosed himself every morning for the English.

For reasons of her own, Ellie had likewise not chosen to em-ulate French fashion to the letter. She didn't need to. She would be magnificent in any clothing ... or in none at all.

Rather than approach her, he kept to the shadows. "Where's your chaperone?"

She idly caressed the petal of a bright orange flower. "With a dozen picnickers, there's no need for individual chaperones."

If only she knew. Cain shoved his hands behind his back to prevent himself from reaching for her. "Then where are the other eleven? Will the tour wend this way at any moment?"

"No, I'm ... alone." White teeth worried at her lower lip. Just when Cain thought she would choose to flee to the flock of humans, the corner of her mouth lifted in a hesitant smile, and she took an inexorable step forward.

She'd be the death of them both.

In warning, he summoned a rakish leer. "If you come much closer, I'm afraid you'll find yourself thoroughly kissed."

"I'm not afraid at all," she answered shyly. "I confess I'm looking forward to the experience."

Cain closed his eyes to block the temptation of her blushing cheeks and only succeeded in heightening his awareness of her scent. Her soap, her perfume, her blood ... If his body had still been human enough to sweat, by now he'd appear the victim of a sudden downpour. He forced his eyes back open.

She was even closer. She had taken another step while he hadn't been watching and was now a mere arm's length away. The only thing keeping her innocence intact was his determination not to move a single muscle. If he allowed himself to touch her, if so much as a red-gold ringlet brushed against his skin, he would not be able to keep his desire leashed. An entire battalion of chaperones wouldn't be able to stop him from kissing her, tasting her, having her.

"Are you all right?" Ellie took another step closer, her eyes filled with concern. "You seem ... out of kilter."

Out of kilter? Cain was breathing heavily, and he didn't even need to breathe.

She lifted a hand, bringing the curve of her fingers near his face as if to check his cheek for fever. At the last second, she dropped her hand back to her side without making contact.

Thank God. His equilibrium had vanished with her arrival. His strength of will was preparing for flight as well. If she had touched him, he would have turned his face into her hand, pressed a kiss to her palm, to the pulse point at her wrist, to her—

Compulsion! He was a vampire; she was human. Compulsion would save him. Would save them both.

Run away, he commanded, letting the ferocity of his desire fill his gaze. *Run now, and run far, or your innocence will be lost right here amongst the flowers. Flee whilst you can!*

A slight frown briefly creased Ellie's brow, but her gaze did not waver. If anything, her expression softened. Rather than run away, she suddenly seemed even closer, as if the hand's width of air between them had been sucked from the conservatory, pulling them together. She tucked a stray tendril behind her ear, but this time her hand did not return to her side. Her fingertips slid from the curl and pushed through the thickened air to graze the side of his face, the rough edge of his jaw.

Cain's entire body trembled from the effort to stay still, to not repay the joy of her touch with caresses of his own. Except he could not help but respond. He had meant to hold himself still as marble, but against his will, his hands freed themselves from behind his back, his entire body inexorably drawn to Ellie's. He jerked away.

"When we were in the kitchens," she said softly, her face tilting up to his, "I thought you were going to kiss me."

"I was," he said, his voice as ragged as his self-control. "I still am."

"Good." She smiled up at him, but her voice was more passionate than playful. "Don't keep me waiting."

Cain brushed the pad of his thumb along the soft curve of her cheek. When she tilted her face into his hand, he sank his fingers into her glorious hair and pulled her close. He dipped his head, intending to cover her mouth with his, but found pleasure in the sweet torture of anticipation.

He slowly feathered his parted lips across hers. Not quite a kiss, not quite a taste . . . just the lightest pressure, to tease them both, just as he had done this morning in the kitchen.

When he angled his mouth for another pass, she nipped his lower lip between her teeth.

The bite was sweet and quickly over, but Cain was as good as trapped. His muscles locked. His cock hardened. And when Ellie ran the tip of her tongue across the very flesh she'd just bitten, Cain's whirling brain relinquished all hope of gentlemanly restraint.

Opening his mouth to the kiss, he surrendered to the moment. One hand cradled the back of her head, keeping their mouths firmly together. His other hand slid along the tumble of soft curls to her waist. He splayed his fingers across the gentle curve at the base of her spine. She clutched his shoulders. He drew her even closer, until not even a whisper could pass between them.

With the tips of her breasts pressed into his waistcoat and the bulge of his cock throbbing against the folds of her skirt, Cain expected reason to intrude upon the innocent young lady nestled against him and send her fleeing. Instead, she wriggled even closer as if she, too, found the friction delicious.

A tiny moan of pleasure escaped her lips, vibrating against his tongue and sending chills along his flesh. Her arms twined around his neck, locking their bodies together. Her increased heartbeat, her rapid breath, the delicious sting of fingernails clawing for purchase against the tailored smoothness of his jacket—the sensations were dizzying, invigorating. Unexpected.

She *wanted* him. She wanted *him*.

He'd been so focused on battling his own desire that he hadn't even recognized the unexpected treasure he'd been bestowed. Rather than his emotionlessly Compelling an equally emotionless blue-blood beauty into the shadows for a nip-and-forget, a young woman whose company he actually enjoyed had sought him, entrapped him, kissed him . . . of her own free will. Her tongue toyed with his because she loved the interplay as much as he did. Her arms locked ever tighter because she, too, had no intention of letting go. And her kisses . . . Lord help him, he hoped they'd never stop.

Cain reveled in the feel of her body against his, wishing he could Compel all this damn fabric to disappear, so he could feel Ellie's bare legs wrapped tight around his hips.

He was feverish. He was shivering. He was strangely, impossibly *alive*.

He kissed her again and again, unable to resist the scent of her skin, the spice of her kiss, the promise of pleasure in the accelerated beat of her heart. He lifted her in his arms, higher, higher, until his kisses fell against the source of the intoxicating rhythm. Each pounding heartbeat seemed to lift the arc of her breast closer, to press harder against his mouth, his tongue, his teeth, until he was no longer aware of anyone or anything except the salty sweetness of her skin and the rich aroma reducing his brain to animal instinct and uncontrollable desire.

Her breath against his neck was an irresistible aphrodisiac. Hot, humid, undeniably human, and erratic enough to expose her increasing passion, if her legs locked around his hips and her fingers digging into his back had not been signal enough. The tip of her tongue touched the sensitive skin hidden behind his ear. In response, he laved his own tongue across the trembling curve of her breast. She pulled the lobe of his ear into her mouth, ran her tongue across the captured flesh, then drove all conscious thought from his mind when she sucked the curved edge between her teeth. He responded in kind and suckled her plump breast, drawn to the beckoning heartbeat beneath that warm, white flesh. This was heaven. This could leave a mark. This could make his—

Oh God. The potent seduction playing out upon his earlobe changed from gentle nibbling to a gasping, carnal bite. Cain couldn't have prevented his instantaneous reaction if he'd wanted to. In the time it took her human teeth to entrap the lobe of his ear, his fangs exploded from his mouth the way his cock longed to leap from his pants. His upper incisors pierced the top of her breast, impaling her flesh, and finally, finally, tasting that hot, sweet blood.

He tightened one hand on the nape of her neck, the other on the curve of her arse, grinding the full length of his imprisoned cock against the frothy waves of silk protecting her innocence from his lust. He suckled her hungrily, dizzy with desire and the addictive taste of her blood. He would rip this infuriating silk from her frame. He would rend his ridiculous vestments at the seams. And when nothing, not even passion-scented air, was between them, he would lock his teeth to her neck and penetrate her with his shaft and his fangs while she moaned in ecstasy.

Ellie gasped . . . but not in ecstasy. She went from fiery blaze to lump of coal in the space of an indrawn breath. She jerked from his arms before he had time to react—he, a vampire with allegedly superhuman instincts—and because she turned before his fangs had had a chance to retract, the retreating tips scraped across her white flesh, leaving twin trails of raw red where invisible pinpricks might have stood.

She clasped pale hands across her mouth, her shocked eyes screaming her fear and horror. The choked sob from behind her palm extinguished his passion more effectively than freezing rainwater.

She knew the truth.

He was a monster.

And he could not let her leave the conservatory with the knowledge.

"Ellie," he said, torn between smiling in an attempt to display a normal row of teeth, and the knowledge that his pearly whites were currently stained pink with her blood. He rallied all the power vested in him to do the one thing that would protect them both: obliterate the memory of the sweetest tryst of his life.

Forget, he commanded silently. *You didn't see any fangs. You didn't feel any fangs. I am not a vampire.* Cain hesitated only briefly before adding, *I made unwanted advances. You gave me a proper setdown. Stay away from me, Ellie. Stay far, far away.*

He reached out to straighten the drooping shoulder of her gown.

She turned and ran.

Cain blinked. First Ellie had seemed all but immune to Compulsion, and now all of a sudden his unspoken command to stay away lit a fire under her hems as if—

Ah, *hell.* As if she'd just discovered her suitor was a bloodsucking vampire.

Cursing whatever it was about her that had distracted him from performing a proper thought compulsion—and cursing himself, his infatuation, and his impulsive fangs for getting him into this scrape to begin with—Cain righted his breeches and gave chase.

Chapter Eight

Ellie fled through the halls with both hands crisscrossed over her gaping mouth. The warm stickiness adhering to her fingers and the telltale coppery sweetness coating her throat were further evidence of the two-pronged proof currently distorting her lips:

She had *fangs*.

"Oh God, oh God, oh God," she panted as she ran, the syllables coming out muffled against the pressure of her hands. Her rational, orderly world had turned completely upside down in the space of seconds.

Batty Miss Breckenridge had been right. Vampires absolutely existed. Mártainn Macane was an incontestable example. She'd kissed the beast. Who had then *bitten* her. The spread of infection was instantaneous. And now she, Elspeth Ramsay, self-professed bluestocking and scholar of all that was mundane and logical, was a godless, soulless bloodsucking monster with razor sharp *fangs*. They protruded from her mouth, for the love of science.

She had to get out of the open. Fast.

Bad enough if someone would have entered the conservatory and chanced upon her and Cain in a compromising position. Unimaginably worse, if someone were to stroll down the corridor and happen across the lowest-born houseguest with a brand new set of *fangs* to augment her perpetual queerness.

Mama would know what to do.

Well, no, Mama would have no inkling what to do. Ellie hadn't the least spark of a plan, and she was the analytical one. But her mother had been Ellie's sole confidante since she was a baby, and as there was no one else to confide in anyway, they would just have to figure it out together. Along with how to rid Ellie of her recent yen for warm blood.

The hope of devising a working plan provided such a rush of relief, Ellie's hand closed around the guest chamber's doorknob before she realized there was no call for the other hand to keep covering her mouth. The strange fangs had retracted as quickly as they'd appeared.

Before she could even begin to puzzle out the reason, the sound of rapid footfalls spurred Ellie back into motion. She pushed open the door, flung herself inside, and very nearly bowled over her own mother as if playing a human game of skittles.

"Mama—" was all Ellie managed before she glimpsed the identity of the approaching observer.

Cain.

She slammed the door shut, slid home the lock, and leapt away from both as if she half-expected him to burst through anyway. He did not. When his footsteps finally receded, Ellie let out her pent-up breath and turned around. The sight of her mother's blanched face sent Ellie's heart into a panic all over again.

"Elspeth." Mama's voice was low, but each syllable thrummed with icy resolve. "You stay *away* from Mártainn Mac Eoin! Do you think he saw me?"

"Macane," Ellie corrected automatically, then blinked to realize her reclusive mother had recognized a ton rake on sight. "And, no, he was looking at me. *I* didn't even see you. How would you even know who he is? Had you met before?"

"Yes." Mama shook her head. "No." She jabbed a finger at Ellie's midsection. "I'm not the one who needs to answer for myself. Since no one has seen me, everything is fine. But what about you? Did you join the picnic? Why are you back so soon? Where were you if not with the others?"

Ellie stared at her mother uncomprehendingly until it dawned on her that her mother's alarm must be of the normal, everyday, overprotective variety. She had no idea anything was amiss. The lace of Ellie's bodice covered the marks left by Cain's fangs. Her own had disappeared before she'd entered the room. If her curls were topsy-turvy or her gown a bit mussed, well, when was it not? Ellie was having an existential crisis, and Mama . . . was simply being Mama.

With an inward sigh, Ellie realized that her hope of puzzling out this new twist in reality together had been a foolish one. Mama believed in the world as she saw it. Her biggest fear was that her baby was not enjoying the house party she'd begged to attend. Mama was safely ignorant of the evil lurking just below the surface of those around her . . . and Ellie was swept with a fierce desire to keep it that way.

Thus unable to confess what was truly bothering her, Ellie smiled as cheerfully as she could. She headed to the tea tray across the room as if she hadn't a care in the world, hoping Mama wouldn't notice her shooting covert glances at the gilded looking-glass above the bookshelf. Ellie's familiar (if ashen) visage reflected back at her. Miss Breckenridge had been mistaken about the mirrors, then. Thank God.

"Everything's fine, Mama." Ellie poured herself a half cup of tepid water. Everything was not fine. Things could not possibly be worse. How could she expect to keep a secret of this magnitude? "I came back because I forgot my parasol."

"So that's what it is!" Her mother rushed to Ellie's side and pressed the back of her fingers to Ellie's cheeks and forehead. "Are you feeling weak? I told you not to go, and now look what's happened. Do you need to lie down?"

Ellie slid out of her mother's grasp. "I'll be fine once I've had a sip of tea. I don't have sunstroke, Mother. I have a dearth of social experience. I don't know how to interact with Polite Society. Our ideas of what makes for interesting conversation are incredibly distinct."

Mama stood for a moment longer, squinting down at Ellie as if searching for signs of trouble using microscopic vision. Apparently satisfied at last that her daughter appeared as normal as she ever did, Mama took a seat on a wingback chair opposite Ellie.

"Oh?" she asked as she settled back without partaking in the lukewarm tea. "What sorts of nonsense are the blue bloods mad about these days?"

Ellie added a lump of sugar to her cup. Now that she'd decided to pretend nothing was awry, she needed to come up with a few details capable of convincing her mother that the High Society houseguests were nothing more than a gaggle of inane fops and fribbles.

"Well," she said slowly. "One gentleman asked me if I'd ever been to Scotland. Twice."

Mama jerked forward, her eyes suddenly intense. "And what did you say?"

"No, of course."

Mama's hyper-focused gaze continued unabated, as if she suspected Ellie of holding back details. "Was that the end of it?"

Ellie shrugged. "More or less. Oh, and he talked about some estate burning to the ground. A castle . . . Foulis, I believe."

"What? *No*. It can't be!" Mother clutched the armrests with trembling hands and stared at Ellie with too-wide eyes. "Why would they . . . When? *How?* Are there survivors?"

"You . . ." Unsettled, Ellie's stomach began to churn with a sick feeling that had nothing to do with stale tea. "You've been to Scotland, haven't you?"

Mama's eyes glazed. "I—"

Ellie put down her cup hard enough to crack the china saucer. "You've been to Castle Foulis. Haven't you?!"

Mama gave her head a violent shake. "I—"

Ellie's eyes narrowed. "If you lie to me, Mother, I shall never forgive you."

Mama's chin lifted in her customary hauteur, then her face crumbled into a wholly unfamiliar expression of guilt and despair. Nothing could have frightened Ellie worse.

"I certainly hope that is untrue," Mama said quietly, "for I have told you many lies in order to keep you safe."

Frowning, Ellie leaned forward. "Safe from what?"

"You wouldn't believe me if I told you."

The tips of Ellie's fingers traced the twin welts beneath the lace of her bodice. "Try me."

Her mother slumped against her armrest, the sorrow in her eyes now tempered by a faraway look of remembrance. "Scotland . . . is very beautiful and very old. Memories are passed down through the generations, and magic is considered commonplace." She shifted her gaze to the thick curtains covering the window. "There are even those who still believe the legends of the vampires of yore. . . ."

"It's no myth," Ellie muttered behind her teacup. Her mother shot up from the chaise. Out of surprise, Ellie did the same.

"Then you know?" Her mother's voice cracked on the final word.

More confused than ever, Ellie ran the tip of her tongue over her sore gums before replying. "I am irrevocably convinced, although I admit to not understanding this conversation in the least."

"Oh, Elspeth." With the tea tray still on the table between them, Mama reached over to briefly lay a hand on Ellie's cheek. "I owe you an apology. And an answer to all your questions. I had no idea you suspected . . . that you *knew* . . ."

Ellie stopped massaging her sore gums as trepidation set in. Whatever she thought she knew was merely the tip of an iceberg she hadn't even known existed. The sick feeling in her stomach increased sevenfold. "Perhaps you should start at the beginning?"

"The beginning?" Mama's laugh was high-pitched and humorless. "A few hundred years are far too many to recount in one sitting. Suffice it to say, I barely recall who I was before I became what I am now. I lived . . . if not happily, then at least contentedly under clan rule until early last century, when I met your father. He was so sweet, so—"

Ellie shook her head to clear the cobwebs from her ears. "Beg pardon, I thought you said . . . early last century?"

Mother nodded abstractedly. "It was forbidden, of course, under penalty of death . . . but a woman in love cannot refuse the call, even if she has the ill fortune of being in love with a human. And an Englishman, at that. He was—"

"You're saying . . . you're a *vampire?*" Ellie blurted as the pieces fell into place. Her flesh grew cold at the obviousness of the truth, now that her empirical mind could no longer disbelieve the signs. Her legs suddenly unsteady, she fell back to the chaise as if awakening from a stupor. "You are!"

Mother perched back on the edge of her seat, her gestures nervous, her eyes guilty. "Was that not what we were discussing?"

Ellie's sudden laugh bordered on hysteria. "No, not at all, but pray continue. It seems I need to know your story in order to better understand mine."

Watching her daughter uncertainly, Mama stammered at first, then let loose with a torrent of words as if a dam had broken free.

Ellie, on the other hand, could only listen and stare, unable to make a sound. Anger, disbelief, and wonder all crashed together as she tried to assimilate the flood of unforeseeable information and unbelievable twists to what she thought she knew about her own life.

Her mother was a vampire.

She'd been reborn in Castle Foulis, centuries ago, where she'd lived amongst dozens more of her kind. There was a clan. A family. A government.

Her mother was a runaway.

Outside of master-and-servant or hunter-and-prey, relationships with humans were verboten. Sexual relations were forbidden above all things, even though mixed-blood procreation was believed to be a myth. A mixed-blood relationship was repulsive and offensive in and of itself. Therefore, the only way for her mother to be with the human man she loved was to denounce everything that she knew and run.

They were being hunted.

If breaking the cultural mores of her brethren weren't bad enough, Mama had also broken a betrothal contract. The vampires of Foulis Castle had agreed to sacrifice their most beloved maiden to the leader of the Pitreavie as a token of peace to end centuries of territorial disputes. Mama had been commanded to submit to the Elders' bidding. But her heart was not theirs to rule.

They were in danger.

Searchers had been sent after Mama to bring her to justice over her transgression, but Ellie was the greater reason her parents had stayed hidden. Even in legends, half-human offspring were considered an abomination. Mama would be sent to the Pitreavie clan or to the castle dungeon. But discovery of the secret behind her daughter's existence would be Ellie's death warrant.

They were rich—but it did not help.

Mama had once been a high-ranking member of her society. She had a hidden cache of precious jewels that had been given to her by family and suitors. But despite its value, the jewelry could neither be worn nor sold because its very singularity meant it could be easily traced. Therefore, every time Mama had been forced to sell a piece for survival money, they'd had to quit town that night and travel as far as they could, before news of the sale had an opportunity to spread.

Ellie's father hadn't died before her birth, after all.

His name was Nigel. He'd been married to her mother for thirty years before Ellie was born, and died of old age decades later . . . while his daughter was barely out of leading strings.

"We thought you were human," Mama explained softly. "He knew what I was, and still we dared to hope. You weren't developing like other children, and I talked myself into believing you were a late bloomer . . . until even I couldn't deny the truth. You didn't grow at the normal pace and ceased aging altogether by the time you gained your current appearance."

Ellie stared at her mother in both hurt and horror. "You *knew* I was a vampire and didn't think it important enough to mention?"

"It came up," her mother admitted. "Frequently. But as long as you were more human than not, you were still susceptible to a thought obfuscation technique we refer to as Compulsion. Whenever you asked dangerous questions, I simply Compelled you to forget."

"You 'simply'—"

"For your own *safety*, Elspeth! What would you have had me do?"

"Tell the truth, for starters!" The teacup tumbled from Ellie's fingers as the full impact of her mother's words hit her. No wonder she had so many holes in her memory! Ellie's head swam as an ugly suspicion sucked the air from the room. "Did you Compel me to forget my own father?"

Her mother reached out a hand. "You would never have believed you were human if you could remember decades passing whilst you were still a tot. I had no choice but to—"

"No choice?" Ellie repeated, choking on the words. She sprang to her feet. "You gave *me* no choice!"

"You hadn't turned yet! You still haven't turned. There was plenty of time for you to have a normal life. There still is. Maybe decades, centuries even. I know this must be difficult for you, but—"

"You know *nothing*." Ellie whirled for the door, her head still spinning with hurt and rage and the desperate desire to flee the one person she had always gone to for comfort and advice. Even as the world tilted off its axis, Ellie could hear her mother scrambling to her feet behind her.

"Wait!" Hesitation shook her mother's voice as she added, "Elspeth . . . I—I Compel you to stay!"

But Ellie wasn't mostly human anymore. No longer Mama's little girl, susceptible to vampiric head games. No longer even herself.

Ellie was out the door and gone.

Chapter Nine

Ellie had barely sprinted free of the guest quarters when an arm flashed out of the shadows, hooked about her waist, and reeled her into a small music room. The obsidian shine of a hulking piano was not what set her nerves afire, but rather the man whose strong arms locked her body to his.

Cain.

"Let me go." Struggling to break free, Ellie pushed at his chest. "Leave me alone."

"I just want to talk." His voice was soft, worried, sincere.

She couldn't have cared less. "I've heard more than enough for one day. I need to be by myself for a while."

Despite the hesitant warmth in his voice, Cain's grip did not slacken. "I can't let you do that. Not after what happened."

Ellie froze mid-struggle.

Not after what happened. He'd seen her fangs! And the fact that he had them, too, could mean only one thing: He was one of the hunters her mother had warned her about. Had been hiding from her entire life. And now that he knew the truth—thanks to her pursuing *him*, of all things—she and her mother were both going to die. Cain wouldn't let her go, now that he had her. And Mama would never stand by and let her be taken.

"Please," she whispered, risking a glance up at him to gauge his anger. "Not like this."

However, he did not appear to be angry. If anything, his expression was stricken. His fingers relaxed, and he took a half step backward.

"I didn't mean for it to happen." His voice was low, but even she could hear the note of self-recrimination. "I just meant to kiss you. That's all. I'd been longing to taste your lips from the moment we met, and I never meant to indulge that desire, much less..." He gave a dry little laugh and continued, "Much less bite you. That's the problem with being...what I am. Less human. Less *thinking*. More instinct. If I could make you forget it ever happened, I would. To be honest, I even tried." He shook his head. "Maybe I've been so long from my homeland, so long without a proper supply of... sustenance, that my powers aren't what they once were. I don't want you to be hurt. I *can't* hurt you. And so I am asking you, not as a vampire but as a man, if you could find it in yourself to please keep my secret."

His face was so earnest, his eyes so candid, his meaning so at odds with anything and everything she'd been expecting, that Ellie stared wordlessly up at him for a long moment before making sense of any of it.

He still thought she was human. He was afraid of her reaction, of what *she* might do. Ellie could have laughed at the sheer irony if she weren't so close to tears.

For the first time in her life, a handsome gentleman actually liked her. Longed to kiss her. *Fancied* her. Right at the moment when she was no longer the girl either one of them thought they knew.

She was a vampire now, but nothing else of import had changed. She was still in the lowest class of her peers. An outcast. An abomination. And instead of simply receiving a cut direct, once the truth became known, heads would roll. Namely, hers and her mother's. She couldn't let that happen. But for how long could she hope to hide the truth from a centuries-old vampire hunter?

"I won't tell anyone," she promised. Years of unflinching honesty made her add in a mumble, "Except maybe my mother."

"Oh, Ellie, you can't. Your mother..." He gazed at her unhappily, as if trying to determine how best to candy-coat some undesirable truth. "I have reason to believe your mother isn't truly your mother. No, don't say anything. Come sit down. You can hear me out and then decide."

He led her to the piano bench and seated her upon the cushion. He stepped back, paused, then stepped forward. He picked up her hands and held them tight. He let go as if her touch had scalded him and shoved his hands into his pockets instead. He sighed.

"Just because I currently find my Compulsion skills lacking does not make it any less real. I'm afraid that the woman you know as your mother cannot possibly be so. You are human. And she is as human as I. The woman you know as 'mother' is actually Agnes Munro, a vampire even older than me." He gave Ellie a hard look, as if half-expecting her to tumble off the bench in a dead faint. When she did not, he took up her hands again and fell to his knees before her. "Listen to me, Ellie. You are in danger."

Ellie shook her head. "She would never hurt me."

"You wouldn't remember if she had."

"I would know."

"Look at me," he insisted softly. "You have a logical mind. Use it. Do you remember your youth? If not, that's because she stole it from you. If you cannot recall your parents, it's because she erased the memory of them right from your brain."

This latter hit close enough to the truth that Ellie flinched involuntarily. She tried to mask the unwanted flash of hurt, but it was too late.

"See?" he murmured sadly. "Some part of you recognizes my words as true. Who knows what else may have been cleaned from your mind. Perhaps you have even served as an easy meal for years, or even decades."

Ellie recoiled so violently that if Cain hadn't been clasping her hands, she *would* have tumbled right off the bench. A source of food for her own mother? What a repugnant idea. Mama would never have done such a horrific thing . . . would she?

"Listen to me, Ellie. Listen to your own heart. If you don't feel safe, it's because you are not. If you don't feel *free*, it is because you are not. And you should be. You deserve to be."

"And my mother?"

"She . . . does not." His spine straightened, and his shoulders seemed to expand. "Besides her crimes against you, she must also answer to her clan for crimes committed in the past, contracts broken in direct violation of blood oaths she voluntarily swore to uphold."

"Are you her judge, her jury, or her executioner?" She tried to jerk her fingers from his hands.

"Neither," he answered, holding fast. "I am a hunter. A warrior whose primary use to his clan is his superior ability to find that which doesn't wish to be found. Two hundred years ago, I was sent to find Agnes Munro. I have found her. And I will bring her home."

"That's it? Your clan just says, 'Go fetch this woman, dead or alive,' and off you go for two hundred years?"

"Preferably alive. And yes, that's what hunters do. Their duty."

Ellie glared at him. "What do you mean, 'preferably' alive? That bit's optional?"

"The elders mean her no permanent harm," he answered carefully.

"Ha. Then why did she run away?"

"She'd broken a cardinal rule, which at that time was punishable by death." The pads of his fingers stroked the backs of her hands. "But times have changed."

Ellie chuckled bitterly. "Have they?"

Cain's brow creased, but his answer was firm. "Yes."

"Then what are the new rules?"

"No more death. There are less of us now than ever before. The elders can't afford to enforce the old ways. Either we change with the times, or we all die."

"So her crimes have been forgiven? Or will she spend the next millennium chained to a dungeon, expected to be grateful to still be alive?"

"Ellie." Cain still knelt before her, Ellie's hands still clasped in his. "Stop worrying about Agnes and start thinking about yourself. You can't go back to how things were. And you can't go back to Aggie. I'm taking her with me. And then I'm going home."

"What are you suggesting I do?" she demanded, as suspicion began to creep back up her spine. "Go with you?"

"Oh, good Lord, no." Cain's surprised laugh was short, but genuine. "When I said vampires were dangerous, I most certainly was not exempting myself. I've already taken a bite out of you uninvited. And here I am, making bad decisions worse by abducting you into a piano room and confessing clan secrets you have no business knowing. As I said, if I could have bade you forget, I would have. So to that end, I am no better than Aggie. Going forward, I want you to do whatever it is that *you* want to do. I want you to be safe."

Ellie shook her head. "But if I'm not with her, and I'm not with you, then I'm alone . . . and how safe is that? I may be legally of age to fend for myself, but with no money and no property and no particular skills outside of reading books and solving riddles, where exactly do you propose that I go?"

Cain dropped onto his haunches and closed his eyes. When he opened them again, his eyes were haunted.

"I don't know," he said simply. "You'll have to decide. I have never been in this situation, and even if I had, I would never presume to make your decisions. I have some money. You're welcome to it. I just need enough coin to return home, which should leave you with more than enough to take up residence somewhere, to be an independently wealthy, thrice-removed cousin of some far-flung nob. For long enough to make a new life, make human friends, and perhaps . . . perhaps even fall in love."

Love. Her hands still rested in his. Ellie nibbled her lower lip and gazed back into his eyes.

Within days of meeting her, Cain was doing the one thing her own mother hadn't done in over a century: voluntarily entrusting her with the truth and allowing her the right to weigh the evidence herself in order to make her own choices about her life.

Unfortunately, he was only in possession of half the evidence. As lovely a picture as his words had painted, Ellie was no longer a simple human girl, if she ever had been. And no matter how angry she was with her mother's decisions, Mama was still the person Ellie cherished above all others. Mama's life was inextricably tied to hers, and there was no way Ellie would allow either of them to face a vampire tribunal over a lovesick girl's rash decision two centuries ago. They would slip through the night, as they'd always done. They would hide from hunters—from Cain—forever, if that was what it took. And none of them would ever go home.

"Tell me about Scotland," she said, surprising herself as much as Cain with the change in topic. Scotland wasn't home, she reminded herself sternly. She had never had one. She never would.

"Scotland is lovely," he answered, his voice wistful. "The countryside is more beautiful than any other place in this world. The men are braw and true. The women are bonny and clever. The food is hearty and the ale even richer. The people are strong and proud. Proud of themselves, of the land, of each other." He dropped his forehead onto her lap. She couldn't help but brush her fingers over his hair. He didn't stop her. "Everyone is happy there. *I* was happy there." He lifted his head to favor her with a crooked smile. "I wish you could see it."

She smiled back. "I wish I could see it the way *you* see it."

"If I weren't a . . . warrior," he said, his smile fading, "I could take you there."

Ellie was shocked to discover she wished he could, too. But he was never going to see his beloved country, since he was never going to capture her and her mother. Ellie tried to ignore the guilty pang caused by the realization, but it was no use. She hated to cause him pain. Which meant she was just as bad as her mother—developing feelings for exactly the wrong man.

He was handsome, strong, charismatic. Loyal to a fault. He liked her body and loved her brain. He respected her. He wanted her to be happy. . . .

And he was a vampire warrior planning to lead her mother to an unknown punishment. And he would undoubtedly abduct Ellie as well if he knew she was a forbidden mixed-blood abomination.

But he didn't know. Not yet, anyway. And if she was addled enough to fall for someone honor-bound to hunt down her loved ones, well, that was her problem. She didn't mind his mischievous run as the most infamous rake in ton history. She didn't even mind that he was a vampire. If anything, now that her true nature had been revealed, she could scarcely fancy a human, anyway. But even more important than all those very logical truths was one very illogical fact: She was half in love and falling fast. And she was never going to see him again.

Ellie's shoulders slumped. She'd never enjoyed running away. Although now that she knew the truth and couldn't agree more with the rationale, her body and her heart still rejected the idea of leaving this man without a second thought. Without a second *chance.* If she was going to be on the run for the rest of her life, then she needed to make the most of this weekend.

She squeezed his hands. "May I beg a favor?"

He smiled. "Anything."

"Wait until tomorrow." Hope bloomed when he didn't immediately respond. "Please," she added for good measure.

His brows lifted, but his voice was good-humored as he said, "Why do I feel like this is a terrible idea?"

"Because it is," Ellie answered honestly. "And so is the part where I come to your chamber after nightfall."

He started. "When you what?"

She took a deep breath. "The house party is over tomorrow. Everyone will go his or her separate paths. If we are going to part ways forever, perhaps we can at least have tonight."

Before he had a chance to respond, the music room door swung open, and Miss Breckenridge stepped inside.

"Get away from her!"

Cain dropped Ellie's hands and sprang to his feet, but not before Miss Breckenridge landed a few good whacks with her parasol.

"I'm leaving, I'm leaving." Sidestepping Miss Breckenridge's attacks, he managed to trade places with her at the door and shoot Ellie a meaningful glance over Miss Breckenridge's head. "I'll be in the conservatory if you need me."

"She won't need you," Miss Breckenridge shot back. She slammed the door in his face, then rushed to inspect Ellie's neckline. "Are you all right? Did he bite you? What on earth possessed you to enter any room alone with him?"

"He didn't bite me," Ellie assured her, before her predilection for honesty forced her to add, ". . . on the neck."

Miss Breckenridge stared at her in horror. "What? When? Are you a vampire, too? Oh, this is a horrible mess, a horrible, horrible—"

"Forget I said anything," Ellie interrupted wearily, rubbing at her temples. "Forget anybody said anything about vampires in the first place."

Blessed silence fell . . . until the noiselessness became more eerie than relaxing.

Ellie lifted her fingertips from her temples and glanced up at Miss Breckenridge, only to find her erstwhile benefactress staring blankly at nothing.

"Miss Breckenridge?"

With a start, her hostess snapped out of her fit. "Miss Ramsay! What are you doing in the music room? You should be abed. May I walk you to your chamber?"

Ellie stared at her for a moment before she realized she'd just

Compelled her client to forget their entire agreement. Now she'd never earn those twenty pounds . . . and now she could better understand her mother.

Mama loved her, and Ellie hadn't given her a chance to explain. Perhaps she'd never meant for Ellie to forget her father. Ellie sighed. Perhaps it happened in a moment too quick to have prevented. And once it was done, it was done, leaving her only with regret. And her daughter.

"I think you're right." Ellie rose from the bench to accept Miss Breckenridge's arm. "I should love to return to my mother."

Chapter Ten

A scant distance into the corridor, Ellie jarred to a halt. She held up a finger to a startled Miss Breckenridge. "Wait."

There was no way she could return to her guest quarters. Mama would be waiting in her chamber. She would wish to finish their discussion. She would wish to explain. Perhaps to apologize, and perhaps not. But without question, she'd insist on running. Immediately.

Ellie could scarce deny the wisdom behind putting as much distance as possible between her outlaw mother and the clan hunter who sought them, but she was not quite ready to pack her bags. She had told Cain she would meet him tonight, and she meant to. Yearned to. *Needed* to.

He truly cared for her, and she him, star-crossed though they might be. He had answers her mother had not shared. He also had expressive eyes, strong arms, and kisses that set her half-blood heart spinning.

That she would never see him again went without saying. After coming so close to capture, they could never again risk so much as a nodding acquaintance with their new neighbors, wherever they landed next . . . much less house parties or dancing or a beau who stole kisses amongst the flowers.

But they hadn't left yet.

"What's wrong?" Miss Breckenridge cocked her head quizzically. "Have you the headache?"

Lifting her brows, Ellie nodded slowly. She had more than enough to make her head ache. The last thing she needed was another confrontation with her mother.

"I think I'd like to be alone for a little while." She gave her hostess a determined smile. "Don't worry about me. Why don't you check on the other guests, or take the evening for yourself? Find something diverting and enjoy yourself. I'll be fine."

Miss Breckenridge's eyes unfocused. Then she nodded once, turned, and wandered off without a word.

Ellie stared after her for a moment, feeling more than a little guilty. Either she'd inadvertently offended her hostess . . . or once again, she'd circumvented her free will with accidental Compulsion. Ellie was definitely going to have to wrangle that skill under control before—No. Mastery over Compulsion wouldn't matter one jot, once she and her mother were confined to some shadowy hovel in the middle of nowhere.

Sighing, Ellie retraced her steps and headed for the opposite wing. Cain had said he'd meet her in the conservatory. Granted, she'd said she wouldn't meet him until tonight, but given that her own guest chamber was no longer a viable retreat, the conservatory would be as peaceful a place to wait as any.

When she arrived, she found herself alone amongst the many blooms. The spicy scent of exotic flowers enveloped her. She wandered up and down the lush walkways, ducking low-hanging vines and pausing now and again to run a fingertip along the satin petals of a particularly breathtaking bloom. She was thus engaged when she sensed, rather than heard, a presence behind her.

"You're early," he said softly.

Smiling, she spun to face him. "As are you."

"I couldn't wait."

She glanced behind him. "No Mac Eric this time?"

Cain shook his head, his eyes crinkled with laughter. "I tried. But we weren't five paces from my door when we chanced upon an unaccountably effusive Miss Breckenridge. Quite a departure from her reception in the music room."

Ellie coughed guiltily. "Amicable, was she?"

"She *hugged* me," her vampire warrior replied as if he'd never suffered a worse indignity. "I asked her if she'd like to pet the puppy, and she said she'd like to keep Moch-éirigh forever."

"So you're letting her watch Mac Eric for a while?"

He shook his head. "I let her keep her."

"But you love that puppy!"

"Trust me," he said with a long-suffering sigh. "I have no difficulty stumbling across loveable puppies. I'll probably find another before we even leave the conservatory."

"Are we leaving the conservatory?" Ellie tried for an arch look, but couldn't help grinning up at him.

His sea-green eyes were nothing short of smoldering. "Aren't we?"

She accepted his proffered arm without hesitation. A delicious shiver slid up her spine. Her shoulders rolled backward in response, causing her breasts to rise and her bosom to tighten. She was acutely aware of every inch of her body, of the thin fabric of her chemise brushing against her flushed skin. She felt oddly naked beneath the oppressive layers of lawn and linen and silk. As if Cain's heated gaze could see right through the lace and flounces and corset to the woman trembling beneath.

Her fingers clutched his arm even tighter. Even voluminous shirtsleeves tucked into a well-tailored jacket could not disguise the strength contained within, the toned muscle of his body. Hard. Strong. Hers.

This was what she'd been waiting for. Longing for. A moment to cherish forever.

The walk from the conservatory to Cain's guest quarters might not have taken half so long, were it not for his inability to refrain from sidelong glances that led directly to stolen kisses. With her curls crushed between her back and the wall, and her hands wound tight about his neck as she eagerly met each kiss with her own, a single passerby would have spelled ruin if she were at all concerned about guarding her reputation. She was not. Her legs were all but twined about him as he spun with her across the threshold and into the dark stillness of his bedchamber at last.

She half-expected him to tumble directly upon the bed and divest her of these confining layers. Rather, that was precisely what she hoped he was about.

But, first, he kissed her soundly before stepping a few feet away to coax the dwindling embers in his fireplace into a softly burning blaze.

The dancing light fell upon a sumptuous master bed, with matching mahogany nightstands on either side. Upon one stood a vase with a single pink camellia. On the other rested a life-size marble bust of what was undoubtedly one of the Breckenridge forebears. Ellie focused her gaze back on the single flower, preferring its natural beauty to the profile carved in stone. The bust's very presence made the general sense of inferiority Ellie had always endured even starker. Not only wasn't she remotely connected to aristocracy, she couldn't even remember her own father, much less have mementos of cherished ancestors. She'd always just had Mama.

Ellie sat on the edge of the bed and tried to push all thoughts of her impending sojourn from her mind. She tugged her slippers from her feet and bent to smell the camellia. As lonely as she had been without a father, how much worse had it been for her mother to have loved and lost her husband? Would this moment shared with Cain bring Ellie years of remembered pleasure, or soul-wrenching dreams of what she had once tasted, but could never truly have?

She shook the foolishness from her head and turned to face Cain. She would have tonight . . . and it would be perfect.

He rose to his feet. The fire's welcome heat eased the chill from the air, and the crackling flames cast a warm glow upon his skin as he reached for Ellie's hand. He stared at her as if *she* were the exotic flower. As if he, too, wanted to sear every touch, every taste, into his memory to relive again and again. Perhaps he did. Perhaps this moment seemed just as tender, just as fleeting, just as vital for him as it did her. He had been a hunter for centuries. Would no doubt continue to be. To him, honor meant upholding the values of his clan. For her, protecting her mother. Both of them put their respective families above all else. Conflicting goals, but shared ideals.

Cain pulled her to her feet, seated himself at the edge of the mattress, and nestled her between his thighs. He seemed content to spend hours thusly, hand in hand, his unreadable gaze never wavering from hers.

Ellie was having none of it.

With a raised brow, she tugged her hands from his. Slowly, she crisscrossed her arms behind her back, conscious of how the action lifted the swell of her breasts very nearly to his parted lips. Almost, but not quite. His gaze dipped. Although she doubted a full-blooded vampire had cause for breathing, Ellie could have sworn she heard a quick intake of breath.

She tugged loose the laces holding her gown together. The sleeves correspondingly relaxed, exposing first one shoulder, then the other. With nothing left to hold it in place, the lace fichu tumbled from her bodice. The triangle of lace slid across one of Cain's parted thighs. He flinched as if the weightless scrap scalded his flesh through his calfskin breeches. His eyes closed as if he were willing himself to withstand pain caused by a wisp of material that had once rested across her breasts and against her nipples.

He opened his eyes. He was a man tortured. Intoxicated. Powerless.

Ellie returned her hands to her sides and brushed her fingertips across his leg where the fichu had fallen. Her shift and her corset supported her bosom, but did not cover it. Her nipples puckered deliciously beneath the heat of his gaze.

He licked his lips. Slowly, teasingly, as if what he desired most of all was to fasten his mouth upon her breast and suckle.

Ellie could hardly breathe for wanting him to hurry up and do so. She eased forward, inclining so slowly as for the motion to be nearly undetectable, were it not for her breasts' trajectory ever nearer to his face.

He was definitely breathing. Hard.

Her right nipple grazed the hollow of his cheek. The side of his mouth. The firm contours of his lower lip. Her insides clenched in pleasure, pitching her forward, sending her trembling breast directly into his waiting mouth.

He laved the nipple once, twice, then began to suckle. He tugged the sleeves from her arms, shoved her gown to her hips, to the floor. His hands slid from the backs of her knees to the backs of her thighs, simultaneously lifting her shift and guiding her forward so that she straddled his hips, the hard length of his encaged manhood pressing against the moist surface of her bare—

"Ellie." His eyes hot on hers, he lifted his mouth from her breast ever so slowly, dragging her nipple along his tongue and across his lower lip to glisten wetly before his parted mouth. "Are you certain you want to—"

Her hands were at his shoulders before she consciously gave them the order to do so, shoving him backward onto the bed. She covered his mouth with hers, stopping his questions with her teeth, with her tongue. She closed her fists over his shirt, rending the fine linen as she exposed his chest to her wanton fingers, to the sensitive nubs of her breasts as she pressed them against him.

His hands fastened about her waist, rocking her hips, slowly grinding her against him until she caught the rhythm with a gasp of ignited desire. Without breaking rhythm, without tearing his mouth from hers, he slid his hands up her spine to her corset. One by one, he loosened the ribbon from the hooks, until the whalebone prison fell away, and with it, what was left of her chemise.

One hand pressed to the base of her spine to hold her in place. He leaned up from the bed just enough to allow her to whip free his jacket, his waistcoat, his shirtsleeves, until nothing was left but his boots and his breeches.

She slid down his body until she knelt on the floor before him. She tugged free one boot, then the other. Her deliberate slowness in doing so must have exhausted the last of his preternatural patience, for he had his fall unbuttoned and his breeches discarded before she had even taken a breath.

He pulled her up, gently, sweetly. Holding her close, he rolled so that she was no longer atop him. He had one arm propped on either side of her ribs, and the naked length of him was hot against her belly. She was now the prisoner and he the captor. But the look on his face indicated she still very much held all the power.

"Kiss my breast," she whispered, arching toward his mouth. "Touch me as I long to touch you."

"With pleasure."

He bent his head to her breast. The knuckles of one hand brushed against the plump curve, then slid to her side, her hip, the inside of her thigh. Once again, her insides clenched with need as he stroked closer and closer to her core, never quite touching the center where she ached for him.

His other hand left her cheek. He splayed both across her thighs, as if preparing to force them apart. No need. Ellie was beyond ready. If he didn't give them both release soon, she was going to scream.

He trapped her nipple with his teeth, biting lightly. Ellie's head jerked upright as she gasped, unsure whether she should push his head away or beg him to do it again.

As if reading her mind, he performed the same sweet torture on the other breast, suckling the nipple to diamond hardness and scraping ever so gently with his teeth as he pulled his mouth away. She nearly flew off the bed.

His hips rising, he bent lower and lower, pressing a trail of hot, slow kisses from the valley between her breasts to the sensitive skin just beneath. He continued lower, along her stomach, over to the swell of her hip, down the impossibly tense muscle of her thighs.

He began to lick. First the quivering flesh of her inner thigh, then just a little higher, and a little higher still, until finally, finally, his tongue reached where his fingers had not.

Her hands shot out to grab fistfuls of his hair, holding him in place. His tongue drew endless lazy circles, as if he had all the time in the world to torture her until she fractured from the inside out. She slid one hand from his hair, gliding her palm up her stomach to hover just above her breast, as if wanting to touch it, to touch herself, but daring not. Her nipple tightened, and the aching tip brushed against the edge of her palm.

As if he sensed what she was doing and sought to tempt her even more, Cain dragged his thumb over her wet core, circling, pressing, until the pad slipped within her as his mouth and tongue returned their attentions to her nub.

Ellie cried out, arching into his face, into his finger, her head tossed backward as her hands found her breasts, rolled her nipples beneath her fingers as she writhed against the climbing pressure in her core.

"C-Cain." The word came out an incomprehensible moan. "I—"

Then his mouth was on hers, drinking every gasp as his shaft filled her. Her fingernails dug into his back as she lifted her legs higher, wrapped him tighter, forced him deeper, faster, faster.

He ducked his head to her shoulder and pressed his open mouth to her skin. As the first contraction of her climax hit, she lifted her head until his shoulder was close enough to taste. With the tip of her tongue, she traced the hard, salty curve. Her inner muscles squeezed tighter with every thrust.

As he gave a shudder indicating his own imminent surrender, the pressure of his kiss increased against her skin. She kissed his neck, his chest, ran her tongue along the bare strength of his shoulder. Their bodies joined faster. He moaned against her skin as another shudder wracked his body. Her release was instantaneous. Twin points painlessly punctured her skin, doubling her pleasure.

Instinctively, she bit down and did the same.

Chapter Eleven

"Liar," Cain choked out, retracting both fangs and shaft from the woman writhing deliciously beneath him as soon as his passion-drunk brain registered the twin points piercing the sensitive skin of his shoulder in exactly the same way his own fangs had fastened upon hers.

He was furious. At her, for having deceived him. At himself, for having let down his guard. At fate, for having gifted him the greatest pleasure of his life with a woman he couldn't help but love and want to protect—only for every facet to have been a lie. She was no innocent human girl in want of a warrior's compassion or protection. She wasn't innocent—or human—at all.

Had she known who and what he was from the beginning? Been mocking him, *managing* him, from the first step of their dance?

Cain flung himself from the warmth of her naked body and off the bed. His every limb trembled in rage. His face twisting, he backed steadily away, even as Ellie's arms reached out to him.

A puzzled frown marred the contentedness of Ellie's expression. A soft, fang-tipped smile marred the humanity of her face. "What is it?"

He turned his head. Despite his fury at having been cozened, despite his self-disgust at having been too distracted to discern the truth on his own, he longed to lick the red smear from her lips while taking her again and again and again. Ignoring the yearning of his traitorous body, Cain refocused on the inescapable evidence before him: The innocent human was actually a vampire.

"Don't even try to play the ingénue," he growled. "Not with my blood still fresh upon your tongue."

Guilt flashed across Ellie's face before she dropped her gaze. "I—"

"Why didn't you tell me?" His hands curled into fists at his sides. He had never felt so foolish, so exposed. So vengeful.

Ellie's glare was defiant. "Why do you suppose?"

"Oh, I don't know," he said as he fastened a button. "Because you're a duplicitous manipulator?"

She shot upright. "That's rich, when *you're* the specter of death come to hunt us and take us captive!"

He crossed his arms and gave her a look powerful enough to send warriors scurrying for cover. She didn't even change expression.

"Judge me for honoring my blood-sworn duty," he said at last. "But I never lied to you about who or what I was."

"I never said I *wasn't* a vampire," she mumbled halfheartedly, then glanced away as if no longer able to meet his gaze.

He didn't even try to hide his disappointment. "Let's not prevaricate, shall we? I think we're a bit beyond that stage."

Rather than reply, Ellie slid off the bed and to her feet. She snatched up her discarded gown as if she could hide behind the rumpled silk. She would quickly learn there was nowhere to hide. No matter how furious she made him, he would never let her go.

"How did you manage to conceal the truth?" he asked at last. "You seem—*seemed*—so convincingly human."

"I am human," she insisted, tugging at her laces. "Sort of."

Cain couldn't believe his ears. "You are a *vampire!*"

"Well, how was I supposed to know?" she burst out, staring up at him beseechingly.

"I don't know," he said sarcastically. "Perchance the fangs and the bloodlust might have been clues?"

Ellie backed into the bedside table. "That just started yesterday."

"Yester—" Cain stared at her in disbelief. "How old are you? Truly?"

Her lower lip wobbled. "I don't know."

"You don't know?"

She lifted a shoulder as if this were a mundane detail only a pedant would concern himself with, but her eyes shone as if battling tears. "Mother . . . Mother says I was born sometime last century."

"Sometime last . . ." Cain gaped at her. "Are you saying Aggie Munro is your birth mother?"

Ellie's chin rose. "I've never said otherwise."

"You've never said anything, confound it!" He tried to reconcile what he thought he knew with what he saw before him. "But if that's true, your father . . ."

"Was human." She ran a finger over the marble bust of one of the Breckenridge ancestors. "I would appear to be half-blood."

He rocked backward as if gut-punched. No wonder she'd smelled human, sounded human, acted human. That side of her heritage would always be part of her. As would that of vampire. It was amazing. *She* was amazing.

"Mixed-blood offspring," Cain breathed, unable to fathom being in the presence of something so rare as to be legendary, yet unable to dispute the truth of it. If the Elders had commanded Aggie's capture for having broken a political betrothal, Cain could scarcely fathom their reaction once they discovered the result of her forbidden liaison with a human.

He hurried forward, reaching out for her in his excitement. "When the Elders find out—"

She moved so quickly, he didn't even have a chance to process the trajectory of the marble bust slamming into his head.

Blackness.

Chapter Twelve

"Mama!"

Ellie crashed through the guest chamber door and skidded to a stop in front of her mother, who had apparently been standing within arm's reach of the threshold, awaiting her daughter's return. If Mama were nervous now, her panic would double once she learned that a very large, very determined, very *angry* vampire warrior would be bursting into the room at any moment to carry them off to a Scottish dungeon. He'd gone down when she'd brained him with the marble bust, certainly, but how long could one expect someone like Cain to *stay* down? Minutes? Seconds? He was most likely already after them—and this time, there would be no getting away.

Ellie grabbed her mother's hand. "We have to go. *Now*."

Forehead wrinkling, Mama squinted at her as if her daughter had grown horns as well as fangs over the past few hours.

"He's coming," Ellie explained impatiently. "Mártainn Macane is—"

But Mama was already on the move, galvanized from the first syllable. "Grab your pelisse. I'll get the jewels."

Nodding, Ellie turned toward her bedchamber. "Our trunk—"

"—will stay here," Mama interrupted. "If Mac Eoin knows, then we have no time."

Well, he definitely knew. The lovemaking had been heavenly—until the end, when it had turned hellish. Ellie hated to leave without trying to explain, without telling him that for her, at least, the lovemaking had not been in body alone. She would never surrender her freedom, though he had already stolen her heart. She'd planned to confess, to compromise, to find a solution to everything. . . . But as soon as he'd spoken the word "Elders," she had known there was no changing Cain's mind. There had been no choice. Just as now, they had no choice but to run.

In the scant seconds it took Ellie to sprint to the wardrobe and shrug on her pelisse, her mother was already at the door, a leather satchel clutched to her breast amid the folds of her cloak.

"Swiftly." Mama led the way through what appeared to be servant corridors. "We cannot call attention to ourselves by ringing for our carriage at this hour."

They arrived at an unmarked door at the far side of the manor, which opened toward the mews. Shivering against the wicked night wind, they raced across the lawn to the stables. Once inside, Mama Compelled the sleepy stable hands to fetch their horses as quickly as possible.

When Ellie was younger, she'd thought their well-worn curricle a foolhardy expenditure for a twosome as poor as they. Now that she knew exactly why they ran, she had a new appreciation for the high speeds possible in the small, light chaise, as well as the wisdom behind owning a carriage that did not require liverymen or a driver.

In short order, Ellie and her mother were settled on the perch, the reins in Ellie's capable hands. With a flick of her wrist, they were off.

The wind was bitterly cold and razor sharp against their cheeks as the curricle sped recklessly into the night, but Ellie barely registered the chapping of her cheeks or the chafing of the leather straps wound about her bare hands. She'd forgotten her gloves. She'd lost her marbles. And now that the initial panic had begun to fade, a sharp twist of guilt chilled her flesh far more effectively than the winter wind.

She'd wounded Cain and left.

She hadn't checked his pulse (presuming he had one) or the blood seeping from his temple, or felt along his scalp to see if she'd shattered his skull. She'd simply dropped the red-stained bust where she'd stood and ran.

What if he was dead? What if she'd *killed* him? Could one even kill a vampire?

He was big and strong and a seasoned warrior, but the mere existence of his clan's death decree meant that none of them were truly immortal. Could a vampire live through a cracked skull? Could he heal without help? Without blood? Without her?

Mama snapped to attention as if she'd been goosed. She grabbed Ellie's leg. "Faster!"

Ellie cracked the whip without question. Seeing the look of pure terror on her mother's face was somehow the most frightening sight of all.

"What is it?" she finally asked, her voice hoarse above the dust kicked up by the horses.

"Hoofbeats," Mama whispered, her ashen face even paler than usual. She gripped the edge of the carriage and bent to peer around the side. With a gasp, she flung herself back inside, slamming the back of her head against the rear panel. "It's *him*."

Ellie was so startled, she nearly dropped the reins. "It is?"

"Halt!" came the familiar voice from just behind the carriage.

Fear at what he might do and foolish, unadulterated joy at Cain's continued well-being collided in Ellie's midsection. She flicked the whip without a conscious decision to spur the horses, as if she were an automaton instructed to do so.

Cain was here. Cain was *alive*. And lovesick or not, she could not allow her mother to be captured.

She leaned forward, urging the geldings faster and faster. But horses pulling a carriage could never match the speed of a single horse and rider.

Bringing his mount abreast of the carriage, Cain leaped from his saddle to their curricle, landing hard on the squab beside Ellie.

"Good evening."

"Good evening," she echoed automatically, then slammed her elbow into his ribs. "Get out!"

He smiled. "No."

Mother closed her eyes and groaned as if suddenly motion sick.

Ellie's own nerves grew more and more tense as Cain's hulking presence continued to tower beside her without further comment or any attempt to wrest the ribbons from her trembling hands.

When she could stand it no longer, Ellie blurted, "What the devil are you about?"

"I thought it obvious." He arranged himself more comfortably. "I'm coming with you."

She tightened her grip on the reins with one hand and sent the other arm flying protectively across her mother. "We are *not* going meekly to some archaic punishment."

"I should hope not."

She sent him a ferocious scowl. "Nor shall we succumb to being imprisoned against our will."

"Very well."

Ellie regarded him uncertainly. "Nor will we return to Scotland, now or ever, until and unless all threats have been revoked."

He lifted a shoulder as if none of those possibilities caused the slightest concern, leaned his head back against the panel, and peacefully closed his eyes. "As you wish."

Just as Ellie found herself utterly and maddeningly at a complete loss for words, Mama pushed away Ellie's protective arm, leaned forward to poke Cain in the leg, and demanded, "What is the meaning of this, Mac Eoin?"

"It means," he responded without opening his eyes, "I'm in love with your daughter."

"What?" Ellie choked out, at the same moment her mother exclaimed, "*What?*"

After a long moment, Cain gave a short nod, as if responding to some argument raging deep within himself instead of at the two women gawping openmouthed alongside him. He squared his shoulders, straightened, and turned to face Ellie's mother.

"As I understand, it is human tradition to request permission to wed from the bride's father."

Ellie blinked at him stupidly.

"As he is no longer present," Cain continued without taking his focus from her mother, "it is my fervent hope that her mother will acquiesce. Agnes Munro, will you grant me the honor of marrying your daughter, Elspeth Ramsay?"

"What?" Mama repeated blankly, the word barely audible above the hoofbeats and howling wind.

Ellie let the reins slacken as she turned to face Cain dead-on. "Is this a jest?"

"Not in the slightest," he answered simply. When the corner of his mouth lifted in an uncertain smile, there was no doubting the sincerity of his words.

A vicious, dangerous, swirl of hope began to unfurl in Ellie's heart. "But you were so angry—"

"I was startled." He gently touched his knuckles against the curve of her cheek. "You breathe, Ellie. Your heart beats. Your human blood rushes in your veins. And you *bit* me."

Mama clutched at her throat. "Elspeth!"

"It was an accident," Ellie mumbled guiltily.

"It was instinct," Cain corrected, "and absolutely incredible. I hope you do it again."

"But you said you would tell the Elders—"

"—that our race may not be on the verge of extinction after all," he said with a self-chastising shake of the head. "I should have made that clearer. You are a miracle, Ellie. Very few of our kind still survive. A handful in Pitreavie Castle, a dozen or so in Foulis . . ."

Mama gasped. "But you said it burnt down!"

Cain grinned at her. "I lied."

"You what?" Mother's voice rose to a shriek powerful enough to rival the wind. "Do you have any idea how much sorrow—"

"Don't pretend you've never told a falsehood, Aggie." Cain's voice was serious, his gaze hard. "I had to know the truth."

Ellie hesitantly touched her fingertips to the back of his hand. "And now that you do?"

"As far as I'm concerned, the terms of an honorable hunt are these: Return with the prey, or not at all." He lifted her hand to his lips and pressed a warm kiss against the back of her fingers. "If it means losing you, then I choose not at all."

Ellie pulled her hand away from Cain's mouth in order to press her lips to his. He responded by pulling her into his lap and sinking his fingers into her hair to deepen the kiss. Ellie didn't pull away until her fogged brain finally realized that the reins had fallen from her grip and the carriage had meandered to a complete stop.

And that she was kissing a vampire warrior in full view of her mother.

Still human enough to be incapable of fighting the blush flaming across her cheeks, Ellie slid off Cain's lap to her own seat. She retrieved the fallen ribbons, cleared her throat, and stared fixedly ahead so as not to witness whatever expression her mother currently wore.

Cain brushed her ear softly with the pad of his thumb and

nuzzled a kiss across her forehead. He settled his arm about Ellie's shoulders, then lifted his head to meet her mother's gaze.

"What do you say, Lady Munro? May I wed your daughter?"

Ellie's entire body tensed to the point of shattering as her mother took her precious time deciding her response.

"You may *court* her," Mama said at last, unable to keep a mischievous chuckle from her voice. "Whether she'll wed you is up to her."

Cain smiled down at Ellie, his gaze shining with hope and vulnerability. "I love you, Elspeth Ramsay. I would like to spend the rest of infinity at your side. Will you be mine?"

With love and joy overflowing her heart, Ellie returned his gaze with a saucy look. "Do you think me such easy prey as that?" she said with mock affront. "You may spend the rest of infinity *trying* to catch me, hunter."

"No," he corrected softly, "it is you who have caught me."

She gazed up at him with a smile. "I love you, too."

This time when he reached for her, she melted blissfully into his arms.